M000204696

HUUT

THE
HUUT

Second Edition

MIKE KENNEDY

Published in the United States of America

ISBN: 978-1-5323-3977-6
Fiction / Thrillers / Espionage
June 28, 2017

Dedication

To my Dad and my brother Tom.
Two people I spent far too little time with.
And my mom, Marie. She would
do anything for anyone

Acknowledgments

Special thanks to my beautiful wife, Andrea for putting up with me during this project. From being struck with the idea for this story through its completion. She let it be—all about me—To my children Shawn, Cameron, and Shannon. Thank you for reading the book early on. Your encouragement and support meant a great deal. Your mom and I are blessed with three fine young adults. To my readers and advisors, Mark Salvatore, Dan Wetherhold, and Kirby Haley. Thank you for keeping me honest while you read and re-read the story. I put you through quite a bit and can't thank you enough. And to all my early readers, a big—thank you—To my writing mentor and editor, Beth Lindley. Over the years, I have read many books. The authors of these fine novels have always spent time thanking their editors. They would give them kudos for their diligence. It wasn't until I put fingers to keyboard, did I realize what an editor and coach actually does. Of course, I can't speak for other authors but for me it's simple. Beth made me a better writer. She is a teacher with a master's in education, well respected within her community. Over the summer months she teaches writing at the local college. I was sure she would find little fault in my ability to write. That could not have been further from the truth. Her first cut of this story came back with so many mark-ups I almost cried. I would sit in my favorite chair, in the comfort of my home making corrections, yelling at her through my manuscript. My daughter would look at me as if I were a crazy person. I commend her for her audacity. She was relentless in her pursuit of my perfection. And it was hard work for I am far from perfect. I have told many people "I'm a story teller, my editor is the writer." I recruited her over Margaritas and my wife had been the witness to many 'back and forths' at our follow-on meeting. But she stayed true, reigning in gerunds and my impatient nature. Of all the people, I have thanked, it is my friend Beth that gets the biggest thank you, and perhaps an apology, for all the not so nice texts. I would also like to thank, Ms. Jody Calkins. She was instrumental in editing and smoothing out this second edition. And finally, thanks to Mary Cindell Pilapil and her team at Raket Creatives. You folks could not have been easier to work with.

Prologue

April 25th 2009
California Interstate 210

The driver glanced down at the dash of his dusty red sedan. The dim glow of the instrument lights washed across the speedometer. *Seventy-three,* he thought. *Not fast enough to be pulled over.* He looked over at his passenger, and as oncoming lights lit up their car, the two shared a knowing glance.

In his peripheral, the driver noticed a flash of movement from his right, but it was too late. He screamed as the tractor trailer hit their car.

Forrest Hanington had struggled with the broken drainage flange just off the I-210 while silently keeping track of the time. Finally done, he gathered his equipment and loaded the truck as he checked his watch for the twelfth time. Not wanting to be late for his son's recital, he slammed the tailgate shut and hurried around to the cab. Forrest shifted his truck into drive and quickly accelerated up the on-ramp. He remembered the box of 2 ½ inch bolts he had left on the bumper the moment they slid off. When he straightened himself in the center lane, they fell from the truck and scattered across the road. Forrest stared in horror at the scene in his review mirror.

* * *

Dave Quinn had been happily listening to Willy Nelson when in an instant, his world changed. Dave tried in vain to control his tractor trailer when the bolts that had been scattered across the road imbedded themselves in his tires.

He felt the sudden jolt in his arms the moment the tires exploded from under him. He fought the wheel but he couldn't stop the trailer from swerving left. Eighty thousand pounds had taken on a mind of their own. Amidst the noise and shudder of the rig, he hardly felt the impact as the trailer collided with what he knew was the car that had filled his mirrors.

In 1983, Dave Quinn, a burly powerhouse of a man, had been backing up his rig when he hit a pole at a TA truck stop in Harrisburg, Pennsylvania. In twenty-five years he had never again scratched a truck.

He looked at the carnage through the side mirror and knew no one had survived. When Dave climbed down from his rig, all he could hear was the ringing in his ears. His hands shook as he wiped them over his bald head. He nearly heaved from the sickening smell of diesel, fuel, and burning rubber. As he leaned against the rig, he saw the crushed and twisted heap of the sedan and almost stumbled to the ground.

Officers Cameron Butler and Shawn Davis were just finishing dinner when they received the call. "Collision. North bound. Highway marker 114. Two fatalities. Officers on scene." This was Cameron's last night as a patrol officer. He was starting with the criminal investigative task force unit in just a few days. With their coffee cups in holders and lights and sirens on, they sped to the scene.

When they arrived, they found nothing unusual. Rescue vehicles were everywhere; the highway was completely shut down. It was a sight Cameron had rolled up to over a hundred times. The driver had lost control of the semi-truck after blowing its left front and rear tires. The accident was horrific. The fifty-three foot, eighty-thousand pound tractor trailer swerved into the fast lane, catching the car between its front and rear tires and drug it forty yards. It had been ripped apart and spit out against the eight thousand pound concrete K-rails before it flipped another thirty yards. The sedan was a crushed and twisted heap when it came to rest on what was left of the hood. Both occupants had been killed in seconds. The passenger had been torn from the car. Her bloody, lifeless body was found sixty feet from the wreckage. One of the responding officers approached and handed Cameron two scraped and torn wallets. With a smirk, he said, "Here, your last night. You do the paperwork."

Cameron handed the bloody one to Shawn. As the new guy, he should expect it. Cameron liked Shawn and knew he'd make a fine officer. A little young, but sharp. His sandy hair was trimmed and his six foot, one hundred and ninety pound muscular frame always sported a pressed uniform. Shawn went through the wallet, and although there wasn't much left of the shredded wallet, he found a driver's license. He tilted it to get better look at the name and said, "Mary Springfield,"

Cameron found the other driver's license. "Mark Springfield. Husband and wife? Or relatives?" Shawn showed Cameron Mary's ID. Her address didn't match the driver's. "Damn! Two from the same family," Cameron mumbled. "That won't be easy."

1

April 24th 2009
Richmond, Virginia

Several times a week a car would make its way to a non descript building in the center of town. Over the entrance, the words 'Coffee Huut' are displayed. The rundown building turns folks away faster than it draws them in. Behind the counter normally stands a very pale, blue-eyed woman in her mid 30s with raven hair awaiting her next customer.

Mark Springfield parked his car at the corner and walked toward the coffee shop. His steel grey eyes and squarely set jaw rarely revealed emotion. He was not one to be reckoned with. His closely cropped graying hair and five foot eleven inch muscular frame typically exuded a sense of confidence, but this morning was different. He was uneasy. As he approached the unpainted door and

15

reached for the knob, he felt the hairs on the back of his neck tingle. He lowered his hand and backed away.

Back at his car, he knew he was being overly cautious, but in his business, sometimes all he had was instinct. He leaned against his car and rubbed the back of his neck but still couldn't shake the feeling. His sister had received a coded message, something really meant for him. *What the hell were they doing? This wasn't a mistake*, he thought. The people he'd been dealing with don't make mistakes. *My sister had nothing to do with this. She has a family for God's sakes.* If they hurt her, he'd kill them.

Earlier, Mary had called and asked him to drop by her house. Something had been left for him. She handed him a piece of jade. Inlaid with gold were the words *the huut.* Concealing his surprise, Mark had asked, "What's this?"

"It's not *what's this*?" she had said. "It's *how* did I get this?"

"Are you going to tell me? Or are we going to toss it in the BBQ?" Mark had tried to play it off, but seeing that piece of jade had almost frozen him in place. His cover had been blown.

"Cole came home first with Ashley. Her bear was sitting on the counter with *that* in its lap. He thought I was putting it together for you, but Mark, I didn't do that. Someone was in our house!"

16

"Were your alarms set?" asked Mark. He tried not to show his unease.

"You know I don't leave the house without setting the alarms. Cole would kill me if something ever happened to his collection."

"And did it?"

"No, nothing was touched, just the bear and this piece of jade."

"Mary, why didn't you call the police if you suspected a break-in?"

"Because of this." She showed him the yellow slip of paper that was wrapped around the carving. *Mark, you have one last chance.*

His blood ran cold. He instantly realized the severity of the events that were unfolding. He was no longer anonymous. Not only did they know who he really was, they knew his family, his only sibling, a sister he loved beyond words, a brother-in-law, and two nieces for whom he would die.

"Mark! What is it? What does this mean? I've never seen you like this! It looks like you're going to be sick. Here, sit down."

"No, Mary. I have to go." Mark turned and headed for the door, feeling sick to his stomach. From behind, Mary yelled his name, but he was gone.

He left his sister's house and headed straight for the coffee shop in Richmond hoping it wasn't too late. If he had been exposed, Danielle may have already been killed.

2

For the first time in recent memory, Mark Springfield was rattled. It was different when he was the only one at risk. He received the best training and backing the United States government had at its disposal. The FBI academy and laboratory at Quantico and training with CIA operatives at Camp Perry were just the beginning of his preparation. He cut his teeth with the SEALS by penetrating the Iranian border on a mission that cost one SEAL his life. Mark was well-equipped to handle high-risk assignments. Not just handle them physically. That was a given. But a good CIA operative needed the mental stability and toughness. This was different. After the death of his mom and dad, all he had left was Mary, Cole, and the kids, and he watched over them like a hawk. They were civilians, and in the unspoken world of espionage, they were untouchable.

He leaned against his car and pulled the piece of jade from his pocket. He stared at the inscription that read, *the huut*. It wasn't really a code but an abbreviation for— T*he Huntsville Units Under Test*, part of the National Environmental Satellite, Data, and Information Service. The HUUT was created by the National Oceanic and Atmospheric Administration to operate and manage the United States' environmental satellite programs. That, of course, was the cover. The Huntsville unit was a whole other story.

Code word, *Cyclone* the Huntsville unit was being extensively tested by the National Reconnaissance Office (NRO). During the fifteen-year development program, its nick name became *the huut*. This satellite has the ability to not only see if a penny was heads-up from space, but also see an image buried deep beneath the surface of the earth. And, unlike portable Ground Penetrating Radar units that have a max range of fifty feet, *the huut* can see three hundred feet. With the three- dimensional aspect being developed, a nation would no longer be able to hide not only their dignitaries underground but also their nuclear weapons and chemical arsenals. The nation that possessed the Huntsville unit would be able to decimate a country.

Normally, Mark reported directly to the director of the Office of Satellite Operations (OSO). They manage and direct the operation of NOAA's satellites and the acquisition of remotely sensed data. The Office has operational responsibility for the Satellite Operations Control Center at Suitland, MD and the Command and Data Acquisition facilities at Wallops, VA and Fairbanks, AK. They command, control, track, and acquire satellite data. In the unclassified world, it's to support NOAA and other known government agencies. However, buried deep in its bowels, in specially built rooms secured behind cyber and retina scan locks, is the heart and soul of the Huntsville unit. In partnership with NRO they operate and maintain the ground based stations. The air force uses its newly operational X-37B for the deployed unit, six hundred twenty-one miles overhead, in its near polar orbit.

3

April 24th 2009
Richmond, Virginia

Mark had learned plenty in the last few months. He had learned someone outside the organization knew of the Huntsville unit, and someone on the inside was talking. He also now knew his family was not safe. He needed to report to the OSO. His boss needed to know his cover had been blown. More importantly, he needed to protect his family. Acting as a double agent may get them killed.

He went off the grid the moment he left his sister's house. Sweeping his car and staying hidden is CIA Tradecraft 101, but leaning against the car a block from the Coffee shop he still felt he was being watched. The Coffee shop was a front. It was bought and converted into a covert communications site to report his progress with foreign contacts. To avoid exposing himself, and risking the safety of the encryption, he'd have to make contact here instead of driving up to Suitland Maryland.

Mark jerked his body off of his car and walked to the coffee shop. Danielle gave no indication there was a problem when he stepped through the door. Their coded entry had been rehearsed, practiced and executed a hundred times. He tried to shake the feeling and headed back. Mark stepped through the door and noticed that this time she was out of place. Normally, she was behind the counter, but this time she was pulling the dusty shades to block out the last bit of sun. Protocol was to approach the counter, and if the place was clean she'd simply say, "May I help you?" If she were in distress, she'd say they were closed.

Danielle stepped round the counter from the side of the shop when the hairs on his neck rose. Through the reflection in the glass counter he saw the last ray of sun flash off something at Danielle's waist. *No!* He watched as she pointed the semi-automatic hand gun at him and fired.

4

September 14th 2008
White House
Washington D.C.

During a visit to the Chinese government concerning tensions in the Taiwan Straits, the Secretary of State was handed a gift, a beautiful jade Geisha with long flowing robes holding an umbrella affixed to a marble base. It wasn't until she was in her hotel room that she really looked at it. In the alternating colors of the umbrella, inlaid with gold, was the word Cyclone. After returning to the U.S., she immediately called for a meeting with the president, who quickly assembled a partial cabinet. Not every cabinet member knew of the top secret project, so the meeting was held in the oval office. With everyone assembled she pulled the statue from its wooden box and set it in the center of the table for the group to view. One by one, gasps were heard around the room as they realized what was sitting before them. Admittedly, the dinner party was very lavish with many dignitaries attending. She couldn't remember who, exactly, in the Chinese government had given it to her. Nonetheless, the fact that the Chinese knew the code word for the Huntsville unit was deliberately and plainly being shown to the United States.

The Huntsville unit was the technological advancement of the century. To be able to see into the earth and find where a country hides its most valuable possessions or technologies had given the United States a huge leg up with first strike capabilities. They could decimate another country's buried command and control centers or arsenals before they even left the underground silos. To protect *the huut* meant everything. The United States would spend, or do, whatever it needed to safeguard its very existence. The enemy not knowing their capabilities meant the United States was one step ahead. In war, when tensions run high and the losing side has nuclear weapons they might deploy, the decision to use *the huut* would give the U.S. the capability to locate and pass targeting information to the Air Force which could then deploy its stealthy B1, thereby dropping the Massive Ordnance Penetrator and eliminating the threat. The fact that another country had knowledge of their most valuable asset was a blow to national security.

Following the meeting, the White House called the director of the CIA. A meeting with the president was scheduled for eight o'clock in the morning the following day. The director, Cliff House, an impeccably dressed, short, wiry, bespectacled man, whose hair line was rapidly receding, spent the next few hours running down his best agent, the cagy Italian, Mark Springfield.

5

September 15th 2008

Usually, just a phone call away, on this day he was a little more difficult to find. He'd been back for two days from an overseas assignment, working with the secret service on a counterfeiting sting. Mark was finally getting some well-deserved rest. With his cell phone sitting on the table just inside the back door, he had missed every call.

He worked quietly on his old, overturned wooden boat, running the hand sander over the planks and readying it for a fresh coat of paint. It sat atop two saw horses which were normally a good height, but now it just irritated the pain he felt in his lower back and reminded him of the fall he took while he had been running down a fleeing suspect.

He was hours outside of Washington at his family's small vacation home which had been left to him and his sister following their parent's death. It sat two rows back from the sandy beaches of Kitty Hawk, North Carolina.

He loved the house. The ocean smell that emanated through the rooms was only bettered by his sister's blueberry pies. They would occupy a window ledge when she and her family were in town. He pictured his mom and dad laughing as they walked across the old creaking wooden floor. It was an old friend. It was his escape from an otherwise hectic life. Since leaving California, it was his only way to be close to the ocean. Mark routinely pushed the old wooden boat through the surf, dropping a fishing line now and then. Often the hook was bare; there were times when catching fish had disturbed his solitude.

Mark used the house on the Outer Banks as an excuse to get away and occasionally to meet his sister and family. To his neighbors, he was simply a government employee who loved to travel. He was friendly but mostly kept to himself. He walked everywhere, using the time and salt air to shake the assignments from his head and the soreness from his body. Wearing cut-off jeans and a long-sleeved plaid shirt, he was easily recognizable when he made the trek to the village for groceries and the occasional case of Carolina Blond.

He took a break from sanding the boat and rubbed his sore back. He wondered if a few days would be enough this time. He took the last drink of beer and silently smiled at the memory of walking a suspect, half his age, back to the warehouse and the surprised look on the secret service agents' faces as he sat him down beaten and bloodied.

They had been counterfeiting twenty dollar bills on the best plates Mark had ever seen, and he was happy to help put an end to it. He slowly knelt and slid open the old cooler when he noticed someone walking along the side of his house. Recognizing the local gray police uniform, he relaxed. It usually took him a few days to unwind and get back into the slowness of the community.

"Mr. Springfield?" the young officer called out in his southern North Carolina draw.

Mark straightened and removed the cap from his beer. "That's me."

"Sorry to bother you, but your boss called our office and asked if we'd run out here and see if you were ok. Says it's important that we find you."

Mark reached in the cooler, grabbed another beer and offered it to the young officer.

He held up his hands and started laughing.

"If I took a beer from everyone who offered me one, I wouldn't be able to drive,"

"Thanks for coming out, I'll give her a call," Mark said as he dropped the bottle back into the slushy ice.

The officer turned and Mark lead him back toward the street.

"I hear you work for the government," the young officer said while they made their way to his cruiser.

"Yup, twenty-eight years."

"What part?"

"Just a small financial division off the beltway. You've probably never heard of it." Mark saw him to his door, thanked him, and said goodbye. He kept the fact he worked for the CIA to himself. He found over the years all it does is cause people to ask questions he couldn't answer.

Mariah Littleton was Mark's immediate supervisor since returning to D.C. He had worked with her in the past and thought she was a very capable agent, but for her to call him so soon after an assignment told him something was wrong.

He went around to the back of the house and trotted up the steps. When inside, he checked his phone, expecting to see her number. But, he instantly recognized the number that displayed and it went all the way to the

30

top. Mark had missed fourteen calls from the director of the CIA.

On the third ring, the director's secretary answered and promptly put him through. "Director House, what can I do for you, sir?"

"Mr. Springfield, I need you in my office tomorrow morning, 7:00 a.m."

Very, very wrong. "I'll be there." Mark had worked directly for the director on several occasions, but never before had the director skipped over his boss. He stood rubbing his back as he looked out the window. From over the kitchen sink he could see the Atlantic. Leaning in, he closed the window and rotated the lock. It would take him another hour to close up the house and head back to Washington.

Mark was sitting in the director's outer office looking at a closed door at 6:45 a.m. His lips grew into a thin smile as his dads' voice resounded in his brain. *Never show up on time for an appointment. Be at least five minutes early or you're late.* He had been fanatical about not only being on time, but also about being early, and had hounded his kids until they, too, thought they were committing a crime if they were late. He sat quietly, smiling at the memory of his dad. Mark thought he was the first one there until 6:55 a.m. when Cliff House opened his door and both he and his secretary exited his office. Mark stood as she excused herself, slid by the men and took a seat at her desk. The men exchanged pleasantries while Cliff turned to his secretary and introduced her to Mark. He then turned to Mark and said, "Join me for a bite at the café across the street?" It came as a question, but Mark knew it wasn't a request.

They rode the elevator to the lobby in silence. Mark could tell the director was in deep thought and held off asking what their day looked like. He was curious as to why the director had called him back to Washington but knew enough not to ask; the director would explain in due time. They sat at a small table at the café and briefly went over Mark's last assignment. It was more for small talk, leaving out the classified details until the conversation turned to Cliff's new and very capable secretary. Mark listened as Cliff explained how her ability to second guess his needs was a refreshing change and a commendable talent.

When they were done, the director had his car brought around and they headed for their meeting across town at the White House, 1600 Pennsylvania Ave.

They gave their names, showed their IDs at the side gate, and were immediately ushered into the White House. The Secretary of Defense the Secretary of State, the Secretary of Homeland Security, and the Treasury Secretary were waiting for the president when Mark and Cliff arrived.

Mark had never been in the oval office, nor had he ever met the president. He was excited but knew something was very wrong. After introductions, they made small talk around the sterling silver coffee and tea decanters. The president arrived at 8:30 a.m. with a very attractive young woman wearing a navy blue business suit, her hair in a tight auburn bun. She was carrying a laptop and several folders. As she walked across the room, Mark noticed his name written across the top of the outer file. Cliff walked Mark over to the president and introduced them.

"Thank you for joining us, Mr. Springfield. I hope you find the tea to your liking."

"Yes, Mr. President," Mark said with a slight chuckle. "It's very good."

"I have been reading about you," the president continued. "Your trek across Germany, Poland, and then into Russia was very admirable. I was very pleased that Mr. House was able to find you. I'm sorry that we had to take you away from your vacation."

Mark was instantly taken back three years to a mission he would tell everyone he had failed at. A lump grew in his throat at the thought of the outcome.

"I know we had lost one of our best agents. But the information he had recovered was, as you know, invaluable." The president lay a gentle hand on Marks' shoulder.

"Thank you, Mr. President." Mark tried his best to fight the lump in his throat. Three years wasn't enough. A lifetime wouldn't be enough for Mark to forgive himself for not getting to his friend Ramous in time.

"Mr. Springfield."

Mark snapped out of his daze and turned his attention to the feminine voice. The young woman was pointing to a table across the room.

"Yes, yes," he said then nodded an *excuse me* to the president.

Mark made a detour to refill his tea cup and then joined her at the table. She showed him a lengthy presentation on her laptop regarding the Huntsville unit. She then had him sign a stack of papers pledging not to discuss the program outside appropriate channels with the threat of thirty years in prison if he did. Mark had been through the drill many times, but this time was different - this time he was sitting in the oval office with the president of the United States.

6

April 24th 2009
Richmond, Virginia

If it hadn't been for the flash of light off the chrome slide, the hunt for the mole would have temporarily ended and Mark Springfield would be dead. But it had given him the split second he needed to turn his head, dive behind a set of tables and chairs, and instinctively reach for his gun. The round hit, tearing away the top of his ear as it grazed the side of his head; it burned like hell. Warm blood slowly trickled down his neck. Mark knew he was in trouble. He had trusted Danielle. They'd been together from the beginning of the hunt, and now, in an instant, he was fighting against her for his life. Lying on the filthy floor with one hand on his pistol, he kicked chairs toward Danielle as he fired back. He grabbed a table and pushed it towards his attacker only to have it splinter in his face when she fired several more times.

Mark crossed the room in seconds. He pushed Danielle towards the counter, shoving the broken table on her small frame. She stumbled over a display rack and fell to the ground. In that instant, as he looked her in the eyes, time slowed. He wasn't looking at the woman he'd known, the woman he had worked with side by side, the woman with whom he had shared a bed. He was looking at someone whom he'd never met. The person he was in love with was gone. He fired twice, he hit her in the chest and shoulder as she fell to the ground.

He steadied himself, stepped back, and automatically scanned the room. He gave her a quick glance, then ejected the almost-depleted magazine and stuffed it in his left pants pocket and recharged his gun. After a quick check of his Glock 23 it was back in the holster. Mark wiped the sweat from his brow. The attack, which had lasted only seconds, was surreal. He had just killed a fellow CIA agent. He thought of all the late nights they had spent going over intelligence while they hunted for a potential mole and the Chinese connection. He crouched down and removed Danielle's wig to reveal her striking red hair. Her smooth skin was fair, and under the contacts, he knew, were beautiful brown eyes. He had been attracted to her from the start, and the late nights had quickly turned into a love affair. Mark stood and again looked around the room feeling very alone. The realization slowly began to register. Danielle had not only been a spy, she was an assassin. Tears welled in his eyes. He shook it off and in a low shaky voice, he muttered, "Jesus, my sister." Just before he stepped through the door he looked at Danielle one last time. She lay there staring up at him, eyes wide open.

7

April 24th 2009
Mary Springfield's Home
Outskirts of St. Charles, Maryland.
Just off Marshall Comer Rd.

Mark spent the last two days off the grid double checking his sister's routine in case things went bad. After their mom and dad died he had became Marys' unknown protector, watching over her family and learning their routines. He had shadowed them on many vacations, but while in Mexico, an attempted kidnapping of his youngest niece by two assailants dressed in Mexican military uniforms convinced him that they needed him more than ever. They never knew of the attempt on their daughter. When he had intervened outside the hotel, it was swift and silent. The two had died a quick death.

Mark checked his watch, 4:30 p.m. Mary would be home starting dinner and Cole would be with Ashley at her dance class. He raced to their house. He pulled alongside the curb and could see Cole through the window preparing dinner. Mark took several deep breaths trying to slow himself down and not show any urgency. He knocked on the door.

Christina answered, "Hi, Uncle Mark! Joining us for dinner? Dad's making breakfast!" she added with a giggle.

He gave her a warm smile. Ever since her birth, he adored his dark-eyed niece. She was the cutest thing he'd ever seen. He had been there for her birth which may have something to do with his affections. He bent down to embrace her four-foot frame in his arms. "Hi, honey, I can't stay, but is your mom home?"

"No, she took Ashley to her dance class."

"Hey, Mark, is that you?" Mark's brother-in-law called from around the corner.

"Cole, I need to talk to you."

8

September 16th 2008
White House
Washington D.C.

"Mr. Springfield, please tell us what you think of our new piece of hardware."

Mark was stunned. From the moment he had started to grasp the capabilities of the Huntsville unit, he knew what it meant. The request from the Secretary of Defense wanting him to give his opinion was more rhetorical than anything. Every person in the room knew that a fully weaponized country would be unstoppable in locating and destroying hidden targets anywhere in the world. Mark glanced at the president who watched from the couch.

"Mr. Secretary, what can the CIA do for you?" replied Mark.

The president, normally a soft-spoken politician, stood and made his way to the decanter. He raised his hand toward the Secretary of Defense indicating that he'd take this question. "Mr. Springfield, Mark, if I may? It seems we've had a breach in our security. The Huntsville unit, actually I hear it's being called *the huut*, may have been compromised." He continued to explain the Secretary of State's most recent experience in China, adding that he didn't believe in coincidences.

The president walked over to the couch and took a seat across from Mark. He opened the box and carefully removed the figurine, and set it on the table.

Mark picked it up and handled it with great care as he studied the statue. *Cyclone* was clearly inlaid in the umbrella, and he wondered aloud if it wasn't just the mark of the artist.

"We checked that," added the SecDef. "There's no such artist either Chinese or other that works under the name *Cyclone*."

Mark looked around the room and could tell he was being sized up.

"And the timing," added the president. "The secretary was given the statue after the first test of the unit, directly after a scan in Iraq. We imaged an area where, years ago, we had found aircraft buried sixty feet in the sand. The test

41

was a success, and the aircraft that had been left buried there appeared in two dimensions right on our displays."

The rest of the room came to life with the mention of the test. Mark could feel everyone's excitement over its success. From the far end of the office a very small, unassuming man cleared his voice,

"Mr. Springfield," the secretary of the Treasury said while adjusting his thick round glasses. "We've spent quite a large sum of taxpayer money on this piece of equipment and the security measures put in place are unprecedented. There, too, we spent more than we will admit." Sounding a little more irritated, he continued. "We've gone to great lengths and expense to vet everyone involved."

Mark kept an even gaze as the man spoke. He knew the Secretary cared more about money than national security. Two words came to mind - b*ean counter.*

The president rose from the couch, went to his desk, and made a quick call. Minutes later, the door opened and three carts, covered with white linens, were wheeled into the room. The sound of jingling silverware broke the silence. The president turned to the group. "Lunch, gentlemen?"

9

April 24th 2009
Mary Springfield's Home
Outskirts of St. Charles, Maryland.
Just off Marshall Comer Rd.

Cole Thomas, a very brawny contractor with piercing green eyes and short wavy brown hair, met and fell in love with Mary Springfield fourteen years earlier. He had started his construction business when Mary was looking for a contractor to renovate her modest home. As a lawyer with a small firm, she had needed more home office space. On her list of companies to consider was CT Construction. It had been at the bottom of the list and she almost didn't make the call. She'd already made up her mind but couldn't stop the voice in her head, *Always check around, never get one estimate for anything.* Her dad had given them the same advice over the years. She had laughed out loud and made the call.

Mary was immediately taken with his rugged good looks. His professionalism and sense of humor put her at ease from the start. They had a connection right away and went round and round over the smallest of details, creeping closer and closer to each other while sitting around the table. During their meetings, Mary would insist that the window coverings should be one way. Then a week later, she would blame Cole for the design and insist he change them. In return, Cole would provide her detailed billing, including the cups and toilet paper that his crew had used throughout the day. The bantering continued throughout the construction. By the time the project was over, they were dating.

Cole knew her brother, Mark didn't like him in the beginning. Mary was a beautiful shapely woman with coal black eyes and matching shoulder-length hair. Cole had watched her turn many heads. Her brother didn't trust him and on some level, he understood. But after many family dinners and get togethers, Cole could sense Mark was warming up to him. And when Cole asked both Mark and their Dad for permission for her hand in marriage, he was welcomed with open arms. It wasn't long before Cole was one of the family. Other than Mary keeping her last name for business purposes, it was a typical Italian wedding. Cole and Mark were soon fast friends.

Cole knew Mark worked for the government, but every time he asked about his job, Mark would expertly change the subject. Cole caught on and never asked again. Tonight, when he heard Mark at the door, he detected an urgency in his voice. Cole had never heard him rattled like he was tonight. No, something was definitely wrong. He rushed from the kitchen. "What's happened to Mary?"

"Cole, we need to talk."

"You said that, Mark, what's wrong?"

"It concerns the piece of jade you found. Do you remember it?" Mark's voice rose slightly.

"Yes, of course."

"Cole, I need to find Mary and Ashley, and get all of you to a safe place."

"Does this have anything to do with your job?" Cole asked as he pulled back the drapes.

"Stand away from the window, Cole" Mark almost shouted the command.

"Holy shit, Mark! What's going on? Why is your face cut up?"

Cole watched Mark study himself in the mirror that hung in the hallway. His face had small cuts on the left side and the top of his white shirt was blackened.

"Cole, as you know, I work for the government. I can't tell you what I'm working on, but tonight..." Mark didn't intend to, but he paused, the image of Danielle lying dead on the floor flashed in front of him. He fought the lump in his throat. He had trouble saying his next few words. "I killed my partner."

Christina looked up at Mark. Did her uncle say he killed someone! Someone was dead? She couldn't believe what she heard. Something was wrong. She wanted to ask but stood and stared. Her eyes welled up and tears ran freely down her cheeks.

Mark glanced down at his niece, her eyes where as big as he had ever seen. He returned his gaze to Cole and said. "Grab some clothes for you and the girls. Cole! Listen to me! God Damnit! Get back from the window!" Cole had turned to stone. He was frozen in the moment. He unknowingly took a step back. He could not process what he had heard. After a few agonizing seconds he slowly turned to Mark and asked. "You... killed someone?" Mark stepped towards Cole to shake him out of it when suddenly, the window exploded.

From within the woods across the road a single trigger press from the suppressed Bushmaster A3, sent a ballistic tipped .223 three thousand eight hundred and fifty feet per second. It arrived before the trigger was even reset.

10

September 16, 2008
White House
Washington D.C.

After a light lunch, they had a plan to set up a counter intelligence operation, to trap the mole, and expose the country that was stealing their secrets. The CIA hatched a plan that involved Mark acting as a double agent. It was risky, but there was no other way they could covertly infiltrate an organization and determine the person who was passing secrets of the Huntsville Unit. Mark suggested he would work from the west coast acting as a disgruntled subcontractor. He suggested the Jet Propulsion Laboratory (JPL) in La Canada Flintridge on the outskirts of Pasadena, California. It had played a part in the relay phase of the satellite. He may be able to spread the word from there.

Cliff pushed his glasses up his nose and looked up from the table. "Mark, let's move you south of here to Richmond and insert you with a small group of folks. They manufacture a power supply used in the Fairbanks Alaska facility. They're called ATEC. They meet routinely with several of our other facilities, but they're a smaller group, and inserting you there will be less noticeable."

Once again, Mark marveled at how much Cliff knew of an operation. One that only hours before, Mark had never known existed. It appeared his new boss had been *read-in* for some time. He was very well versed on the players involved and the best place for him to start his hunt. Mark would be reporting directly to Cliff and the director of the Office of Satellite Operations for unfettered access to the top men.

The Secretary of Homeland Security cleared her throat. It was apparent she wasn't fully convinced there was a leak. "Mr. President, gentlemen, we may have to concede that we may not have a problem and all of this may be for naught. The statue given to the Secretary may not be as sinister as we think." Jordyn Kennedy had an undeniable presence. She was fit, impeccably dressed, and her shoulder-length hair was always in place, despite its graying at the roots and wisping at the ends. The recently divorced fifty-five-year old woman had thrown herself into her work; 'the huut' was her top priority.

The president rose from the couch and turned to Jordyn. "Ms. Secretary, I do not believe in coincidences. The gift was too well-timed and we have too much at stake to compromise the Huntsville Unit. I hope in the end this was all for naught, as you say, but in the meantime we will fully implement the plan. Mr. Springfield, Director, you have the full support of my office."

Mark knew that, technically, the CIA could not operate covertly in the United States. But at the moment, sitting in the oval office, they had just been given permission to do so.

The president walked back toward his desk, then turned and addressed the group. "Thank you, gentlemen, Madam Secretaries, for coming on such short notice. The sooner we can determine if we have a problem, the sooner we can mitigate the risk." Looking at Mark and Cliff, he continued. "I'm sure our friends at the CIA will have the answer soon."

11

September 17th 2008
CIA Headquarters
Langley, Virginia

The last three days were hectic. They had spent hours poring over maps and records of Richmond, ironing out the details, and trying to find a defunct business close to ATEC to use as a communications site. The director was keeping the number of people involved to a minimum. With the help of only one other agent in the records department, he finally found a mom and pop coffee shop close to the center of town on 15th Street. It was up for sale.

Three days later, Mark was on the road to Richmond, Virginia. It had taken his boss a while to set up his alias, register a Chevy Malibu under his new name, and insert him into ATEC. Since Mark had been recruited into the CIA directly out of college with his electrical engineering degree, it was easy to find him a place in ATEC with the cover that he would be trying to miniaturize their power supply for the space-born unit. They were more than happy to pick up the additional work and with a recommendation from the Office of Satellite Operations, they welcomed Mark with open arms.

He used the two-hour drive down I-95 to unwind. He thought how nice it had been to be back in Washington close to Mary, Cole, and the girls. Los Angeles was too far. And with his busy schedule, the visits were becoming more difficult. They lived in St. Charles, just outside Washington down I-95. Living in Washington, he could be at her door in a little over an hour, and he could pop over to her house for dinner a few times a month. This gave him the opportunity to catch up on the girls' activities and any upcoming trips.

Mark had never married. He had dated plenty over the years. A few times, he thought he might have found "the one" to settle down with for good. But in the end, the last thing he needed was to worry about someone at home while he was flying all over the world in and out of precarious situations. His sister continued to tease him every time he was with the girls. "You'd make an excellent dad," she would say repeatedly. A smile grew on his face as he made his way towards Richmond.

His stomach told him it was time to eat and he rolled the sedan to a stop at a diner outside of town. He was a breakfast person and as usual, he ordered scrambled eggs, home fries, and all the meat varieties they offered. When the bill came, he paid for it using his new credit card.

"Thank you, Mr. Salvatore," the waitress said when she returned.

Hmm… that shouldn't be too hard to get used to. That's more Italian than my real name. He smiled to himself at the thought.

The other Springfield is the gun he wears in the small of his back. The sub-compact XD9 carried in a modified inside the waistband holster was an excellent back-up weapon. His primary firearm is a Glock 23. He carried it on his waistband in the fastest holster he could find, a Blade Tech. Firearms training with the agency was a snap since he had been shooting before he was ten years old. But it was the explosives training that he could've spent years doing. He loved it, from detonating commercial energetics and commercially available fertilizers to the formulation of explosives using common household items. Mark couldn't imagine working for anyone else, and now felt he was on the most important assignment of his career.

12

September 22nd 2008
Richmond, Virginia

Mark sat in his car and punched the address of the coffee shop into his GPS. He accelerated onto the I-95 and before he knew it, he was pulling off the freeway. He turned onto 15th Street and found the coffee shop minutes later. While he was walking up to the door, he studied the neighborhood and surrounding businesses. It was an area of town less traveled. The business seemed well kept; they just lacked people. Mark had seen this in his own hometown. A new strip mall goes up and everyone flocks to the latest fad.

He stepped through the doors and wasn't disappointed. Other than the young lady working the counter, he saw only one customer. Mark ordered tea and tried striking up a conversation with the very cute counter girl. He figured she was a high schooler working part time. "Nice location. I'm surprised it's not busier this time of day."

Before the young lady could say a word, Mark heard someone from behind the counter say, "It was a lot busier before they put that Starbucks in, and to make matters worse, they put another one in not three damn blocks away." Mark moved around the corner to get a better look at the voice. "I don't know why they needed two within three blocks. Who can stand their coffee anyway? I tried it once and threw it out."

"You own the store?" Mark asked with a laugh. He liked the woman's direct, staunch voice.

"Sure do. My husband and I opened up years ago, but he's tired of all the crap with the city and tryin' to compete with the chains. We've made our money, and like the sign in the window says, it's time to go."

Mark walked around the counter with his outstretched arm and said, "Name's Rick Salvatore."

She dropped her rag on the counter and took his hand, "Helen Wieger. Nice to meetcha, Richard."

"Please, call me Rick. My wife's been talkin' 'bout buyin' a place like this, but if you're havin' troubles, might not be a good idea."

Helen Wieger's short, white hair framed her thin face. She wore a hint of lipstick, had stark blue eyes and wore a flowered apron wrapped around her plain gray skirt and loose white blouse. Though she was thin in the face, her stocky 5'4" frame made her look the picture of Germany. "Well, we've been doin' this for quite some time. Truth be told, I'm tired. My husband and I are sixty-five years old and we're ready to go. This place just needs new blood," she said with a thin smile.

"Mind if I have a look around?"

"Not at all."

Mark strolled around the shop. He took notice of outside walls, vents, plumbing, phone lines, and anything that ran through the walls or floor that someone could access from the outside. Feigning a phone call, he stepped outside and walked around the grounds. *With some work this place would work just fine.* He popped his head inside and pointed at his phone as if there was an important matter needing attention. He thanked Helen and waved his goodbye.

His next order of business was to drive to ATEC on Valley Road. It was a short trip from the Coffee shop, but enough distance to detect whether he was being followed, something he may need later. He wasn't slated to start for another week but he wanted to get a feel for Richmond.

After his drive past ATEC offices, he headed to the house that had been recently purchased by the agency, a single story, just twenty minutes across town on Pepper Avenue. The agency had decided to purchase a single family house rather than lease, rent, or use an apartment. This would keep prying eyes away. They legitimized his move to Richmond without drawing any suspicion. The one-hundred ninety-two thousand dollars it cost for the house was a drop in the bucket compared to the cost of *the huut*. He slowly pulled his car alongside the curb outside his new home. The blue, house was neat as a pin. A well-kept lawn with a low white picket fence surrounded the house. He got out of his car and walked to the side gate. From what he could see, the lawn in the back was just as nice as the front. In one corner of the back lawn was a small windmill rising up from a flower bed. In the other corner stood an old blue metal shed, and stretched between two poles, was a very long clothesline. Mark heard a car door slam but continued to study the backyard and what he could see of the surrounding houses.

"Can I help you?"

Mark turned and saw a short, well-dressed man holding the For Sale sign that had been stuck in the front yard.

Mark gave his best startled geek look, turned, stumbled a little, and started towards the realtor. "Hi, I'm Rick Salvatore. My wife and I just bought the place."

"Mr. Salvatore, so very nice to meet you. Welcome to the neighborhood. We were wondering who would buy the place sight unseen," he said with a big smile.

"Oh, no. I've been by for one of the open houses, but kinda stayed to myself. Went back and told the missus we just gotta have it and here I am."

"Well, again, welcome."

Mark looked around and asked, "Is this a quiet street? Cause the one we're on now is next to a freeway, and it's cars and trucks all the time."

"Yes, sir. The only thing you'll hear around here is the occasional dog barking, or some of the neighborhood kids on their bikes." The realtor paused and took a slow approving look at the adjacent houses. Then he asked. "Are you working in the area?"

"Just took a job with ATEC and have to start soon. My wife won't be along for a few months," Mark said while walking towards his car. "When can I pick up the keys?"

The agent handed his card to Mark and said, "With all the money upfront and the inspections waived, it'll close in a week or so. Then she's all yours."

"Great! I'll give you a call in a week and check on it." Mark slowly made his way to the car as he studied the neighborhood. He opened the car door and paused to lookback at the house. The fall leaves were turning color and he noticed a pleasant aroma wafting through the cool air. *This feels nice*, he thought. He sat in the car, smiled, and said, "Man, I'm getting old." He closed the door and took a slow drive down the street.

13

April 25th 2009
California Interstate 210

Cameron Butler, an eighteen-year veteran of the California Highway Patrol, took his profession very seriously. As the senior officer on the scene, it was his duty to oversee the events that were unfolding before him. Cameron had been to countless accidents throughout California, and this one, though more gruesome, was another sad loss of life. The smell of gasoline, diesel, rubber, and burnt asphalt were smells which had become common to him. But the smell he would never get used to was the smell of death. He walked to what was left of the sedan and pulled back the white sheet which covered the body. Identification would not be easy. Then, he walked to the passenger lying some sixty feet away. He knelt down and pulled back her sheet. "This *is* bad," he said to no one in particular.

Cameron stood and walked over to the driver of the semi-truck, deliberately placing each foot on the pavement so as not to slip in any of the diesel or oil that had spread over the highway. "Mr. Quinn, sir, do you need medical attention?" Cameron could tell the big man in front of him was shaken. His broad shoulders which normally filled his cab were now slumped over the patrol car's hood. Dave was in a trance. He looked defeated.

He turned his head and looked up at the brown eyes of the fair-skinned, red-headed patrolman. His voice broke as he replied, "I'm ok."

Cameron patted his shoulder to reassure him. "I just spoke with Officer Hunter. He gave me the quick version of what happened. Can you fill me in on the details?"

Dave tried to stand. His ankle gave out and he fell on the side of the car. "Damnit! Must have twisted it in the cab." He pushed himself up, started to turn toward the wreckage, and asked, "No one survived?"

Cameron shook his head and said, "I'm sorry, no. Both driver and passenger." He helped turn Dave towards the crash.

"I hit something in the road, must have blown some tires. I lost control just after the on-ramp." Dave half pointed down the highway. As he looked at Cameron, his eyes welled up. His throat constricted and his voice trembled as he spoke. "Those poor folks had no place to go. They put those damn K-rails along the inside. When you're in the fast lane you have no place to go. I tried, I just couldn't get 'er under control." Dave leaned back against the patrol car and almost fell as he slid down the side. Realizing he had just killed two people was more than he could bear. He sat hard on the ground, buried his face in his hands, and cried.

Cameron walked over to the ambulance crews and made sure they tended to him. He found Shawn and walked back to their cruiser. "Shawn, I noticed something," Cameron said as they approached the hood of their car. "The driver, Mark Springfield, the hair color on his license says black. I'm sure it's brown. I want you to take the license you dug out of that purse and try and match it with the passenger."

Shawn looked at Cameron like he had just asked him to arrest an alien. The woman lay in a bloody twisted heap. Moving body parts around was not a task with which Shawn had much experience.

"Part of the job, my boy," Cameron said. From the trunk of their cruiser, they retrieved pairs of blue latex gloves and performed a field identification.

Matt Hunter, a ten-year veteran of the CHP and the one who had first approached them, helped pull back the sheet on the driver. Cameron hated this part. On a few occasions, when it had been a small child, it had brought tears to his eyes. He scanned his light over the body. The driver definitely had brown, not black, hair. He knelt down, and even though the face was disfigured and full of blood, he was able to pull up an eyelid and get a clear look at the eye. The pupil was fixed, but he could see that the iris was clearly brown.

"Hmm..." Cameron murmured as he leaned back on his heels. "Matt, what do you guess his height to be?"

Matt looked at the driver and said, "Don't hold this against me if I'm wrong, but I think he's well over six feet." At the same time, Cameron was looking at Mark Springfield's driver's license which showed his height as five feet eleven inches.

He looked over at his partner. Shawn, who was standing back with a confused look on his face, looked up and motioned for Cameron.

"What did ya find?" asked Cameron as he walked towards his partner.

"Her license says five feet ten inches, black eyes, and black hair. I haven't verified eye color, but the rest doesn't match."

"Well, let's dig deeper. I want you to pull up her eyelid and verify the color."

Shawn had responded to a few scenes but he had never dug this deep. This would be a little more difficult to do than it had been with the driver. Her head was twisted at a macabre angle, and to move it would require Shawn to pull it from under her body and twist it against her broken neck. Under the watchful eye of Cameron, he carefully positioned her head. Feeling the neck bones grind against one another caused bile to rise in his throat. Concentrating, repressing the urge to vomit, he lifted her eyelid. He looked up at Cameron, shaking his head. In a broken voice, he murmured, "It's brown."

"The passenger was short with blond hair and brown eyes, the driver tall, with both brown hair and brown eyes," Cameron remarked. He turned and handed the driver's license to Matt and told him to run Mark Springfield's name for any aliases and to run the vehicle registration.

Five minutes later, Matt returned. "Mark Springfield lives in D.C, drives an F150, and has no aliases, but get this, he works for the CIA. This car, however, belongs to one Martin Powell."

Cameron stepped back and looked at the traffic. It was finally moving. Even though the accident wasn't blocking the entire road people still had the tendency to rubber-neck and back up traffic for miles. At least they had one lane open.

On his last night as a patrol officer he would make an unpopular decision. He had his men pull the tow trucks and all rescue vehicles. "Shut it down," he told Matt. "I want this whole area taped off. Halt all movement around the vehicle. This is now a crime scene."

14

September 22nd 2008
Richmond, Virginia

Mark made his way back to the coffee shop around closing time. He had hoped to sit and talk with Helen.

"Come for another cup of tea?" From behind the counter, Helen was counting her register. The place smelled of disinfectant and had been wiped down. The pastries that had once filled the case were no longer there.

"Did I come at a bad time?"

"Well it's just about quitting time, young man, but I'm sure I can rustle up some tea."

"That would be great, and maybe we can sit down and talk about me making you an offer you can't refuse," he replied with a smile.

Here, I'll sweeten the deal with these," Helen said as she set two cups of tea and a few scones on the table.

Mark chuckled and asked if she needed to call her husband.

"I make all the business decisions. Right from the start, he handled the store maintenance and hiring, and I ordered and paid the bills."

"Then let's get to it," Mark said with a raised scone.

"A man after my own heart," she said. "No messing around."

They hashed out the details and settled on a price. Helen offered to have her husband continue with maintenance. She was willing to stay on for a few months to help with the ordering.

"Thank you for your offer, but I think we're ready to jump in with both feet and take our lumps along the way," Mark countered.

"Well, Mr. Salvatore, if that's the way you want it, then so be it. I wish you the best of luck, but if you ever need me, please don't hesitate to give me a ring."

"Helen, my wife has come into a sum of money. Hopefully, we can close our deal within the next week. We'll have our banker call and transfer the funds when the lawyers finish up the fine print." They stood, and Mark held out his hand, but he wasn't fast enough. Helen leaned in and gave him a big hug.

Mark walked out of the coffee shop. He had been in this spot many times, sitting across from someone pretending to be somebody else. The stories he has had to fabricate during a covert operation, and their effect on civilians, had stopped bothering him a long time ago. He knew he was working towards the greater good. He liked Helen. She was a good example of what the nation was made of. She was a hardworking, honest, decent business woman who loved her country.

Mark headed back to Washington. He had been able to look at the house, meet his new employer at ATEC, and close the deal on the coffee shop. It had been a very productive day. A detour was in order. He called Mary from his cell to invite himself over for dinner. He loved seeing the girls and they loved seeing him. He needed a break from the hardened CIA operative he had become. He needed a moment to be his nieces' big teddy bear.

15

September 24th 2008
CIA Headquarters
Langley, Virginia

Mark met with Cliff House, the day after he closed the deal with Helen and finalized the details for the store. He turned the whole financial transaction over to the legal department who would act as Richard Salvatore's lawyers. Cliff ordered the architectural drawing of the coffee shop from their records department, and they went over the communication details with one of their best communication men, Jeremiah Thompson.

JT was like no other CIA operative Mark knew. His bowl-cut hair sat on a very round face, and his glasses were always perched on the tip of his nose. Mark often wondered how he ever passed the annual physicals with his short, pudgy stature. He would never make the CIA clandestine recruitment poster, but when it came to communications, he was one of the best.

They decided to convert one of the storage rooms into a secure lab, complete with an encrypted satellite communication uplink. The Satellite Communication room wouldn't need much space, and as JT pointed out, the smaller and more out of the way the room was, the easier it was going to be to pawn the whole place off as a decrepit coffee shop.

Cliff leaned back in his chair with a sly grin on his face. "Mark, we'll need to get you an assistant, someone to man the coffee shop and keep an eye on things while you're at ATEC, and I have the perfect person."

16

October 2ⁿᵈ 2008
CIA Headquarters
Langley, Virginia

After lunch, Danielle Minium stood before the director of the CIA looking nervous. Cliff introduced himself, Mark, and JT. She had no idea why she was there. She was put on the fast track for the vetting process and had been cleared that morning. The director stood, offered her a seat, and placed a phone call. Minutes later, the same woman who had had Mark signing papers in the oval office made her way into the room and sat with Danielle. Thirty minutes later, papers were signed and she was gone.

"Miss Minium," started the director, "thank you for joining us on such short notice. We have an assignment for you. You come highly recommended and your work on the Iranian communication project leads me to believe that this is right up your alley." Cliff turned towards Mark and JT, explaining how Danielle had almost single-handedly tapped the phone of the Iranian oil minister's mistress' which had helped the president determine how well the embargos were working. Danielle looked at the men and felt a little embarrassed. She hadn't realized her work had caught the attention of the director. "We're setting up Mr. Springfield in Richmond to try and trap whoever is leaking information on the Huntsville unit. Your job is to mind the store while he's out, and at night, you two will sift through secure communications."

Mark watched Danielle for several minutes. He could tell she was uneasy about being in the director's office. So in a matter-of-fact tone he proceeded, "Danielle, the shop's a front. Your job is to keep it open during the day and keep an eye on things. It should be pretty straightforward." They spent the next few hours explaining the work that had been done, Mark's infusion into ATEC, and the necessary specifics needed to carry out the plan. When they were finished, they asked if she had any questions.

"I have one. I'm to travel to Richmond, be away for maybe months, possibly a year, and if I have this right, I'm going to be a barista?"

The three men looked at each other and spontaneously broke into laughter. Danielle had taken the last two hours of detailed planning and accurately reduced her part to its simplest job.

17

April 24th 2009
Mary Springfield's Home
Outskirts of St. Charles, Maryland.
Just off Marshall Comer Rd

If it weren't for the dual pane windows Cole had installed two years earlier, Mark Springfield would be dead. The work expended by the bullet when it punctured the window increased with the thickness of the glass. The deflection of the bullet by the glass decreased its accuracy. The angle at which it hit the window caused the entire pane to explode sending glass shards across the room.

The muzzle energy of a .223 is one thousand eight hundred and ten foot pounds. Thanks to the shot angle and dual panes, something less than that had hit Mark. The deformed round raked across the bridge of his nose whipping his body to the right. Christina, who had been standing quietly with tears streaming down her face, suddenly screamed with an earsplitting intensity.

Mark had been moving toward Cole and was in front of Christina when it felt like he'd been clubbed in the face; his entire body toppled to the right. His training and instincts kicked in. Before the second shot was fired, he had recovered enough to throw his body over Cole and Christina. He heard the sound of glass crunching as Cole hit the floor. Christina continued to scream, and Mark quickly reached over and covered her mouth. "Shhh. It's going to be okay. Uncle Mark's got ya."

Christina's screams turned to uncontrollable sobs. She grabbed his shirt and pulled herself close to him. Mark stroked her hair while turning his attention to the outside, straining to listen. He watched Cole reach for Christina. But the look of pain on his face told him he was hurt. Cole lay back down.

The shooter took careful aim and pressed the trigger a second time sending the round through the same space as the first shot. If it hadn't been for Mark's quick reflexes, it would've been over. The round penetrated two interior walls and came to rest in an exterior stud. Cole, Christina, and Mark lay motionless on the floor.

In the distance, Mark heard sirens. They were faint, but he knew only minutes remained to get out. "Cole!

Listen to me. The police are on their way. Tell them you both need protective custody." He brought himself to his elbows and grabbed the pad of paper off the telephone stand. Another pane of glass suddenly exploded and the entire telephone shattered as the .223 passed through it and into the wall.

"Son of a bitch!" Cole screamed as shards of glass rained down. He tried to get up.

"Stay down!" Mark yelled. Mark glanced at Christina. She was lying in the fetal position, staring off into the distance, still sobbing. He was glad she wasn't trying to run but rage burned inside him as he watched her slowly rock back and forth. The sirens grew louder. He was sure the shooter would soon leave. He wrote a number and handed the pad to Cole. "Here, have them call this guy."

Cole's voice shook as he asked, "Who's this?"

"The director of the CIA."

Cole looked up at Mark and his jaw went slack. For the first time, he noticed the collar of Mark's shirt was caked with dried blood and the top of his ear was gone. His face was cut up from the glass, and there was a gash across his nose. A well of emotion hit as he looked at Mark and gasped, "Oh my God! Mary, Ashley..."

"Cole, listen to me, I'll find them." Mark moved carefully around Christina. He crawled towards the back door. Mark made it out the back before the four St. Charles police cruisers skidded to a stop. With his Glock in hand, he methodically moved through the back yard. When he was at a safe distance, he hunkered down, and waited for the police to enter the house. Once they did, he headed north for the train tracks.

18

October 14th 2008
Richmond, Virginia

Soon after he returned from Richmond, the house deal was finalized. A week later, the Coffee Hut was in their names, Richard and Colleen Salvatore. Since his wife would never make the trip to town, he would hire someone new, a young, black-haired, blue-eyed barista named Danielle Walters. Things were falling into place, and soon they would be operational.

Mark and Danielle took a crash course in running a coffee shop with the intent of sabotaging it. One way to keep most people away was to keep the place looking unkempt. The next step was for Mark to move to Richmond, start with ATEC, build and set up the communications room in the coffee shop, then open the shop for business. It was during this time that Mark and Danielle became close. He started referring to her as Dannie, and she started to spend more and more time making dinner at his house. Keeping a low profile outside the business was important. They couldn't draw any undue attention to themselves. They couldn't afford to be talked about by the local townsfolk. She altered her appearance anytime she was in public in case she was needed later for an additional role.

Jeremiah Thompson pulled up at the Coffee Hut in a green van with a *Richmond Plumbing* logo on the side. Mark met him at the front door, and in a purposefully loud, yet friendly voice, greeted him with rambling exclamations about how they had a huge plumbing problem. JT's cover was perfect. He looked more like a plumber than an agent. Wearing beige coveralls, sporting pens in his pocket, and carrying a large red tool box, he exclaimed, "I'm the man for the job."

Once inside with the door closed, Mark turned to JT. "Good morning, you remember Danielle?"

"A young lady who's hard to forget," JT said with a grin. "Looks a little messy in here Danielle."

"Then our goal has been met." Danielle chuckled. "Follow me,"

"Hey, Mark, nice touch outside. You never know who's listening."

Mark had made sure the door was locked and the *Closed* sign was in full view outside, then he followed them to the storeroom that he and Danielle had been converting into their communication site. Once inside, JT went about his work. He started with setting up the security system for the room. They needed to know who was outside the coffee shop and around the perimeter of the building whenever the room was being used, and it needed to be locked down when not in use. JT was a perfectionist. His security system could rival the Pentagon's. His camera system was expertly hidden in the sprinkler system and the retina scan was placed just before the door on the right, hidden inside the electrical breaker panel. It had a three-second delay in order to scan, then open the door.

Day two brought a secure satellite phone complete with the newest crypto engine with the strongest and most secure algorithms available. Once his power supplies were installed, the SAT phone was up and running, and his alarms activated, he turned to Mark. "I have a surprise for you tomorrow."

"You're not done? What else is left?" Danielle asked, half laughing.

"You'll see tomorrow." With that, he grabbed his tool box and headed for his van. As he drove off, he said, "I'll see you at 7:00 a.m." He drove back to Washington, D.C.

Mark waited for Danielle to call. They had a standing date every Tuesday at his house for dinner. To the outsider, it might look like he's having an affair so she would park at Upper School and walk the block to his house in the shadows. When she didn't show up, he became worried. And she still hadn't shown up by the time JT arrived the next morning.

JT pulled up at exactly 7:00 a.m. in a very old pickup truck that looked like it had trouble making it across town. On the door was written *Ernie's Handyman*. JT jumped out, and pulled low over his head was his *Ernie's Handyman* ball cap. Mark met him outside the door. They shook hands like they had never met. "Good morning, Mr. Salvatore. I have that new door for ya."

"Come on in, Ernie, and I'll show ya where she goes."

Inside the shop, Mark turned to JT. "Door? You brought us a door?"

JT motioned Mark to follow. "Join me. It's heavy." Out at the truck, he pulled down the tailgate and flipped a side of the tarp to reveal an old brown door. "Mr. Salvatore, I'll pull this out, grab the other end, and we'll get 'er in."

JT left the tarp on as he pulled it from the truck. Mark damn near dropped it when he grabbed the end from the tail gate. By the time he made it to the coffee shop, he was out of breath.

"Why's your face so red?" JT asked, laughing. He knew he was carrying the light end.

"Don't be a smart ass. I didn't expect that."

Inside, JT looked around. "Where's Danielle?"

"Not quite sure," Mark said hesitantly.

"Well, here's your surprise, a brand new, old-looking, seven rod steel security door."

"Holy shit, it looks like wood!"

"Supposed to," JT added, still smiling over Mark's red face. During the next few hours, they removed the old door, reinforced the hinge side, hung the new door, drilled and installed the steel rod sleeves, and powered up their new security door. Just as they were testing the room and setting the locks, there was a pounding on the front door. Mark looked from behind the counter and let out a low groan. It was Helen Wieger.

"JT, I need you to tell the woman at the door I'm not here, and she can't come in. She's the old owner, and I'm sure she is simply curious about what's going on here."

"Okay, but whatever you do, do not close this door."

Mark gave his partner a small grin. He knew JT liked electronics and his gadgets; he did not like talking to people. Mark stayed in the back while JT met with Helen. All he could hear was mumbling, then in a clear voice heard, "Well, Ernie, I'm comin' in! If Mr. Salvatore was using my husband I wouldn't worry, but I'm gonna make sure he's getting his money's worth!"

Damnit, Mark turned and ran to the storage room. Moments later, a sound resonated through the coffee shop that made JT's heat sink. Seven steel rods engaged their sleeves from a door that had not yet been programmed to open.

19

April 24th 2009
Behind Mary Springfield's Home
Outskirts of St. Charles, Maryland.

Mark ran inside the tree line on the opposite side of the train tracks. From this vantage point, he was able to see if someone emerged from the wooded area. Next stop was to Ashley's dance class, but staying alive was his first priority. One thing he had learned over the years was patience. "Never be in a hurry to get killed," was the motto he had heard over and over from his instructors at Quantico.

He stopped, turned in the opposite direction, knelt down, and took a deep breath. Up until then, his training and experience had kept him focused, compartmentalizing the events. Now, kneeling in the woods, he was able to assess the last few days. His cover was blown, he'd been attacked by his partner and lover, and now he'd been shot while at his sister's house with no regard for anyone else. As he rested, he started to feel the pain. Adrenaline had carried him this far, but now he would have to will himself further. He knew that if he were to be seen in public bloody and with cuts on his face, someone would surely call the police, but he had to make it about five miles to Ashley's dance class. He pulled his phone from his pocket and called his boss - no answer. Not unusual. But, what *was* unusual was that the phone rang two times then disconnected, and it happened every time he tried. There was no way to leave a message. Next, he tried to call the director of OSO. Same thing, two rings and a disconnect. Without trying anyone else, he called his house. Nothing. "My phone's being jammed," he said quietly to himself. Suddenly, the tree next to his head exploded.

The round slammed into the tree inches from his head. He was hit, not only with pieces of bark, but with the concussive force from the impact of the .223. It knocked him off his feet. He rolled down a small embankment. Staying low, he crawled behind a cluster of trees and lay there. Not only was his phone being jammed, it was being tracked. Mark had been on the defensive from the moment he walked into the coffee shop. He'd been shot at before, just not so many times in one day, and he was tired of it. He pushed the emotions he felt for his family to the farthest recesses of his mind and focused on the task at hand.

Without making any sudden movements, he carefully removed the battery, wiped it on his sweaty arm, and replaced it. He dialed his home number then quietly pushed the phone into the ground covering its cooling vents, and crawled about twenty feet. He cautiously turned back towards the tracks and waited. He kept his Glock holstered the entire time. He knew a shooter with a long gun had the advantage. Trying to make a shot under duress with a handgun over long distances, was a waste of ammo, and in a gun fight, there were two things that there was never enough of - ammo and time. Better to save them both until he had the tactical advantage. The shooter, whoever it was, was a professional. It would take all of Mark's self-control to wait it out, but it wouldn't be long. Neither of them was leaving until one of them was dead.

Snap!

Mark heard a small tree branch breaking under the shooter's foot. He strained his ears, listening for anything. Nothing. He waited. Seconds seemed like hours.

"Stand up, Mr. Springfield." Mark looked over his shoulder. A very tall, thin man held a rifle aimed at Mark. "Only when I kill you, will you fall."

Forcing himself against the pain, Mark pushed himself up, turned, and faced the shooter.

"I watched you kill Danielle. It will give me great pleasure to return the favor."

"Why didn't you kill me in Richmond?"

"It was not time, and if it wasn't for your nieces screams and their neighbors calling the police, I would've killed the three of you back at the house."

"You would kill civilians? My family?" Mark ground out the question with clenched teeth.

"It would've given me much enjoyment. Like you, Mr. Springfield, Danielle meant a great deal to me."

Like me! Mark thought. *Was this man Danielle's lover.* In the moonlit night he could see the whites of the shooter's eyes. Everything else was a dark silhouette against the night sky.

"Where's my sister?"

"Doesn't matter. I will kill you and send a photo of your dead body to my partners, who will show it to Mary."

Mark's jaw clenched at the mention of her name. He wanted to lunge at the shooter's throat and squeeze the life out of him, but he knew that was suicide. He had to wait and hope a chance presented itself. Then he would silence this snake.

Mark taunted him, trying to stall. "Do you know who made love to Danielle every night?"

With a sneer, the man answered, "Do you know who will make Mary scream tonight?" He was bluffing. Mark was sure of it. If nearly three decades with the CIA had taught him anything, it was how to read people.

First, a loud *ping*, then a long sizzle, followed by an intense red glow caused the shooter to glance over his left shoulder. When he did, he lowered and slightly swept his Bushmaster to the left.

In that instant, a lifetime of training paid off. By the time the shooter realized his mistake, Mark had already swept his jacket, presented his weapon, and had it pointed at the center of mass in four-tenths of a second.

The shooter froze. They both listened to the cell phone's overheated battery fizzle out. Mark, one of the CIA's most-respected agents, prided himself on not using much profanity, but on this night, in this moment, he uttered a hard "Fuck You" as he pressed his trigger.

Two solid reports could be heard across St. Charles as the .40 caliber hydra-shoks slammed into the shooter's torso. He felt like he had been hit with a battering ram. The energy expended from the rounds threw him ten feet. He dropped his rifle and the shooter was unconscious before he hit the ground.

Mark cautiously walked up and kicked the rifle off to the left then stooped low to check his pulse. It was faint with shallow breathing. His shirt was already soaked with blood. *He'll be gone soon,* Mark thought. He pulled off the ski mask. Mark instantly recognized the sandy hair and blue eyes from the coffee shop as one of three who had been sitting at the table. It was clear now. Danielle had been passing information the whole time.

Mark scanned the area and listened intently for anything out of place. Other than his breath and the faint sounds of the distant city, the tree line was quiet. He relaxed a bit and leaned against a tree. Exhausted and hurt, he slid down the trunk. His survivor euphoria was short lived. He was sick about Mary. Now, he was sure they had her. Sitting on the ground in the still of the night, he could think. He had to make it to Ashley's studio and find out if she was ok, contact his boss, and find Mary. But first, he had to take care of his friend.

The shooter was wearing black cargo pants, a long-sleeved black t-shirt, gloves, and a ski mask. Mark didn't expect to find much, but looked anyway. Extra magazines and a phone were all he found. Clipped to one of his lower pockets was a device that displayed his cell number. *This is how you followed me and jammed my phone,* he thought. He knew Danielle must have given him his number.

How could I have missed it? Mark thought as he stood. That morning when Danielle didn't show to help set up the room with him and JT. Her excuse claiming she was sick hadn't felt right. And she had become distant when they were in the final planning stages. Once, she even disappeared outside. He would blame himself for missing the signs he should've picked up. They had been there in front of him. He was romantically involved and had let his guard down.

Mark stared at the tracking device while flipping it over in his hand. Looking down at the shooter he said "And who were you to Danielle?"

He clipped the tracking device to his pocket. A thin smile crossed his face. Mark reached down and grabbed the shooter's belt with both hands.

Walking away, he looked back to see the body lying across the tracks. A slow menacing smile emerged on his face. Mark knew a train would be along anytime.

20

November 18th 2008
Richmond, Virginia

The steel door that JT and Mark had hung in the coffee shop made a very mechanical sound when it closed. The noise from the seven locking rods engaging startled Helen. She turned to JT, "What was that?"

Thinking fast, he retorted, "Well, that was probably the cooling units in our counters. Been acting up lately. I think it's the refrigeration. Been making quite the racket the last few days."

"My husband's been keeping this place ship-shape for a while. Maybe I should tell him to stop by."

JT gave her his *I'm offended* look. "No, ma'am. That won't be necessary. That's what I'm here for. Been makin' small repairs here and there and that's my next project." He slowly walked her towards the door and was very relieved when she finally stepped out onto the sidewalk.

He closed the door, locked it, and then breathed a sigh of relief. Leaning against the door, he muttered, "I hate people." He walked across the shop and grabbed his tool box. He smiled as he pulled out a satellite phone and wondered what Mark would do when he heard the phone buzz in the room. Hopefully, he would remember how to answer it. He punched in the encryption, then the number, and waited.

*　　*　　*

When Helen came into the coffee shop, Mark had needed to hide fast. He ran into the communication room and closed the door. He remembered that JT had told him if the power failed, the door would automatically lock. Not knowing how to lock it, he had pulled the power supplies and the bolts engaged. After about 10 minutes, he heard the satellite phone buzz. He picked it up, punched in his code, hit SECURE COM, and heard laughing on the other end. "Damn you, JT! How do I get out of here?"

"I heard the bolts engage and thought, now we'll have to take my beautiful door apart." For the next twenty minutes, JT explained how to disassemble the lower door exposing the back-up battery and locking mechanism.

91

Once there, Mark disconnected the solenoid that actuates the rods. Using a wrench from JT's tool bag, he worked the retract cam until the rods were pulled back into the door.

Mark stepped through the door sweating and waving his hands. "Fans," he said. "We need fans in there!"

They spent the rest of the day putting the door back together. Then they set the retina scan, and JT showed Mark how to arm and disarm the alarms. Seconds before they were ready to leave, Danielle came through the door.

"Where the hell have you been? We've been here all day and could've used the extra help. Get your butt over there and grab those spools of wire and get'm out to the truck."

When JT walked out of the shop, Danielle turned to Mark and gave him a knowing grin. She knew they had to keep up appearances even with JT.

When the three of them had finished loading the truck, JT opened the door to the cab and slid inside. He looked at Mark and said, "Well, I'd like to stay and have you buy me dinner, but it's back to school night for my son and I can't be late."

He gave JT a puzzled look through the side window. "I didn't know you were married?" In all the time they had spent together, he had never once mentioned his family.

"Sure am, eighteen years." JT leaned forward and reached for his wallet, proudly producing a picture of his wife and a young man who appeared to be about thirteen years old.

Mark gave him a confused look. The woman in the picture was extremely attractive. JT was a squat bald-headed man who didn't exactly exude an aura of sex appeal. Mark cleared his throat and said, "JT, she's beautiful," while handing the picture back.

"Andrea and Thomas John, the loves of my life. Don't know what she sees in me." He laughed as he tucked his wallet in his back pocket. JT stuck his head out of the side window. "Ok, you can get that stupid look off your face. Happens every time I show someone her picture."

Mark started laughing. "Well, you tell them the guy you've been spending so much time with sends his best." Mark slapped the side of the truck to send him on his way.

"I'll do that." JT smiled as he accelerated down the road.

Once JT had ambled down the road in his rickety truck, Mark turned to Danielle as they walked into the coffee shop.

"And where have you been, young lady?" he asked quietly.

"I'm sorry, Mark. I felt sick last night and lay down, for a few minutes. I fell asleep." Mark looked at her with a raised eyebrow. "I should've called, but I pretty much stayed in bed all day. I think I'm just too run down."

Mark grabbed her shoulders squaring her off, "I will *not* be out of communication with my agents. If you need time off, ask. What we have going on here is far too important. The last thing I need is to worry about my team." He turned, headed back towards the back room and went through the entry procedures to unlock the door.

Danielle followed. Once they were away from the front of the shop and out of view of the windows, she grabbed him, spun him around, and kissed him hard on the lips, pushing him into the door. Mark, taken by surprise, pushed her away. His stare pierced her with the intensity of a new lover. Her perfume was intoxicating. He was about to cross a line and couldn't stop. "My house," Mark had heard himself say.

Danielle leaned in and whispered into his ear. "Thirty minutes."

Mark felt her hot breath wash over his ear and down his neck as she kissed it softly.

Mark gently pushed her away. "This is wrong. We should stay focused until we finish this up."

Danielle shook her head. "I don't care. I'll see you in thirty minutes." Mark looked back at the door, then once again at Danielle. He reached out and opened the door. Then he closed it to reengage the locking mechanisms. They took the next day off.

The following Monday, Mark had started with ATEC. He spent the first day filling out paperwork and getting familiar with the grounds. He decorated his small cubical with diplomas. Richard A. Salvatore was written on every one. There were even a few wedding and family photos showing his fictitious wife, Colleen. All compliments of the CIA's Director of Intelligence Division Multimedia Producers. At eight o'clock the next morning, his boss showed up carrying a roll of drawings and introduced himself. "Hi, I'm Mike Vanns."

"Good morning. Rick Salvatore," Mark replied as he extended his hand.

"I understand you're going to help miniaturize our power supply?"

Mark watched his new boss while they made small talk. He instantly liked him. He seemed friendly. He was a few inches shorter than Mark, had black curly hair, broad shoulders and if his crushing handshake was an indicator, he was in fair shape.

"Well, I've done some work with other aspects of the program. Apparently, they like what I did, and thought I could help here. So, here I am."

"Anybody who's a friend of the OSO is a friend of ours. This could mean quite a bit more business if we can figure this out."

"I'll do what I can."

"Thanks, Rick. Take a look at these drawings and tell us what you think." As he turned to leave, he asked, "Hey, what else have you worked on?"

"You know, I can't say. I left with some bad feelings so it's just as well." Mark had just cast his first net.

21

November 24th 2008
Richmond, Virginia

Mark heard Danielle let herself in the back door as she had done so many times over the last week. She parked down the street close to the local elementary school. It was an easy walk in the shadows of the low-hanging trees that lined the path to his house. It was a fiery new relationship and they spent most of their free time under the sheets in intimate exploration. Mark knew that starting a personal relationship with Danielle might seriously complicate the investigation. He had liked Danielle from the start and had tried to keep his libido in check. He had never seen himself with a redhead before, but her sexual energy was overpowering. He had actually been relieved when she had made the first move.

She flipped her hood down when she walked in the house, removed her wig and contacts, and laid everything on a shelf in the outer room. "Hellooo..." she shouted.

"In the kitchen," he yelled back.

"How was your first day at work, dear?" she asked jokingly as she wrapped her arms around his neck.

"Great. Met my boss, a few coworkers, and worked in my cubical. I couldn't do that for twenty years!" he said. "I took some information from the power supply I'm supposedly working on. I'll need it transmitted to Cliff so he can have the guys look it up and help me find a way to miniaturize it. I'm in way over my head with this stuff. I'm sure there've been lots of changes in the electronics field since I've been in school."

She leaned in and gave him a long, soft kiss. "I'll take care of it first thing tomorrow," she murmured in his ear.

"How was your day?" he asked as he turned back towards the counter.

"Well, let's see... I made a few drinks and sold a few pastries. That about sums it up. However, I am getting pretty good at this barista thing."

"I bet you never knew you'd be putting your college degree to such good use. Join the CIA and work in a small, out-of-the-way coffee shop."

"Nope, that wasn't in the job description," she retorted.

"Yes, it was. It's under *And Other Duties Assigned.*" They both smiled at the old *catch-all* phrase.

Over the next few months, Mark worked diligently on the power supply. Of course, he had help. The teams at CIA headquarters were some of the best, and even JT took an interest. With the advancements Mark was making, the folks at ATEC thought he was a genius, and that helped him with his story. He spent many hours in the lab testing his designs, often with coworkers. Without being too obvious, he would quietly complain about not being appreciated for his contributions.

At night, he reported to the OSO, kept them apprised of any information they may have collected. The head of the OSO was a good source for rumors, but it was always the same...no one knew anything. Mark started to wonder if he'd ever get a bite or if there was a leak at all.

Mark left early Thursday and headed to the coffee shop for an early visit to 'the room'. He and Dannie would go over communications that were sent to them which had been collected from the different embassies and whatever the spooks pulled out of the air over at the NRO. Since Mark was working within the ATEC organization, he would often meet with engineers and technicians from different locations as they tried to integrate the power supply. After hours in 'the room,' he was tasked with reviewing data and paid specific attention to the Chinese Embassy transcripts.

Mark parked his car and walked the block to the coffee shop. He happened to look up just before he entered and saw the sign. It read *Coffee Huut*. What the hell?

He walked to the counter and was greeted with, "May I help you?"

All clear, he thought. As he walked in, he observed three people sitting at a table and instantly took notice of their features. Tall male, Caucasian, brown hair and eyes, pointy noise. Short female, Caucasian, blond, brown eyes, nicely dressed. Tall, skinny male, Caucasian, sandy hair. He took notice of everything and ordered a hot tea.

Mark took his tea to one of the round tables by the window and opened the newspaper he had grabbed from the stand. He half-heartedly read it until the others left. He looked at Danielle and motioned with a nod of his head to 'the room' as he started to go that way. Danielle locked the door, put up the *Back in One Hour* sign, and followed Mark.

"They've been here long?"

"Not too, why?"

"They seemed to become a little uncomfortable when I walked in."

"Sorry, didn't notice." She pointed to the breaker box. "Shall we?"

Mark opened the door, leaned in, and scanned his eye. Once he was in, he punched in his encryption code and the secure fax started spitting out pages of data. Danielle checked to make sure he didn't need anything else and went back out front. He spent the next two hours going over communications and was eventually joined by Danielle after she closed up shop. When inside the room, she took off her wig and shook out her hair. Mark thought she looked stunning. He soon forgot about the three customers at the table and his feeling of unease.

No matter how he read the communications, no matter what slant he put on them, he could not find a hint of a leak concerning the Huntsville unit. He did, however, uncover several affairs at the diplomat level. He simply noted it and moved on. He glanced at the time, 11:30 p.m. It was time to call it quits. As they walked outside, Mark looked up at the sign above the door, 'Coffee Huut', then at Danielle and raised his eyebrow.

Mark assumed that earlier Danielle had taken down the sign and repainted it. Unbeknownst to Mark, Danielle was testing him. She had added the extra 'u' to the word Hut. She knew Mark would never allow the word Huut to be displayed for all to see, unless his emotional attachment to her was starting to cloud his judgment. She needed to know how far she could go, how much she could get away with.

"Thought it appropriate," she shrugged while suppressing a smile. They went their separate ways.

22

March 10th 2009
Richmond, Virginia

Mark sat in his cubical looking at his fake wedding photos and started to think that it might be time for him to truly settle down. As he thought about what could've been and what could be, his thoughts drifted towards his sister. *They're able to make it work,* he thought. *If I apply for a more stable position, I could get out of the field and stop worrying about never being home.*

"Excuse me, Rick. Rick!"

"Oh, I'm sorry." Mark turned and saw his boss standing at his cubical entrance. "Good morning, Mike."

He laughed. "I think I caught you daydreaming."

"No, just wondering how my wife can spend so much money."

"Trouble?"

"Not really. What can I do for you?"

"Wanted to know if you're ready for the test this afternoon?" Mike inquired anxiously.

"I think so," Mark said as he rolled back in his chair.

"Rick, I can't believe the progress you have made in such a short time. How about I buy you lunch today?"

"I'm in!" Mark worked in the lab most of the morning preparing to test the smaller version of the power supply. Actually, he realized, the unit was, indeed, going to be useable, and he was proud of his and the agency's accomplishments.

* * *

Sitting in a high-back wooden booth in the corner at the pizza place, they shared a pitcher of beer. Mike was a different person in the seclusion of the booth. He became a little too attentive. "Rick, how come I haven't met your wife?"

"She was just here. Went up to visit her mom in D.C."

"Sorry to be nosey, but earlier you said she spends a lot of money. Everything ok? I hate to have a good man distracted because of home." Mike kept pushing the point.

Mark took a long drink of beer and cautiously hesitated before he answered, "Yeah, we're ok, thanks."

"You've been doing a great job for us, and I think we can sell this power supply of yours to the OSO. That'll mean big dollars for the company and maybe a bonus for you!" He grinned and lifted his beer slightly in a toast.

"Well, I could use the money, for sure, but I won't hold my breath. I helped make a huge leap for the last place and all it got me was a pat on the back and a dinner certificate. I worked my ass off! Of course, my wife had to buy a new dress and shoes and have her hair done to go to dinner. Jesus. Mike, does your wife have a closet full of hats, dresses, shoes, scarves, and God knows what else? All kinds of shit? I love her, and she loves shopping, but I'm not made of money!" Mark leaned forward and groaned, grabbed the pitcher, and poured another.

At the same time, Mike stood, excused himself, and headed toward the restroom. Mark looked over his shoulder. When Mike was out of view he poured the beer in the planter next to the booth. He grabbed the pitcher and slowly started pouring another. He hoped his ramblings were doing the trick.

"Hey, slow down there! We have a test this afternoon," Mike said as he came from the back.

"Sorry, Mike. I think I've had too much. I guess it's been bothering me more than I thought."

"Well, let's finish up and get back. I'll get the bill and meet you out front."

As Mark walked towards the door, he knew this had not been merely a friendly lunch with a concerned boss asking personal questions. This felt like an interrogation.

23

April 24th 2009
Outskirts of St. Charles, Maryland.

The shooter drifted in and out consciousness. He became slightly conscious while feeling a hum through his entire body, no, a vibration. He forced opened his eyes. In the moonlight, the train tracks faintly came into view. Slowly, he became aware that he was lying on the ground. He smelled the creosote-soaked wooden ties. In a horrifying instant, he knew where he was. He tried to move, but couldn't. His blood loss was too great. His mind screamed, "Move!"

The light came into focus. His mind was still screaming, and the vibration felt like thunder.

Yuri Kovaleskiaka's quest for 'the huut' was over.

24

April 24th 2009

Mark headed away from the train tracks, into the housing development and back towards the street. He cut through backyards and found one with a swimming pool. Mark took the opportunity to clean up. He brushed the dirt off his pants and carefully pulled pieces of glass from the shattered window panes from the cuts on his face and arms. He took the handkerchief from his breast pocket and dipped it into the swimming pool. After ringing it out, he wiped his face. When the chlorine hit his cuts, it burned like hell, but a thin smile crossed his lips when he heard the train go by. He took off his shirt and shook out the glass and debris. He wiped his arms and again dusted off his pants. He thought he must look homeless, and that gave him an idea.

He made his way to the street and hitched a ride in the back of a pickup. When the truck slowed for a stoplight close to Three Chopt Road. and Patterson, he jumped from the truck and ran behind a grocery store where he found a cart. He rummaged through the dumpster and filled the cart with odds and ends. He took off his jacket, rolled it, and placed it in the cart along with his shoes. He wrapped his tie several times around his forehead and pulled out his shirt tails to cover his firearms. He looked down over his disguise. He was hiding in plain sight.

Sluggishly, and without purpose, he began to walk to the Village Dance studio. He pushed the cart across the street, paying close attention to everything and everyone. As he rounded the building, he saw, at the end of the plaza, no less than a dozen police and agency cars.

He ambled along aimlessly, checking trash cans and picking up the occasional can or plastic bottle while singing softly to himself. To the general public, the homeless were typically invisible. Mark was able to get close to the scene without being noticed. By the time he arrived, the cops were wrapping up. The last of two ambulances was driving off. Cole and the girls were sitting in the back of one of the cruisers with two burly police officers in front. One of them had his head turned. He was smiling, and joking with the girls. Cole was slumped forward, his head in his hands. Behind their car sat a black Suburban with blacked out windows. Mary was nowhere to be seen. Mark's fears were realized. He felt ill. Knowing Mary was not there made him want to vomit. *Stay focused*, he told himself.

He turned and headed back towards a Target store he had passed earlier. He took his clothes from the shopping cart and walked into the store. He went directly to the restroom where he put himself back together the best he could. It was time for a little shopping. Jeans, T-shirt, black sneakers, and a blue baseball cap completed his ensemble. Until he could figure this out, he had to lie low and stay off the grid. When he checked out, he paid cash. He tossed the cap on his head and headed towards the door. On his way out, he noticed a phone impression in the front pocket of an employee's smock. He accidentally, on purpose, bumped into her, easily lifted the phone and dropped it into his bag. Once outside, he walked through the plaza, scanning the area to see who was nearby. When he was sure he was not being watched, he opened the phone and placed a call to his boss.

The phone rang and went to message. Mark breathed a sigh of relief. At least this time he got through. He knew Cliff wouldn't answer a number he didn't recognize so he left a very generic message. "Mr. House, I need to talk to you." He knew the number would appear on Cliff's phone and ended his call.

Mark had been on the move all day. He had been damn near killed, and was physically and mentally exhausted, and hungry. He walked into a coffee shop, which he thought ironic and ordered a hot tea, with a ham and cheese croissant. He sat at a table in the far corner where he could watch the door and sipped his tea trying to make sense of the day.

He had killed Danielle. His family had almost ended up the same way, and Mary was missing. He pulled the shooter's phone from his pocket and looked at it while he turned it over in his hand. He had turned it off so it was of no use. Maybe if he were somewhere with a poor signal he could turn it on and go through it. It was probably password protected, so he ruled it out. The risk of it being tracked was too great.

Twenty-four hours ago, he was ready to tell Dannie that he loved her, he had had a good lead on the mole, and his sister Mary was safe and happy. It had been too much, too fast. He sat back, thinking, *Hang in there, Mary.* Then, to no one whispered, "Why, Dannie? Why?" Mark stared at his croissant. As he started to unwrap it, the phone began to ring. As he reached for it, he noticed he was being approached by a police officer.

25

March 10th 2009
Richmond, Virginia

The test at ATEC was a success. The miniature power supply provided enough volts to run the Aim Point Antenna in the space-born unit. It was still dropping too much heat for the surrounding mounting surface, but for the most part, it was a success. His lab partners thought he was a genius. Mark sat back glowing in his, and the agency's, accomplishment. After months of digging through hours of communications, there was still no leak, and Mike was turning out to be simply a concerned boss. Mark and his co-workers broke down the set up and cleaned up for the day. Mark stayed late to finish the paperwork, formalize the results, and note the calibration dates of the equipment.

As he was logging off his computer, Mike walked into his office, grabbed a chair, and sat close to Mark. "I've been thinking about your situation, Rick. You should talk to someone." He handed Mark a yellow piece of paper. "Take a look at that when you get home." Then as suddenly and abruptly as he had appeared, he stood and left.

"No shit," Mark mumbled as he stuffed the paper in his pocket. This was either a marriage counselor or my net may have something in it. He liked Mike and hoped it was a counselor.

Mark sat in his car a block from the Coffee Huut and opened the yellow piece of paper. 81834126.154511810186713 was all that was written.

After four months of looking, it was his first confirmed contact. He had a hit. In the coffee shop, he approached the counter and was greeted by Dannie with the normal, "May I help you?"

He smiled. "I'll have the usual." He took a seat at the table, scanning the room and what he could see of the outside.

She set the tea on the table and quietly said, "Your mood has changed."

He stood. "I need to make a call," gave her a wink and headed for 'the room'. Once inside, he loaded his encryption and called his boss. "Cliff, we got a hit."

"Finally! I was beginning to think I sent you on a vacation complete with a car and a house."

Mark pulled the paper from his pocket, copied it, and then faxed it to his boss. "We'll need to run these numbers through Ramous." Ramous was their code breaker, a machine that processed number and letter combinations faster than any machine Mark had ever seen. It was named after, Ramous Bohdan, an operative who was killed in the line of duty in Russia. Mark couldn't say the name without getting choked up at the thought of his old friend. Ramous was to have been contacted by an officer from the Russian Navy with plans to photograph their submarine communication codes. Mark had been working with other agents to plan his escape through Germany. Days before the extraction, Ramous was found and killed in the town of Murmansk, just south of Severomorsk, headquarters for the Russian Northern Fleet. It was an operation of which the American people would never hear.

For Ramous' service, his wife received his pension and Ramous got a star on 'the wall.' The CIA Memorial Wall is one of the first things visitors see when entering the original headquarters building lobby. Located on the lobby's north wall, it stands as a silent memorial to those

CIA employees who gave their lives in the service of their country.

It had been a hard blow to the department and to Mark personally, but there was nothing he could do about it. He had been in Germany ready to receive his friend and fellow agent when they lost contact. Mark, too, had narrowly escaped when agents from the Sluzhba Vneshney Razvedki (SVR), Russia's External Intelligence Service, had bled into the surrounding countries with the intent of tracking down Ramous' contacts. The KGB was dissolved in 1991 and replaced with the SVR, but it was purely for show. They retained the same leadership and mentality and continued to be as ruthless in their pursuit of foreign agents. Many were not taken alive. When he had returned to the states, Mark had had to debrief his superiors and help bury his friend. Without a body to lay to rest, it had left a gaping hole inside of him. An abyss he would look into every day. It was hard for Mark to face Ramous' wife and children. Even though they didn't know the details, he felt responsible. He made a silent promise to Ramous that he would take care of them until he died.

Three days went by and nothing had been resolved with the numbers. Why would they pass a code that is so hard to break? He had been sure Ramous would have it deciphered in a matter of minutes, but minutes had slipped into hours, and hours into days. Something about the number was familiar, but Mark couldn't put his finger on it. He was baffled. Ramous had thus far been unable to break the code.

"How 'bout we take a trip to St. Charles, and I meet your sister while we wait," Dannie suggested. "I'll close up shop, and we'll take a day or two off."

Mark gave Danielle a munched eyebrow stare. He didn't know how to answer. Many nights they had lain in bed, and on occasion he had talked about his sister and family. He and Dannie had been getting along great. He had never met someone to whom he had been so attracted. But to introduce her to his family? To give his sister hopes of her brother finally meeting someone he cared enough about to bring by to meet the family? The idea made him laugh. In the minutes he thought about his sister, he mulled it over. *It might not be a bad idea to get away for the weekend,* he thought. Then he said, "Danielle Minium, that is an excellent idea. We have been at it pretty hard. I will notify the powers that be that we're taking a few days off. If they need me, I'm just a cell phone call away."

Two hours later, they were headed up I-95 to St. Charles.

He called Mary and sheepishly asked if she would mind company for the weekend. "Cole and I were taking the girls to the Air and Space Museum in D.C., but this is rather epic. I'm sure the girls would love to see their uncle, and without a doubt, Cole and I want to meet your *friend*. We'll visit the museum another day."

Traffic on I-95 was light. It was a crystal clear day. He liked the idea of spending time with Dannie away from work. This was exactly what they needed. "Remember, if they ask what you do, you're my secretary," and with that, she punched him in the arm.

"How about I just say I'm your coworker?"

"Ok, you can be the *head* secretary," he retorted, and they bantered all the way to St. Charles. The thought of the hunt for the mole faded away temporarily, though still lingered at the recesses of their mind.

They pulled into the driveway at dusk and were met by both girls yelling and jumping on their uncle the moment he got out of the car.

"Uncle Mark, come look at my new bear Mommy got me."

Mark loved his nieces. Ashley, with her long black hair, smooth features, and long neck, was the spitting image of her mom. Mary and Cole didn't give Mark the time of day. They went straight for Danielle and welcomed her with open arms. They spent the next day taking in the sights of St. Charles, complete with a boat ride on the lake. At night, they sat outside on the patio soaking up the aroma from the ribs on the BBQ. The talk of the day on the lake turned to the boating trip they had taken to Catalina Island during a summer that Cole, Mary, and the girls had visited Mark in Los Angeles. Mark had routinely sailed when he worked in Los Angeles. It was a hobby he had picked up from one of his coworkers, and he had perfected it over several years. He had loved it and would find himself out in the Pacific every chance he got. Suddenly, it hit him, he knew why the numbers had seemed so familiar. The latitude was off but the longitude is what did it. It was close enough to be familiar and that gave his mind the piece of the puzzle that it needed. He had been subconsciously working the numbers the moment he had seen them.

Mark looked over at Dannie with a new look on his face. He had a telling look in his eye and from the look she returned, he knew she picked up on it immediately. The last two days he had been relaxed and having fun, something he hadn't seem to do outside of the bedroom. Normally, it was all about work. But this was an insightful look, and he wanted to share with Danielle. Danielle stood, excused herself, and went to the bathroom. Several minutes later, she called Mark into the house.

When he returned to the patio, he apologized to Mary and Cole and explained that Danielle wasn't feeling well so they would be leaving. Cole made a comment about Mary's cooking which Mark laughed about all the way to the door.

"You can't go, Uncle Mark!" yelled Ashley. "We haven't had our ice cream yet!"

He smiled, gave them all a big hug, and walked Danielle towards the car. She smiled weakly and put her hand over her midsection as she feigned symptoms of an upset stomach. Mark helped her into the passenger's seat.

As they drove down the driveway, he turned to Dannie and said, "We need to get to Richmond."

"Ok, tell me what you figured out."

He looked at her with a big smile.

"Oh, a smile even." She chuckled.

"I may have figured out the number, but I need a few minutes with a computer and a map I can pull GPS coordinates. It hit me when we were talking about boating and Catalina. I used a GPS every time I went sailing. The GPS coordinates for Two Harbors Catalina, which I saw every time the GPS was turned on, are 33-26'24" N 118-29'57" W. It was the 118 in the string of numbers. For some reason, it had been familiar. Maybe because it was preceded by the 34, I don't know. I couldn't put my finger on it, and then sitting on the patio, there it was. It occurred to me from out of nowhere."

"Slow down, Mr. Chatty, you haven't talked this much in a week," she said, laughing.

"Ok, ok... Let's get to 'the room' and a computer. I'll take a look and try to put it together."

"Do you plan on calling Mr. House?"

"No, not until I have something more than just a hunch."

Danielle pointed to a restaurant when they were four blocks from the coffee shop. Before she could say anything, Marks said. "That'll have to wait. I have to check this out." Danielle looked at Mark and stuck out her lower lip. Mark laughed and said. "Okay as soon as we're done." A few minutes later he parked in front of the coffee shop.

Mark sat in the room looking at the number 81834126.154511810186713. He was on his second attempt. Then, he simply started at the 118 and moved forward to 10' 18". He wrote the 6713 below the rest. Next, he backed up to the 34 and again moved forward for the minutes and seconds, 12 and 6.1. The number

818 545, and the number written below, 6713, were left. He put it together, and it was obvious - a phone number, 818 545 6713. What was left were GPS coordinates 34° 12' 6.1"

N, 118° 10' 18" W. Mark basked in the moment. He had figured it out. All he had to do was reference the number on the map to find out who owned the real estate.

Danielle was with him the entire time he had worked the numbers. She had made flattering commenting how nice it was to know such an intelligent person. "The agency only picks the best."

He finally looked at her. "If you're bucking for a raise, forget it!"

She laughed as she excused herself and headed for the restroom. She knew Mark would be preoccupied with the map he had just pulled up, so she headed for the door. Once outside she walked out of view of the surveillance cameras and placed a text, "He's figured out the numbers," and hit SEND.

Mark was just finishing up a call to JT when she returned. "You went outside?" he asked.

She looked at him a little startled. Suddenly worried she wasn't far enough away from the cameras. Then she thought, *how do I explain the text I just sent?*

"I know, you probably really don't feel well and needed some air," Mark said matter-of-factly.

Holy shit, he didn't see it. She went from fear to elation in a matter of seconds. *He really doesn't suspect anything,* she thought. She gave him a little peck on the cheek.

26

April 24th 2009
Coffee shop
St. Charles, Maryland

Mark's mind went into overdrive. Seeing the approaching police officer, he immediately ended the phone call.

"Excuse me, may I grab this chair?" asked the officer.

Mark kept a friendly look on his face but was concerned that being caught off-guard would show. "Yes, you can." S*hit! That could've gone bad,* he thought. Mark was rattled and it bothered him. He couldn't allow himself to be arrested. He had no idea who else was trying to kill him and he had to find Mary.

He exchanged some brief pleasantries with the officer and a few minutes later stood and left. A light rain was falling. As he walked through the plaza, he heard the wet leaves squish under his feet. It was spring, his favorite time of year, but he had no time for the luxury of dwelling on such pleasures. He had to find Mary. Again, he called Cliff.

"Hello," came a voice after one ring.

"Was that you in the Suburban?" asked Mark

"Yes. I gave your brother-in-law the unclassified version of your job. We're debriefing him now, then taking all of them to a safe house.

"Where's my sister?"

"Your niece, I believe Ashley, said her mom never showed up. I'm sorry, Mark."

"They're going to use her to get to me and if I find them..." Mark stopped himself. He wasn't about to express his next thought to the director of the CIA. "I need a new ID. I have to go to California."

"Mark, listen to me. Come in. We'll find Mary together."

"Can't. Set me up with a new ID and credit card. Have JT bring them to me. This phone will be turned off soon. It's hot. I stole it from a Target employee. Have him go to my sister's house. I'll meet him there tomorrow at four in the morning."

After a long pause, he heard, "Consider it done." It had taken Cliff thirty seconds to agree with Mark. Clearly he knew that short of throwing Mark in jail, there would be no way of stopping him.

"There's one more thing," Mark continued. "Danielle was turned." Those last three words caused Mark's voice to break.

"What!?" Mark imagined Cliff rising out of his chair. "She was recommended to me by Mrs. Littleton. Where is she now?"

"At the coffee shop in Richmond. Cliff, I killed her."

"Jesus," he gasped as he sat back down in his chair. "Your brother-in-law mumbled something about you killing someone, but he's in shock and hard to understand. The shop will need to be sanitized."

"It was loud. The police may have already been there."

Cliff heard the strain in Mark's voice. "Meet JT tomorrow; follow your gut to California. Do what's needed to get your sister back. I'll take care of Richmond."

By the time he made it back to Mary's house, his car was gone. He had figured as much. The agency didn't like loose ends. They had cleaned up the house, towed his car, and replaced the shattered panes that very night, as if it had never happened. Too bad, he had had a bug-out bag and extra ammo in the trunk.

Mark didn't like the fact that Mary's house sat on a dark road. But tonight with the moon low in the sky, it would be perfect for staying hidden. He waited just inside the tree line across the road. He'd been there for over two hours watching the house. Mark knew that early in the morning not many people would be out and was surprised when two cars quietly passed him heading towards St. Charles. He saw a dark sedan pass Mary's house. The driver looked unsure. He pulled off the road forty yards past Mark. Mark watched closely as the driver stepped from the car and look around. Mark scrutinized his movements. When the driver reached inside his coat, Mark knew he had drawn a firearm. The driver slowly and cautiously started walking back towards the house just off the road. As the person got closer, another passing car briefly lit up a small, heavy set man who was wearing glasses. "JT," Mark said in a hushed voice. JT was startled, but recognized Mark's voice and headed across the road. Mark led him into the trees and out of sight. "Am I glad to see a friendly face! Mind putting that thing away?" Mark said, pointing at JT's gun.

"Oh my God, Mark. Your sister, and Danielle?" JT said as he re-holstered his Glock. "The boss is digging up everything he has on Danielle. She's been on some pretty risky missions for the agency. Our boss had recommended her. Apparently, Danielle had caught her attention after the Iranian oil information was passed. The director thinks she must have been recently turned," he whispered as he handed Mark a slightly used wallet.

"Or it was all staged. She was building trust within the agency. She played me right from the start, had me introduce her to my sister on a supposed weekend getaway. We even had the occasional dinner together."

JT gave Mark a questioning look. Though curious, he had never asked about their relationship outside of work. JT was more comfortable with his electronics, not so much with people. He let Mark talk. It's what he needed to do.

"I just didn't see it coming, I just didn't see it…" Marks voice trailed off. He opened the wallet. Inside was a driver's license, a Visa and Mastercard, an AAA card, a few fictitious pictures and three hundred dollars in cash. "Let's see, who am I today? It's a strange business we're in JT, here one day, gone the next." Both men nodded in agreement. "What else do you have?"

"Yesterday, the agency got a hit on you."

"Where?"

"Seems the Highway Patrol out in California ran your name," JT said as he pulled out his notebook. "Ran your sister's as well. The officer that requested it was… Matt Hunter," he said, flipping through his notes. "The boss checked into it. Seems there was a major accident westbound on the I-210. Both driver and passenger were killed. Apparently, they had your driver's licenses." JT looked up at Mark's ashen face and grabbed his shoulder. "Wait, Mark, let me finish. Neither one of the people in the car matched the description on the licenses. That's why they called it in."

"Jesus, JT! How did I get my sister involved in this?"

"Here's the name and address of your driver while you were in California. We've had him under surveillance ever since. There's the name and number of the agents, office and cell numbers. The boss also wants you to have the patrolman's numbers." JT wasn't quite sure Mark was ready for his next bit of news but he needed to know the entire picture. "There's something else. The person behind your sister's house, on the tracks, was Yuri Kovaleskiaka. He's on a work visa from Russia and before that he had a student visa. He has a master's degree from Webster University." JT didn't have to say more. Mark instantly made the connection. He knew from the nights they had lain in bed talking that Danielle had attended Webster. Mark swallowed hard against the lump in his throat, but he quickly composed himself.

"Who else is involved in this? China? Now Goddamn Russia?!" Mark asked. "Thanks, JT, tell the boss nice work."

"Yeah, I'll do that. He also wanted to know how the shooter got across the tracks. He thought perhaps that was how he fell when you shot him."

Pulling someone across the train tracks to let them be cut in half was conduct unbecoming to an agent and was borderline murder, but this was covert war against a foreign power. No civilian court or jurors could ever understand what agents go through, nor would they ever. He knew exactly what his boss meant without actually saying it. That was the story and he was passing it through JT. "Strangely enough, JT, that's exactly what happened."

"Mark, can I have the device? The boss wanted me to take it and kill the encryption, then deliver it to him." JT knew the answer before he had asked the question.

"Sorry, that won't work for me. Tell the boss I'll keep it safe." JT looked at Mark from under his brow and gave him a nervous grin. "How about a ride back to D.C.?" Mark continued. "Drop me at Dulles. I don't trust leaving from Richmond. I also need to stop at any sporting goods store. I need a lock box."

"Sure, hop in! Oh, one more thing, the boss wanted you to have this." He handed Mark a slightly used cell phone. "We don't think you should turn it on until you're ready to check in."

Mark shook his head as he closed the door, and JT started down the road. Looking out of the window, he didn't see the trees that had given up their leaves for the season or the sky beginning to lighten, or the pavement that stretched before him. All he could see was the look on Danielle's face staring up at him as she lay sprawled on the dusty floor of the coffee shop, dead.

27

March 16th 2009
Richmond, Virginia

Mark drove into his parking spot at ATEC at seven in the morning and walked directly into his boss's office. "Mike, I'm stumped. I have no idea what that yellow piece of paper means." Mike looked up from his desk and studied Mark as he took a long sip of coffee.

"Rick, how about we meet for lunch. Let's say ten thirty this morning?"

"Sure, but that's a little early."

"Be in my office at ten thirty," Mike said, pointing down to the floor of his office. The morning flew by, and at precisely ten thirty, Mark was in the doorway.

"Let's go," Mike said as he whisked his coat from off the hook. Mark followed Mike through the door as he put on his jacket. When they got close to Mike's SUV, he asked, "Pizza?"

"No, Rick. I have a surprise for ya," Mike said as they both slid in and closed their doors. "We're headed to the Richmond International Airport. Rick, you're on the 1:00 p.m. flight to Los Angeles."

"What?"

"You passed the test, my friend."

"Test?"

"Yup, if you would have come to me with the answer, I would have known you'd had help."

"What the hell are you talking about?" Mark's eyebrows rose. He cocked his head to one side and mustered up an incredulous look.

"It's a risk we take, and no one's been able to figure that out even with help from an automated source," Mike explained.

Mark was relieved. It had played out as he had hoped. He wasn't sure at first, but he was in and knew exactly where he was going. Mike stopped the car alongside the curb outside the United terminal. He quickly exited and headed towards the trunk.

"Mike, I can't just leave for California. What about work? My wife?" protested Mark.

"You said, the other day that your wife's in Washington. Let me take care of work. You're simply on a trip to L.A. for a meeting."

Mark looked stunned.

"Here, my friend, just a few things so you don't have to stop anywhere," Mike said handing Mark a blue backpack with the ATEC logo on it. "I made a reservation right after we spoke this morning."

Mark took the bag and looked inside. "You thought of everything."

"Just a few essentials. Have a good trip. See ya in a few days."

Mark stepped onto the curb and strolled through the glass doors heading towards the counter. He swiped his driver's license and checked in. With no bags to check, he turned and walked towards security. As he was getting in line, he looked down at his boarding passes. "Seat 1A, first class, nice," Mark mumbled to himself. A smile crossed his face as he thought of all the times he had traveled on business sitting in the back of whatever contract carrier had been authorized by the government. *Crime may not pay in the end*, he thought, *but it sure starts off well.*

He could not contact Cliff using the cell phone, so he waited until he was close to the gate. He found a payphone, made a very short call and left a message for Cliff, "Flying from Richmond to Los Angeles. United Flight 4498. Arrive 6:30 p.m."

133

He picked up the cell and made a call to his house in Richmond, in case someone was listening. "Honey, if you get home before I get back, I had to take a trip to California for business. See you in a few days. Love you."

Two rum and cokes, a hot meal, and a warm chocolate chip cookie made flying in first class a real treat. When the wheels chirped on the runway, it jarred him awake from a light sleep.

As he rode the escalator down to baggage, he saw a middle-aged gentleman in a black suit with brown hair sticking out from under his black chauffeur's hat holding a sign with his name, Richard Salvatore.

"That's me, I'm Rick Salvatore," said Mark.

"Mr. Salvatore, sir, do you have luggage?"

"Nope, just this backpack."

"Please follow me."

"Where're we headed?" Mark asked as he stepped alongside the black Lincoln.

"I'm to take you to the Jet Propulsion Laboratory in Pasadena."

"JPL!" he gasped, showing surprise.

Mark took out his cell as the chauffeur closed his door. He was leaving a message for his wife by the time the driver started the car. He never knew who might be watching. He had to play his part and calling his wife after leaving abruptly was the thing to do. He left a very apologetic message and sat back to enjoy the ride, pondering the possibilities of what lay ahead.

Mark felt at home as he was driven through L.A. up the I-105 to the I-5 to the I-210. Set in the hills was the JPL. Traffic was light for a Monday. The trip only took forty-five minutes, but by the end of it, he was hungry. The car pulled to the west entrance and stopped in line with the main entrance doors. He took his backpack and started to open the door, but before he knew it, the chauffeur had it opened and was helping him out. As he reached for his wallet, he was stopped. "Everything has been taken care of Mr. Salvatore," the chauffeur announced and handed him his business card. "Please call when you are ready."

Mark thanked him, then turned and stepped through the large double doors. He was greeted by a man who stood well over six feet. Mark picked up that he was prior military right from the beginning. The man had a commanding presence, but Mark also felt an easiness about him. Mark looked up and held out his hand, "Hi, Rick Salvatore."

"Good evening, Mr. Salvatore. Ken Benner. If you would, please follow me. Thank you for coming all this way. Sorry for the late hour, but there's not so many folks around after five.

As they walked towards the elevator, Mark questioned him. "May I ask what this is all about? Mike just gave me…"

"Rick, how about we hold all questions until later," Ken said, cutting him short. With a slight shrug, Mark raised his eyebrows and shook his head as they waited for the elevator. The elevator doors silently slid open and as both men stepped inside the doors closed with a hiss. Mark flashed a confused look towards Ken.

Kenneth Benner was a dark-skinned goliath of a man who had worked as a communications specialist with the Rangers. He was turned against his country when he was approached by his commanding officer after he had intercepted and broken an Iranian code during the first Gulf War. Ken's ability to not only sniff the code out of the air, but to translate and decipher it had impressed the colonel. His handling of the communication and his ability to brief the field commanders had impressed him further. After the colonel returned to the States, he dug up what he could on Ken. He had found a young man from a broken family who had joined the military four years earlier to get away from home. He had an above average IQ and had scored high on his enlistment tests.

Because of his physical prowess, he had set himself apart during boot camp and was asked to join the rangers where he excelled in language and had an aptitude for communications. At the end of a ten year enlistment, he was approached by his now-retired commanding officer and offered a job. He was ripe for the picking. He had been twice passed over for rank and had left the military disgruntled. In very much the same way that Mark was being recruited at this very moment, so had Ken Benner.

The trip down in the elevator was quick. After being led down a long hallway, they turned towards a narrow door. Ken leaned in, scanned his eye, and then punched in a code. The door clicked open. Mark walked in first and was followed by Ken who closed and checked the door. Sitting in a room that wasn't much bigger than a jail cell was a man of Asian descent. He sat at a small table in the center with a few chairs. In the corner was an oak cabinet with a vertical push button combination lock. Mark quickly scanned the room and noticed two very small cameras, one pointing at the cabinet and one at the table. What was hard *not* to notice was the platter of food in the center of the table.

"Good evening, Mr. Salvatore. May we interest you in some dinner?"

A big smile formed across Mark's face. "I guess if you're gonna feed me you can call me Rick." He stuck out his hand. His host stood, took Mark's hand, and shook it with vigor.

"So very pleased to meet you, Rick. Steve Chang at your service."

One thing about this group, Mark thought as he sat down, it sure was a polite bunch.

"Rick, mind if I talk while you eat? I want to tell you why you're here."

"I'm all ears,"

"We brought you here to offer you a job. You were recommended by a friend at ATEC. He's been telling us some great things. Seems you almost have the power supply miniaturized."

"Sure do," he said with pride, "It's all I think about. Once I put my mind to something, that's it."

"I bet your wife hates it?"

Mark sensed he was fishing. "She likes to shop and visit her mother in D.C. I don't think she notices."

"Hmm, that's why we haven't seen your wife," Steve commented.

Mark glanced between the two men. "Seen my wife? When would you've seen my wife?"

"Well, we like to know the people we employ and their families." An alarm went off in Mark's head at this odd remark and he detected a rather sinister tone. "Occasionally, someone may drive by a residence and make sure everything's ok. What we had seen is a very pretty girl at your house."

Show time, Mark thought. "Hey, wait a minute!" he said as he started to stand. "What's this really all about? And how do you know she's not my wife?"

"Is she?" Chang asked slyly.

Mark sat down and quietly said, "No. She's someone I met in town. Look, my wife's never home and I enjoy female company."

* * *

Steve Chang had turned people for years. He was the first generation born in the U.S. His parents were immigrants to the United States from China fifty-five years ago. With the help of the U.S. government, they had taken jobs in manufacturing. They had given their son an American name hoping to give him every advantage. He had excelled in school and had been awarded many grants and loans. He had graduated from Massachusetts Institute of Technology (MIT) with honors. The companies that had courted him were numerous, but in the end he had picked the JPL. At fifty-two, he now sits as deputy head of their propulsion division.

Before his father died, their family made many trips to China. Ten years ago, during one of their trips, he was approached by a military attaché who managed to spend some time with him. Steve spoke fluid Mandarin and his family had continued to practice Chinese customs, so connecting with the attaché was natural.

The attaché was a spy. His professional expertise was turning Chinese Americans, and he was good at it. He knew that the closer to mother China the family was, the less allegiance they had to America. He had told Steve there would always be a place for him in China, and that he could be part of the greatest military build-up ever. Stealing technology from other countries would get them that much closer to global domination, especially over the U.S. With his feeling of allegiance still in China, Steve was easy to turn. The attaché told him they were beginning to hear about a satellite system with unusual capability. It was a closely guarded secret and coincidentally, part of it was being developed at the JPL. They only knew that it operated in the near polar orbit. They had to know more. Steve had been instructed to spend whatever he needed, do whatever was necessary to collect information on the system. Steve was flattered that they had come to him. He looked at the smuggling of top secret information as a game, a game with an unlimited budget. So, for ten years, Steve had built and conducted covert operations right under the nose of the United States government in a small room at the JPL.

Mark sat in the small room across from his adversary. He knew Chang had to break him. He also knew that to turn someone required just a few elements, money, sex, and blackmail. Right now, Steve could offer Rick Salvatore all three.

"Rick, don't worry. With us, you can have it all, depending on what you can offer our organization, and we hear you can offer a lot. We will pay you a tidy sum, and your wife, Colleen, will never hear of the girl. Rick, you are very smart and deserve to be paid for your contributions. Your companies never appreciated your work like we will. You'll be compensated handsomely and will be able to give your wife the things she loves."

Mark sat in front of Steve and Ken looking dumbfounded. He hung his head. *So, this is how it happens,* he thought. *They try to break you by showing they know you and your family, then throw in a little blackmail. Build you up, inflate your ego, and then make an offer you*

141

almost can't refuse. They know you only have to give them one thing, one act of treason, and you're theirs.

Mark sat shaking his head, looking defeated. After a few moments, he slowly raised his head, met Steve's gaze, and grinned. "How much money?"

The hand was played. It had to be convincing.

Steve Chang turned just about everyone who had sat in front of him. He knew he was close to breaking his newest quest.

The one that got away was a retired navy captain, Daniel Rico, whose creditors were knocking at his door. With his kids in the best colleges, it had been hard to keep up. His navy retirement was good and his salary at the JPL competitive, but he still found himself using his credit cards more and more. When those ran out he had refinanced his home. Steve had watched him for months; he had been ripe for the picking. When he thought it was time, he had Ken invite him to this small room. In very much the same way, he had made an offer that couldn't be refused. But refuse he did. His loyalty to the United States government had been deep. He had become visibly upset during their meeting and ended it abruptly. Steve had reminded the captain of his family, the schools his children attended, and their activities. Captain Rico had abruptly stood, left the room, and headed for the elevator with Ken close behind him. When they reached the doors he had turned and held his hand up to Ken. Not wanting to draw any attention, Ken stopped. They knew it would take time for him to digest everything. Would it be worth the risk to his family? But they only had days. It was a risk they had been unable to take.

In front of Captain Rico's house a black Lincoln had pulled alongside the curb. The chauffeur and a very pretty blonde dressed in a black suit had gotten out. The blonde had walked to the door while the driver had opened the trunk. It had been just another normal early morning in the Captain's neighborhood. With him traveling so much, a chauffeured car was not unusual. The young woman had approached the house and rang the bell. Dan, just getting ready to leave for work, opened the door, and greeted her. "Good morning, young lady."

"Good morning, Mr. Rico. We have a pickup for you today, Sir."

"I'm sorry, there must be some mistake," Dan had said pleasantly.

The young woman had retrieved the order from her suit jacket and stepped through the door to show Dan. As she had leaned in, she slowly wrapped her right arm around his neck and quickly injected him with a hypodermic syringe, which she had palmed while she had reached into her jacket. Daniel Rico, retired navy captain had died before he hit the ground. The organization was well aware that a pretty girl can go just about anywhere, even into the house of an unsuspecting man.

Now, Steve Chang watched Rick, waiting for what he knew would be success. He'd been reading people for years. This was a textbook case. Rick Salvatore was underappreciated, underpaid and already having an affair. He had come almost gift-wrapped. Chang watched as Rick mulled it over. When Rick had looked up and asked the number one question, "*How much money?*" Chang knew it was a done deal.

"What can you offer?" Chang was quick to counter.

"Of course the miniature power supply and related software."

"And?" Chang pressed.

"To tell you the truth I have to think about it," Mark said a little uneasy. Even though he wasn't actually selling out his government, it still felt, strange. Though it was a covert operation, he still felt like he was about to commit treason, and that didn't sit well.

Steve read it as nerves. However, if Rick Salvatore would give them the power supply, they had him.

"Mr. Salvatore, we'll settle on the power supply for now. Later, we'll talk about what else you helped the OSO with."

Inwardly, Mark was relieved. He didn't have to come up with anything else and slowly leaned back in his chair. The two men stared at each other for several long minutes. Steve reached into his folder, pulled out an envelope, and slid it across the table. If it wasn't for the circumstances, Mark would've laughed out loud. This little scene resembled every spy movie he had ever seen. "Money?" he eagerly asked as he reached for the envelope.

"No, a simple communication. When you get back to ATEC, give this envelope to Mike, unopened."

Mark took the envelope, unzipped his bag, and placed it in an inner pocket. "What do I do now?" Mark asked, looking at both Ken and Steve.

"You enjoy a few days in southern California on us," Steve said with a wide smile. "Your plane leaves Los Angeles on Thursday morning, United Flight 1244 at eight-thirty in the morning. Until then, use our chauffeur. He knows where to take you. When you get back, see Mike."

Ken stood by the door waiting for Mark to retrieve his backpack. When Mark turned to leave, Ken was ready to open the door, but it wasn't until Steve raised his hand that he actually keyed the door. Mark took notice of the organization and dedication of the men. In fact, he noticed everything. Steve Chang was Chinese, Kenneth Bremer was prior military. The room had cameras so it was being watched from somewhere else. The room was small with a secure cabinet in the corner. The group was well organized and funded, complete with a driver.

As he rode the elevator with Ken, he asked, "How long have you been with Mr. Chang?"

Ken looked at Mark and just before the door opened, he replied, "Eight years."

"Must pay well?" Mark's comment came out as more of a question.

"Enjoy your time off, Mr. Salvatore."

Mark took his phone from his pocket, intending to call his driver. Before he could key in the numbers, the black Lincoln was pulling alongside the curb.

Kind of like a cult, no time to myself, Mark thought as he stepped through the lobby doors and into the waiting car.

28

March 18ᵗʰ 2009
Hilton Hotel
Richmond, Virginia

Danielle met with her handler while Mark was gone. From the surveillance report, he had been dropped at the airport, checked in through the United kiosk and gone through security. Danielle drove to the center of town and met her contact in the lobby of the Hilton. She was passed a small envelope, then she rode the elevator to the room that was written on the back of the envelope. She swiped the key card and entered. Standing by the table was the same tall, skinny man with sandy blonde hair that Mark had seen at the coffee shop. In his hand was an H&K semi-automatic handgun.

"This is a lot nicer than the coffee shop," he said, setting the gun on the table.

"Business first," she replied as she sat on the bed and took off her shoes.

"I'm not so sure the time you spend with Mr. Springfield is all business," he quipped coldly.

"That's absurd. He means nothing to me. If you develop a relationship that's not about sex with someone like Mark, he won't let his guard down. Add in a little sex and you can lead a man around like a puppy dog."

"I don't think you've been adding just a little."

"Jealous?" Danielle retorted with a smirk.

"What do you have for me?" Yuri asked harsher than he had intended. He could tell she was growing fond of the CIA agent and the order he was about to give her pleased him.

Yuri Kovaleskiaka *was* jealous. They had worked together since her recruitment over ten years ago. They had both attended Webster University. He had been on a foreign student visa from Russia and was placed in the heart of the United States for the sole purpose of espionage. Webster was visited by both the CIA and the FBI for recruitment. It played out better if they came looking for you. There wasn't a better place than Washington, D.C.

Danielle was young and from a poor neighborhood and had been away from home for the first time. She had been on a partial athletic scholarship that rarely paid the bills. She had not met the requirement for student aid and it had put a financial burden on her already broken family. The constant struggle had left her bitter. Yet, all around her, illegals were getting a free ride and it made her furious. Yuri had taken note of this, her activities, her papers, and more importantly the Webster Conservative Society club to which she had belonged. They promoted the principles of limited government under the constitution. He had sat many times in her government classes and watched as she had argued recent events. The fact that Congress fought all the time inflamed her even more. Danielle's disenchantment with the government had drawn Yuri to her. She had been impressionable and Yuri had taken full advantage of it.

Yuri's meeting with Danielle had been calculated. He had positioned himself so he would run into her throughout the week. Finally, he had introduced himself.

"Hello, I'm Yuri," he had said nearly running to catch up to her as she had left class.

Danielle had turned and given him a quick look. Yuri was five years her senior and extremely good looking. His sandy hair was a mess. She smiled. "Hi. Danielle."

"I couldn't help but agree with your arguments about Congress. Those guys have their heads up their asses," he had said.

"Thanks." She had kept walking but at a slightly slower pace.

"Maybe we should elect you to Congress. I'll vote for you. Danielle for Congress!"

"They don't want me there. I'd fire the lot of them!" They had continued walking for a while without saying anything more. There had been an awkward silence. Danielle had thought it was rather cute. "Yuri. What kind of name is that exactly?"

"Actually, I'm Yuri Kovaleskiaka. It's Russian. I'm here taking advantage of what your country has to offer," he had said smiling.

"Your English is very good."

"Thanks to my parents. They insisted I learn the international language, the language of trade." Yuri had known that to be effective, one must learn the language of their enemy well.

Yuri had been a young agent, a new breed from Moscow, very versed in the English language and very loyal to the old Soviet Union. His western looks and family history had made him a desirable agent who had the coveted job of a Sluzhba Vneshney Razvedki (SVR),

Russia's External Intelligence Service agent. They had been placed in U.S. schools to befriend potential future leaders. It was found that he had a talent for spotting the not so loyal westerner. He would develop and pay them handsomely to pass information from the different agencies he would push them towards. This had been his last year in school and the twenty-nine year old was finishing his Master's degree in business. He had attended school as long as he could without drawing any suspicion to his visas. The plan had been for him to return to Russia for a complete debrief, apply for a work visa and return to the U.S. He would then reconnect with the contacts he'd developed over the years. He had had several prospects but knew he only had time to develop one more. He had chosen Danielle. The young red head had excited him. And had purposely manipulated their relationship so it would turn sexual, and on a Friday night after a frat party, it did. They had spent days in bed and eventually became inseparable.

Yuri had constantly spent money on Danielle. He had bought her clothes, and dinners, had taken her to movies, to plays and on a trip to Disney World. He had gotten her comfortable and used to having money. Since she hadn't had it for so long, this aspect had been an important step in luring and seducing her into his organization.

After they had attended a CIA recruitment drive, he had made her the offer. They'd been together for almost a year and talking to her was easy. They had been hiking through the Appalachian Mountains and had camped for the night. Yuri knew how to pick very secluded areas. He was always cautious. They had both been huddled around the campfire late at night. The only noise had been the sound of the forest and the crackle of the campfire. "Danielle, how about we go into business together?"

"Business? Well, whatever it is I hope it pays well!" she said with a grin.

"What if I told you that I have acquaintances who pay very well?"

She turned away from the fire and looked at him with a raised eyebrow, "For?"

"There are friends of mine in Russia who like to know what your government is doing, just to keep the balance of power."

"Balance of power? What do you mean 'balance of power'?"

"They use information I provide so they don't overbuild their military. We're not a wealthy country, not like the U.S."

It had taken several long seconds for her to understand his implication. "Wait a minute. You're asking me to be a spy? Spy for Russia? Yuri, you're a spy? Is that what this is? You want me to spy?"

"Wait a minute, Danielle. Slow down. I simply pass information that can already be read online or in that magazine, *Jane's Defense*. I only try to verify it."

Danielle had reached for the bed roll that had been sitting next to her and shook a blanket from its center. She wrapped it around her shoulders, and then moved closer to the fire. She sat quietly for a long time staring into the flames. She had watched as they seemed to come to life and dance around the logs, slowly consuming them. She listened to it pop and crackle as she occasionally waved the smoke from her face. The more she had thought about it, the more intrigued she had become. "A spy," she had said to herself still gazing into the fire. Then she had turned to Yuri. "A spy?"

Yuri had pressed a little more. "Let's say you become employed with the CIA or FBI and you start at forty thousand dollars a year. My friends will match that just for an occasional piece of foreign policy information, more for technology. It's not like television. You'll actually be put on a payroll, and just as you might move up in a regular company, so too will you with us. Also, you'll be helping my country catch up to yours without starving our people. It's only to balance the power." He tried to soften the sound of it. "Have you ever wondered why I don't seem to have money problems?"

"I just assumed you have a wealthy family," she had said a little slyly.

"I do, Mother Russia."

29

"As I reported in the text, I have the location of the facility in California, the JPL of all places. I have the name and position of his contact at ATEC. When he returns, I'll have the name of the contact in California. It will probably confirm our suspicions that it's the Chinese," Danielle said while lying across the bed.

"Very good, my dear." He stood, walked towards the bed, and lay next to her. "I miss you," he said, pulling her hair close to his nose. "I don't like sharing you with other men."

"I said business first!" She pushed him away playfully. "What about you? Who am I sharing you with?" she asked with a flip of her hair.

"You should know I've grown very fond of you over the years," he murmured in her ear as he pulled her closer.

Danielle and Yuri spent the rest of the night in bed. In the morning, they went over a few details. Yuri brought Danielle an order from Russia. His bosses were uncomfortable about the reports Yuri and his colleagues had given them. They were afraid Mark Springfield would soon become suspicious of Danielle. Russia had recently been made aware that the United States had developed a satellite with unique capabilities. They couldn't risk losing their spy network which Yuri had spent so many years developing.

It was fortunate that Danielle was brought into the Huntsville program. With Danielle part of the program, they were now starting to learn its capabilities and determine which facilities were parts of the system. If they could get their hands on the technology, they would save billions in developmental costs. Danielle knew she would likely make a large sum if she could lead her handler through the maze of technicians and engineers who would sell what they knew. But she may be in over her head, operating with agents with so much experience. If they found out that Danielle was a mole, she could bring down their network. Danielle left the room at 11:30 a.m. As she rode the elevator, she tried to remember how she had let it get this far. When the door opened, she stepped out and paused, then walked across the lobby and sunk into a huge overstuffed gold chair. She sat there for several long minutes contemplating her next move. She remembered back about ten years ago when Yuri had first made her an offer. He had said, "It isn't like the movies."

Now, sitting in a hotel lobby after a covert meeting, as a spy for Russia, she knew it was just like the movies. Once they had her, they would never let her go. The more well-placed she was, the more they wanted. They became relentless. They knew that one act of treason would get her twenty-five years in jail and would brand her a spy for life. Just like Walker and Ames, her picture would get hung on the wall of every security room on every U.S. military base in the world. She stood, smoothed her dress, and walked toward the door, hating herself. Danielle had been given the order from Yuri to kill Mark Springfield.

30

March 19th 2009
Los Angeles, California

It was Thursday morning when Mark boarded the United flight to Richmond. He had spent a few days in California under the watchful eyes of the chauffeur, yet he felt rested. As he sat in first class, sipping his rum and coke, he started to understand how someone could turn. Showing people a lifestyle normally reserved for the rich and famous makes it hard for them to go back. With some risk, they could have it all. As he relaxed in his oversized cushioned chair with his foot rest extended, he closed his eyes. He wondered what *his* price was. What would it take for him to turn on the U.S.? But it was a moot point. Mark Springfield would always remain fiercely loyal to the United States.

Mark hoped the call he had placed from the pay phone to his boss before he had boarded his flight to

California would prove to be fruitful. After the code had been broken, he had given Cliff and JT the GPS location and phone number. They had hoped it wasn't a ruse, but it was all they had. They had been standing-by for their next move, which had come with the unexpected trip to California. He would have to wait until he reached the Coffee shop to contact Cliff again. He couldn't risk using an unsecure phone. He hoped Cliff had been able to arrange something on the other end.

Mark held a fresh drink in his hand. A thin smile crossed his face as he thought, *I'm glad I'm not driving home when we land.*

The Huntsville Unit was scheduled for another imaging test. It was being programmed and moved around in its polar orbit and would be in position soon. This test, like all tests, was a closely guarded secret. Not everyone was privy. The mere idea of a mole had the top brass worried, and they were keeping techs and engineers who didn't have a direct role in the upcoming test out of the loop. With the exception of a modified solar array and mirrored tracking ball assembly, the huut had been packaged in a 1960's satellite. This had been done to avoid visual identification of the space-born unit. But a country could gather information from any suspect satellite by simply pointing their antennas at it.

The power being emitted, the relative angle to earth, and the frequencies on which it may operate were all aspects of the satellite. The information collected was valuable in determining capability. But more importantly a country with advances in space, which knew what satellite was part of the Huntsville system, could destroy it and later suggest that it had been hit by space junk.

Mark knew about the tests, and the flight across the country gave him time to think. He didn't get a sense that either his boss at ATEC, Mike Vanns, or Steve Chang knew anything about the upcoming test. He did get the impression that their organization was very well connected, and he was concerned about how far up the chain of command their connections went. He wondered what was in the envelope that had been given to him at the JPL. Was he accepted? Or was it something more sinister?

"Excuse me, Mr. Salvatore, may I refill your drink?"

Mark looked down at his empty glass and up at the flight attendant, a very pretty brunette, with her long hair wrapped up in a lose bun. "As a matter of fact, you may, thank you."

"I'll have that rum and coke right up," she smiled at him and her hazel eyes twinkled as she took the empty glass and gracefully managed her way down the aisle. Mark leaned slightly into the aisle. Her long shapely legs made up for her drab United uniform. She returned promptly, and as she bent down to set his fresh drink in front of him, he could smell the faint hint of perfume. It lingered as she smiled with that gleam still in her eyes.

"Thank you," he said, and chuckled to himself as he sipped his third drink. He'd admonish himself later for drinking on the job.

The reginal jet Mark had connected to offered little resistance to the turbulence over Pennsylvania. Other than a few bumps, the flight had been uneventful. Sliding out of his seat Mark removed his backpack from the overhead compartment of the small plane, already missing first class. Briskly he made his way through the terminal and rode the escalator down to baggage where he saw a familiar face, Mike Vanns was waiting.

"How was the flight?" Mike asked with an outstretched arm and a smile on his face. He knew Rick had flown first-class.

"I particularly liked the brunette. She made a mean drink," Mark replied as he shook Mike's hand and gave him a wink. They walked to the car in the parking structure.

"Rick, I have some great news. Our friends at the OSO are very interested in your power supply. We met on the side during the funding meeting and I mentioned that your test, except for the heat exchange issue, was a success. Hopefully, I didn't misspeak when I told them that you would probably have that solved in a few months." Mike looked over his shoulder as they walked through the structure and in a low voice murmured, "There may be others interested as well."

"I have something for you," Mark said nervously. "An envelope."

"We're right over there." Mike pointed to his green Ford Escape. Using the fob, he clicked open the door. Mark tossed the backpack onto the backseat, retrieved the envelope, and then closed the door. Mark handed the envelope to Mike. Mike held it up to the light as though he were looking for some type of indicator that it had been opened. When he seemed satisfied, he fished his knife out of his pocket and sliced it open. He pulled out a yellow slip of paper. Mark hid his surprise but instantly realized what was going on. *That's how they communicate. That's why the boys over at the NSA can't sniff anything out of the air. They flew me to California to feel me out, make me an offer, then used me as a messenger. It's expensive, but not detectible. They are skirting technology to achieve one of the most advanced pieces of hardware on the planet.* Mark understood what that simple piece of yellow paper meant. Unlike modern organizations that communicate over secure lines and airways, they were using one of the oldest forms of communication to pass information, the written word.

"Well, it seems the guys at the JPL like you," Mike quipped with a big grin.

Mark stole a glance and saw there was a great deal of writing on the paper but from what he could see, it was unreadable. It was in code.

"Mike, I don't know what to do here? I feel like I'm being watched," Mark looked out of the windows of the car apprehensively.

"Listen, Rick. We take a lot of precautions. All we ask is that you follow a few rules for which you'll be compensated handsomely. Don't talk to anyone at ATEC but me, ever! Never tell anyone you've come into a windfall as far as the money is concerned. We don't need anyone snooping around."

Mark shook his head with a bewildered expression.

"We'll set up an account for you offshore. It'll look like you've invested in foreign stocks. Occasionally, we'll withdraw some of the money so it looks legit."

"Mike, is there anyone else involved with this at ATEC?"

"As far as you're concerned, no. So, remember rule number one, talk to no one. One more thing, relax. We've been doing this for a while. Oh yeah, you'll be given some cash. Deposit a little of it but hide the rest. Don't go off buying a new car. The key is not to draw attention to yourself."

"Who does Steve Chang work for?" Mark asked in a hushed voice.

"Rick, I honestly don't know. I assume it's the Chinese, but I can't say for sure. I will say one thing, the money's damn good." Mike noticed Rick fidgeting. "After a while, you'll relax. In the beginning, I was always looking over my shoulder and peeking through the curtains. It drove my wife nuts," he said with a chuckle, trying to calm Rick's nerves.

"Mike, this is a place I never thought I'd be, spying for another country. I don't even know who it is. I don't know. I may be having second thoughts."

Mike laughed. "Rick, I was the same way, but when I saw how much they pay, those worries went right out the window." Mike knew the consequences, and he also knew it was too late for Rick to back out.

"Ok, ok. I won't do anything drastic, Mike. I'm just a little nervous. Sorry."

Mike started his car and slowly made his way out of the parking structure. Mark sat quietly, like he was contemplating his next move. However, he knew his next move. He would get to the coffee shop and make a call to his boss and the head of the OSO.

"OK, what now?" Mark finally asked. "I need a lesson in Spying 101? Or Spy Craft 101? Or Trade Craft 101? Oh hell, I don't know what I mean." He looked over at Mike to gauge his reaction. "How do I get the power supply and software out of the building? How do I make copies?"

"It's simple, Rick, just like the movies, a camera."

"A camera? Just walk in with a camera and take a picture?"

"Yup, it's that easy. In fact, if you'll open that glove box, I have a surprise for you."

Mark opened the glove box and found a camera and a little something else, an envelope. He fished it out, half expecting to find a piece of yellow paper inside, but from the impression made on the envelope it was obviously cash.

"I was going to wait, but consider that your first installment."

Mark opened the envelope and slowly thumbed the money. "Man, Colleen's going to like this," he said with a smile. He looked over and noticed Mike's shoulders drop. Apparently, he had been worried about his new apprentice, but now seemed to relax.

Mike did relax. He had started to second guess his choice, but with Rick's enthusiasm over the money, he felt better. All he needed was one act of treason, and they had him.

They drove in silence until he had slowly pulled up and stopped outside of Mark's house. "This seems to be a very quiet neighborhood," Mike said as he looked around.

"A few kids now and then but for the most part, I like it."

Mike turned in his seat and faced Mark. "Look, Rick, it's real simple. Go in tomorrow, go to your desk, and work on the Aim Point Antenna power supply like you've been doing every day for the past several months. Continue to work during lunch. At exactly 12:15 p.m., photograph what you can starting with the first page. Don't get out of order, and take your time, what you don't get today, you'll get tomorrow and so on. Stop at exactly 12:18 p.m. and put the camera back in your briefcase. The room cameras will be off for exactly 3 minutes and 30 seconds. That'll be enough for one day." Mike didn't want to spook Rick so he gave him this simple task. *One act of treason,* he repeated to himself. That was all they needed.

"Then what?"

"Meet me tomorrow night at six. The same place we've been having lunch, in the same booth."

Mark looked at Mike and then back at the envelope. "This is kind of exciting," he said as he tapped the envelope. "See ya tomorrow." He closed the door and strolled up the walkway looking over his shoulder, then up and down the street.

Mike smiled to himself and drove off.

Mark watched Mike drive down his quiet street, stepped through the front door, turned, and locked it. He walked straight to the refrigerator, grabbed a beer, made his way to his La-Z-Boy chair and dropped down with a loud thud. He tossed the envelope on the table next to the chair, and sat back. He felt the stress of the last few days wash over his body. He had thought he had been relaxed when he flew home from California, but it wasn't until that moment that he realized how stressed he had really been. Before he knew it, he was up and peering through the curtains. He picked up the envelope, turned it over in his hand while looking at the impression made by the stack of money. After several more swallows of beer, he sat back, thinking, of all these years with the CIA, he had never before been in so damn deep so damn fast. He opened the envelope, removed the bills, and spread them out on the coffee table as he counted them. "Twenty thousand dollars," he said aloud to himself, "twenty... thousand...dollars." He needed to get to the secure room and bring Cliff up to date, but it would have to wait. He needed another beer.

31

March 19th 2009
Richmond, Virginia

Mark looked around his house for a place to stash the money. His first thought was to take it to the secure room in the coffee shop, but thought better of that, just in case Mike came by looking for it. He decided it was best to keep it at the house.

He was happy his car had been brought back from ATEC to his house while he was in California. Mike took care of having the car moved then tossed the keys through the mail slot which was one less thing he had to worry about. Just before he stepped out of the house, he pulled the curtains back and looked up and down the quiet street, then made his way to his car. As he backed out of the driveway, he thought *what a recruitment program.* On the way to the coffee shop, he called and left a message for Danielle to meet him. Then he placed a call to Cliff.

"It's about time you called, Mr. Springfield," Cliff said with a hint of sarcasm.

"Sorry, boss. I needed a moment alone," he said with a short laugh.

"Did you contact the director of the OSO?"

"I did, before I called you. I wanted to check the rumor mill and test schedule. He hasn't caught wind of anything and the test is on track. It doesn't surprise me. If they can keep communicating the way they do, it'll be hard to get ahead of these guys." Mark then explained their simple form of communication.

"Ok, let's talk about your friends at the JPL. After you called me from the airport, I called our office in Los Angeles and put two agents on you for the entire trip. Knowing the location ahead of time was nice. I was able to stage the team. It made it easy for the agents to follow you since they knew where you were going. Good job figuring out that code. The phone number rang the lobby of the west entrance of the JPL. Here's the interesting part, the chauffeur dropped you off, then parked just around the corner and went in the same door as you did. After a while, he came out in a hurry, moments before you did, and headed straight for the Lincoln."

"He was watching me, I left in a hurry. So who is he, I wonder?"

"I was waiting for you to ask, my boy. His name is Martin Powell, and he's not a nice guy. Spent a little time in the marines and was kicked out for fighting. He couldn't shake his gang affiliations."

"What'd he do in the Marines?"

"Made it to Sergeant, was training for the 1st. Intelligence Battalion Division, Expeditionary Force, out of California. Too bad. His trainers say he's very smart. But, he just couldn't keep his temper in check."

"He seemed so professional," Mark said, a little surprised.

"I'm sure they were sizing you up from the time they picked you up until they dropped you off. Good job staying focused and on cue."

"I have to admit, I was a little worried at times. Thought I might be overplaying it."

"You did well. It seems you're in," Cliff replied.

Mark paused. He didn't take compliments very well. He let the last few days and his acting ability sink in. "The question is, how do you want me to handle the power supply?" He sat back in his chair and put his feet up on the desk.

"Let's work it exactly how they want and see how it plays out. Now that we know some of the players, we can keep an eye on them. We have a man on your boss at ATEC, Mike Vanns. So far, he's done nothing out of the ordinary. In fact, he's got a clean record."

"I'll go in tomorrow and start my photography career and report back tomorrow night. One more thing, Cliff. I taped the envelope to the bottom of my La-Z-Boy." he said matter-of-factly.

Cliff seemed a little surprised "What envelope? What La-Z-Boy?"

Mark waited to tell Cliff and thought he might have some fun with the head of the CIA. He knew this was happening fast and Cliff had been in the dark ever since Mark had left for California.

"The envelope containing twenty thousand dollars. It's taped to the bottom of the La-Z-Boy in my living room."

"Twenty thousand dollars!" Cliff spit.

He grinned as he pictured Cliff coming out of his chair.

When Mark left the secure room, Danielle was just pouring water over a tea bag. She greeted him with a seductive grin. He had checked the cameras before he left the room and knew no one else was there. He walked over and stood close. He rested his right hand on her lower hip and nuzzled her hair just above her ear and whispered. "Good evening, Dannie." It was late, but Danielle's fragrance invigorated him. He missed her when they were apart. "How about I make us a late dinner?"

"Sounds great." Danielle's tone was one of submission. She glanced towards the door and assured no one was around. She turned back towards Mark and threw her arms around his thick neck. She leaned in, pushing her chest into his. Mark grabbed her around the waist. Pulling her in even closer, he kissed her.

Danielle pulled away and asked, "Dinner, are you sure that's *all* you want?"

The question caused Mark to return a sly grin.

"Well, maybe later." He grabbed the back of her head. This time he lightly pulled her hair as he kissed her.

Danielle let out a deep pleasurable groan. She leaned back and stared intently at Mark. "You don't have to be so gentle." Then lightly bit him on his lip.

32

March 20th 2009
Richmond, Virginia

"Good morning, Mike," Mark called as he passed by his boss's office.

Mike waved from inside and shouted, "Good mornin', Rick."

After going into the secure area, Mark made his way to his office. He carried his briefcase with the camera inside as he read the signs which stated *No Cameras or Cell Phones Allowed. All items are subject to search.* He couldn't blow his cover. He had now been accepted and it was crucial at this point that he not be discovered. Working as a double agent was a precarious juggling act.

At exactly 12:15 p.m., he pulled out his camera and started to photograph the plans laid out on his desk. He started with the cover sheet. He kept an eye on the time and at 12:18 p.m., he stopped and returned the camera to his briefcase. He turned and headed for the water cooler. He was sweating.

He took a paper cone-shaped cup, filled it with water, and looked back at his office. He had copied a lot in three minutes. It was an unnoticeable amount of time. If anyone ever reviewed the security footage they would write off that time loss as a glitch. He stood there for a few more minutes allowing his heart rate to return to normal. He walked back to his desk and went back to work as though he had done nothing unusual.

Mark entered the pizza place at 5:15 p.m. and headed back to the booth. No one was there. He took a seat and waited. Feeling restless, he got up and ordered a pitcher of beer. Before he sat down, Mike walked in and met him at the counter. They ordered a medium meat lover's pizza and walked to the booth. Mark continued to project the part of a new spy, appearing jumpy, constantly scanning his surroundings.

"Ok, it's done," Mark said in a hushed tone.

"Rick, if you look and act suspicious, people will pay attention to you. Relax."

Mark sat back for a minute, took a few deep breaths, then reached in his briefcase and produced the camera. He removed the SD card, handed it to Mike, and said, "Here are the pictures from our fishing trip."

Mike casually reached over, gave Mark a wink, and thanked him. He reached into his pocket and produced another SD card. "Since I'm taking yours, I owe you one. Thanks," he exclaimed. Mark slid the card back into the slot in the camera and placed it back in his briefcase.

Mike took a long drink from his beer and leaned back with his hands on top of his head. He gave Mark a grin. One act of treason, just one, that was all he needed. In front of him was his newest addition. Rick Salvatore was a good find.

For the next month, taking his time cues from Mike, Mark photographed the miniature power supply at different times of the day and always for no more than three minutes. Although the signs were posted, no one ever checked his personal belongings and he became very comfortable with his task. He had a normal, pocket-size Kodak camera. It was nothing special. If he ever got stopped, he would simply say he had forgotten it was in his brief case. After every session, he removed the SD card and slipped it into his pocket.

Mike thought his new protégé skilled, almost too skilled.

33

April 10ᵗʰ 2009
Richmond, Virginia

Mike Vanns was well paid by ATEC. It wasn't unusual for him and his wife to visit California and spend a few days on the beaches in Ventura. He hid his *extra* money well. His wife had no idea of her husband's covert activities. After he returned from a recent trip with his wife, he met Mark at their usual spot. "Rick, I met with our friends in California and we're going to hold off on the overseas account for a while."

"Wait, I thought that was part of the deal!" Mark said a little flustered. "In fact, I was hoping for another envelope, Mike."

Greed, Mike thought, it *was a great thing.* Rick Salvatore was motivated by money, and keeping his wife, Colleen, happy was apparently not an easy task. Mike knew Rick was *all in.* He'd been handing over information for weeks. He'd committed his act of espionage and now he was stuck.

"Twenty thousand dollars is quite a sum, Rick, and we plan on paying you more, much more. We need to get some information on the work you've done for the OSO."

Mark pushed himself back in the booth, irritated, as he stammered for the right words.

"I don't know, Mike. I think I should be paid more for what I've already given you. You have almost the entire package. Now you want my OSO work?"

"Slow down, Rick. I know. I know." Now it was Mike's turn to speak in a low, hushed voice. "You've been passing classified information to me for a month." Mike chose his next words carefully. He didn't want to use the word treason. He didn't want to be combative; he knew Rick would figure it out. "We plan on giving you another installment and soon. We just want to know what you have worked on for the OSO."

"Ok, Mike. Give me a few days to come to terms with this."

"Rick, take the weekend," Mike said as he took a gulp of beer.

Mark left work and drove home. He'd planned on meeting Dannie later at the Coffee Huut but needed time to think. He also wanted to make sure he wasn't being followed, something he'd been watching for since returning from California. As he stood in the hot shower of the steam-filled bathroom, he wondered what would be next. How could they flush out the top man? How could someone so new to the spy game get to meet the boss of a well-connected organization, and was Mike the guy who could set it up? He stepped out of the shower and toweled off. Wiping off the mirror, he scrutinized his reflection. "Jesus, what does Danielle see in you?" he said aloud. He grinned, got dressed, and headed downtown.

Mark entered the coffee shop, and after their rehearsed greeting, headed to the back room. As usual, the shop was empty.

Mark and Cliff had been talking for a while on the phone when Danielle rang the access buzzer. She had been brought into the program to provide support but was being relied upon more and more. She single-handedly had been ordering inventory for the coffee shop, running the counter and ensuring all the classified faxes and transmissions had been coalesced and filed. Mark checked the surveillance cameras, then pressed the button on the control console to open the door. Danielle stepped in, took a seat next to Mark, and set a cup of tea in front of him. He looked up and gave her a wink.

"So, to bring you up to speed, we think we have a way for Mark to meet the higher-ups," Cliff informed her.

"It's dicey," Mark interjected, "but it's something they'd kill for."

"You're not going to give away the farm, are you?" Danielle asked hesitantly.

"We're giving them the crypto code to communicate with the space-born unit," Cliff said.

Danielle stared wide-eyed at Mark. If he knew what she was thinking, she'd be thrown in jail. Not only was it a stroke of luck that she had been chosen to participate in 'the huut', now it was going to be possible to get the grand prize. She tried desperately to control her excitement, and then, her heart sank with Marks next few words.

"Well, at least that's what they're going to think," Mark chuckled.

"There's no way we can chance risking the actual code," Cliff said.

With that remark, she decided to take a chance and plunged forward saying, "What if someone versed in writing code looks at what we're passing and suspects something?"

Mark looked at Danielle with a raised eyebrow.

"Miss Minium, we're very good at what we do," bellowed Cliff. "We cannot, by any means, let the crypto get out in the clear. If it falls into the wrong hands, all this secrecy, billions of tax-payer dollars, and our leg up on national defense will be for nothing."

"I'm sorry Director. We've come this far. I just want us to be successful."

Danielle fought to sound convincing. She did not want to jeopardize her work with Mark. She had gleaned so much.

Several more voices could be overheard on the speaker phone. One voice Danielle recognized as JT. The others were unknown to her. From what she could tell, they were having a discussion about the crypto, and then she clearly heard Cliff's agitated voice, "But how do we guarantee it's not compromised?"

"Danielle may be right. If Mark passes the code to someone and they have a way to review it before he leaves, which they probably will since they're not going to believe it in the first place, they'll kill him, and then go underground. It may take years before we get this chance again." JT, a man of few words, never blurted out anything with such conviction. Mark and Danielle looked at the speaker phone in stunned silence, then looked at each other and smiled.

"Mark, what do you think?" Cliff said in a low tone.

Mark had half expected the question. "I don't like it."

"It's not my call anyway. It's the president's," Cliff replied, sounding relieved. "For now, the plan is to tell them you have access to the crypto for the space-born unit. Once they pull their jaws off the ground, tell them you'll only deliver it to, and get payment from, Steve Chang's boss. This will tell us if he's at the top of the food chain. In the meantime, I'll brief the president with our findings and the concerns over the code. Mark, JT makes a valid point. I want you to think of the best way to protect yourself should the decision be made not to use the code."

There was mumbled agreement from the team. Danielle stayed quiet. For now, killing Mark was out. If there was a way to get the crypto for the satellite, he was the way. Killing him would have to wait. She wondered who would pay the most for such a coveted piece of hardware.

34

June 14th 2006
White Sands Missile Test Range
New Mexico

Danielle Minium had killed Ahuv Levi, an Israeli Engineer, at White Sands Missile Test Range, New Mexico, while they were working on Iron Dome, a top-secret missile defense project used to defend Israel from rockets fired from the Gaza strip. She was one of four agents given the assignment of watching over a group of Israeli scientists and engineers while they worked at White Sands.

She had had access to all phases of the program as she monitored their movements both during and after hours. Occasionally, she had socialized with the men and they had built a relationship of trust and confidentiality.

This had been her first attempt to steal technology. She'd been supplying Yuri with foreign policy information but had found that task to be mundane. Although she was being paid well, she knew there was more to make. Iron Dome information could prove very profitable. Clipped to the inside of her holster was a camera, and it was always there. She wanted to prove to Yuri that she could take the next step. The ability to supply drawings, schematics, or wiring diagrams went a long way in proving her worth.

After an unsuccessful intercept test, the engineers had the guidance system plans spread out all over the control room as they tried to figure out what had gone wrong. When they had taken a short break Danielle had volunteered to watch the drawings so they wouldn't have to lock them up while they were out. This had been the perfect opportunity for Danielle to use the camera she'd been carrying around for months. Her heart had skipped a beat as she pushed the heavy door closed when the last agent walked out. She had quickly removed her camera and started to record the plans. She had paid close attention to photographing the entire page with each shot including the legend. She was quick and efficient. Her heart pounded in her chest. It was different than passing a policy or a few copied papers here and there. She hadn't realized how this would affect her. She had paid strict attention as she continued to work and focus on the plans. She had, indeed, been too focused. Before she knew it, there was a loud clunk at the door. It broke her concentration, and as she looked up from the plans, the door was opening. In an instant her world had collapsed. She knew her mistake, and it was a rookie mistake. She had been caught.

Ahuv Levi mingled with his friends in the break room for several minutes before he realized he'd left his heart medicine in his briefcase. He had gotten permission from one of the agents to walk down the hall and get it. He thought nothing of walking through the door and picking up his medicine, but as he stepped into the room and looked towards the desk for his briefcase, he had seen Agent Minium standing over the plans with a small camera in her hands.

It had been surreal to see someone standing at the door. Danielle knew she would have to kill the Israeli. Ahuv paused, then stepped all the way into the room. The automatic door closure, a standard in all secured rooms, did its job. No one heard him yell, "Stop!" as he raced towards Danielle to stop her from photographing the drawings. She instantly drew her weapon and shot Ahuv, hitting him twice in the chest. The two rounds hit less than one second apart and threw him across the room, slamming his body into an adjacent wall. His body crumpled to the floor.

Danielle was shaken but knew she only had seconds. She ripped her blouse from shoulder to waist, stood over Ahuv, grabbed his bloody hand, and raked his nails across her face and neck. She stood, dropped the camera inside her jacket breast pocket, and headed for the door.

Abe, the agent standing at the entrance of the break room, had heard the muffled gunshots and turned towards the sound. As he looked down the hallway, he saw Agent Minium walking swiftly towards the security station. The guards were already on their feet. Abe drew his weapon. Methodically, he walked down the hall and stopped just before the control room.

Danielle was shaken, but couldn't lose her focus. She had just killed a man, was about to ruin his name and strain relations between the U.S. and Israel. More importantly, she had to keep herself out of jail. The information she carried in the camera would be passed to Yuri and would net her a tidy chunk of change.

"Call 911!" Danielle yelled as she walked towards the security station.

A guard grabbed the phone and punched in the numbers. Danielle, visibly shaken, walked back towards the room and approached Abe in the hallway.

"Abe, I shot Ahuv!"

"Holy shit! What happened?!" Abe, the other agent assigned to the Israelis, looked at Danielle in disbelief. They had been with the Israelis for seven months and had gotten to know them very well. The security guards slowly made their way past Danielle and Abe into the room to check Ahuv. Danielle and Abe followed. They found him slumped over on the floor near a corner in the room. One of the security guards stooped down to check his vitals. Danielle hadn't considered that he could still be alive, and for a brief instant became terrified. An eternity passed as she waited.

"He's dead," announced the security guard as he rolled back on his heels and looked up at the small group.

Those two words brought immeasurable relief to Danielle. Abe looked at Danielle sympathetically. Never, would he ever suspect his fellow agent of any wrongdoing.

"He opened the door and attacked me," Danielle's voice shook. She struggled to maintain her composure but felt the tears well up in her eyes. The minutes following a shooting were critical. She was on the verge of confessing. The emotional ramp-up of taking another human life, especially an innocent one, was overwhelming. She battled her instinctive emotions and kept herself focused. She was either all-in or would confess right now. "It all happened so fast. I was looking at a magazine when the door opened. He said something in Hebrew and lunged at me. I pushed him off and yelled at him to stop, but he came at me again. I drew my weapon, but it did nothing to stop him. So, I fired."

"That was your training. It kicked in," Abe spoke compassionately.

Relief flowed over her as she realized that he had drawn that conclusion.

"I checked him," she said in a low shaky voice. "He was alive, and reached for me again," she continued as she rubbed her fingers along her neck. "When I grabbed his arm he went limp. That's when I left for the guard station."

Abe holstered his firearm and walked Danielle back out into the hallway away from the emergency and base police that were starting to arrive. He held Danielle by the shoulders and pushed her back a bit to get a good look at her. "You're scratched up. You'll need medical attention."

"No, I just need to sit."

"Danielle, I need to follow protocol and relieve you of your weapon, then I'll have an EMT take a look at you."

Abe slowly pulled her jacket aside, withdrew her firearm, cleared it, then handed it to one of the other agents. Danielle was checked by the responding EMTs and her scratches cleaned on the scene. She gave her statement to the local police and spent hours on the phone answering questions by her management.

As the days passed, she felt more at ease with killing Ahuv. Her account of the incident raised no suspicion or questions. She had committed murder and no one was the wiser. Dropping the camera in her pocket had been a good call; it could've been seen when Abe had taken her weapon. She was in the clear and couldn't wait to see Yuri.

She had returned to Washington and spent three weeks on a desk while the attack was investigated by her department. Three weeks to the day, she had returned to full duty. Case closed.

Danielle had waited for one month before seeing Yuri. She had watched her environment to assure she wasn't being scrutinized. She knew that the CIA could be very shrewd, and one thing she had learned over the years was patience.

35

April 13, 2009
Richmond, Virginia

"Mike, can we take a drive after work?" Mark was standing at Mike's office door with a sheepish look.

"Good morning, Rick," Mike said spinning around in his chair.

"I have some personal things I need to talk to you about," Mark continued.

"Sure, I'll meet you in the parking lot at 5:30 p.m."

Mark nodded, turned on his heels and walked slowly back towards his office, rubbing the back of his head. He spent the rest of the day acting distracted, working slowly, and being short with everyone.

Mark purposely waited until well after 5:30 p.m. to start towards the parking lot. As Mark walked through ATECs fenced lot, the security lights came on. It was about 6:00 p.m. and Mark was approaching Mike's car when he heard. "Ready to take that drive?"

"Sorry I'm late, Mike."

"Well, jump in and we'll go for a drive."

They pulled out of the parking lot. Mark was constantly looking over his shoulder. "We're not being followed, are we?"

Mike laughed. "Rick, we're not being followed, but whatever you have for us must be good. I've noticed that you've been jumpy all day."

"What I have is different than just the micro power supply. What I have is going to give someone the *whole* thing," Mark replied solemnly.

"The whole thing?"

Mike's startled reaction was exactly what Mark wanted to hear. He turned in his seat and looked at Mike.

"It's the reason I was so pissed at those guys," Mark explained. He could tell Mike was getting excited and at the same time trying to hide the excitement. He dragged it out a bit more. "I don't know, Mike. I feel a little sick." Mark shook his head, looking straight out the window, waiting, letting the anticipation build in his boss.

"Rick, have you been drinking?" Mike suddenly asked.

Mark *had* been drinking. He had taken an extended lunch to help sell the part knowing his actions would be noticed. As he sat in Mike's car, he could smell the alcohol on himself. It was a nice touch. He dismissed the alcohol question with a wave of his hand and said, "I can give you the code used to communicate to the Huntsville Unit - the satellite itself."

Had Mike heard Rick correctly? He drove in silence, processing the claim while looking for a place to park.

Mark wasn't sure of Mike's reaction. He had either shocked Mike into silence, or he had over-played his hand and was in deep trouble.

Mike took several sideways glances at Mark as he drove down a secluded street. They had been slowly driving around in the industrial area to avoid the business and noise of the highway. Most people had gone home for the night and Mike easily found a place to park. He became visibly animated as he twisted in his seat. "Wait, are you telling me you were part of developing ICE?!"

Mark was thrown a bit but he didn't show it. This was the first time he'd heard the name ICE and had no idea what it meant. He was on his own. If he miss-stepped, it was over. One thing he did know, he'd been reading people for twenty-eight years and Mike Vanns was truly excited.

"I had a small part at first. They gave me the antenna interface to work, and I worked it all the damn time.

191

It was all I thought about. My wife wasn't very happy. She rode me constantly. I was miserable. I poured my heart and soul into that thing and only got a pat on the back." Mark stopped himself. He knew he was starting to ramble and slowed himself down.

Mike read it as being, disgruntled. "It doesn't sound like you were very happy."

"I wasn't. I thought it was all behind me. Working on the power supply was therapeutic. The envelope you gave me," he said, looking around the car, "helped, too."

"What do you have for us, Rick? I mean, I doubt you have the actual code, but what do you have?"

Mark hesitated. He had no idea what ICE was. He had to be generic with whatever he said, but he had to be believable. He could feel himself starting to sweat. "That's just it, Mike, I know how they communicate with the Huntsville unit. I know the code. I know how they generate it. I know how they generated the random frequency." In a low, shaky voice he finished, "I can deliver the satellite."

"Jesus Christ, Rick! Are you screwing with me?!" Mike knew exactly what this meant and struggled to control himself. If they could communicate with the Huntsville unit, they could reprogram it. The United States would lose control of the satellite. This was everything they'd been working towards. "Do you know how much my employer would pay for this, Rick? This is big. ICE of all things! Rick, we may never have to work again!" he said, laughing. Mike started shaking his head. A huge grin broadened across his face.

"Mike, there's one thing. I have to be the one who turns over the code. If I'm going to do this, and I'm not saying I am for sure, but I need to know who I'm selling out to. I need to know what country is getting it."

"Now wait a minute, Rick. I don't think that's going to play well. It's a very secretive bunch. I don't even know who's at the top. Hell, I don't even know for sure if it's the Chinese."

"No, I've given this a lot of thought. I'm going to be the one that hands it over or it's not going to happen. I'm tired of being shit on. If I'm giving up ICE, it's going to be to the boss," Mark said with conviction.

Mike let out a heavy sigh. "Ok, let me contact the higher-ups and I'll let you know how they want to handle this." Mike paused and looked for several long moments at Mark. "Oh my God! ICE of all things!"

Mark had done it. He had pulled it off. Whatever ICE was, they'd been trying to get it for quite some time and he was their answer. He still had one question. What the hell is ICE?

36

April 13th 2009
Coffee Huut
Richmond, Virginia

"Integrated Cyber Engine," Ryan announced excitedly.

Mark sat in the secure room with the phone pressed to his ear going over the events of the day. Cliff, JT, and their best software engineer, Ryan Swimer, were on the other end of the line.

"It was a breakthrough in communicating with encryption," he went on. "It's based on communicating with land facilities using random coded encryption based on time cues, all synchronized around GPS time. It's dependent upon which hemisphere 'the huuts' located and which GPS satellites are cueing. We apply an algorithm in..."

"Wait a minute, Ryan. I think that'll be enough. We don't need to get into the nuts and bolts," Cliff interjected, clearly agitated.

Mark started to laugh but stopped short and hoped it wasn't picked up on the other end. Engineers are the worst when it comes to security. They have an analytical mind and security measures are not part of it.

"Mr. Vanns and his cohorts are in deep," Cliff said. "The security around ICE is like no other. The fact they know it exists, tells me they may have someone in Alaska at our Fairbanks facility, where they command and acquire the satellite data or the satellite build-up itself. Jesus, they could even have someone in the X-37B program. I haven't gotten anything back from the president concerning the code, so you'll have to stall. We've got to figure this out, Mark. If it's not going to be you, then eventually it will be someone else. We have to get you to them first."

Mark could hear the strain in Cliff's voice but there was nothing he could do until they got the go-ahead from the president as to whether they would use a fictitious code or the actual cyber for 'the huut.'

Danielle met Mark for dinner during the following few nights as he waited for the president to make a decision. She had also spent the night, an unspoken invitation. Mark was anxious. Not knowing who would contact him first made him uneasy. She sensed his anxiety and was careful not to seem too eager. She could not draw any suspicion to herself. If she could acquire the encryption for the satellite, it would change her life. She had decided to sell it to the highest bidder. However, the order to kill Mark Springfield had already sealed her fate.

37

April 16th 2009
Richmond, Virginia

I dodged another bullet, Mark thought as he drove out of ATEC's parking lot. He'd been feeling like he was in limbo, but at least Mike hadn't asked him for anything.

Mark parked a block from the coffee shop and made his normal trek towards the front door. From the outside, it looked like any of a thousand places that had sprung up across the country. As he stepped into the shop, a very pretty blonde was on her way out. He held the door open as they exchanged pleasantries. He looked around. There was no one else in the store. As he strolled over to the counter, he asked Danielle, "Has she become a regular?"

"She's been in a few times. I'm surprised you recognized her."

"Faces stick with me. The first time I saw her, she was sitting with two guys right over there," he said, pointing to a table close to the counter.

"Next time she's in, I'll get her number," Danielle said with a devilish grin. Inwardly, she was surprised Mark had noticed but didn't show it. She was, however, impressed with Mark's recall and made a mental note not to get caught with what Yuri called 'his scouts.'

Mark smiled, walked over to the fuse box, opened the door, leaned in, and scanned his eye. At the sound of the click, he walked into the room. He was early and spent his time going over transmissions from the NRO guys. After a while, the buzzer went off. One check of the cameras showed that Dannie was waiting with a cup of tea. Mark smiled, pushed the button, and let her in. She walked over, placed the tea in front of him, and looked up at the clock. "Almost seven," she said as she took a seat next to him.

Mark had been meeting over the encrypted line with Cliff in the secure room for the past few nights. Like the previous nights, he was ready for his 7:00 p.m. update. While surfing the web at work, he had learned that the president was on the move. He was making a rare visit to CIA headquarters. Rumor had it that he was personally presenting special recognition awards to agents who were instrumental in uncovering terrorist attacks against the United States. Mark wondered if it had anything to do with the encryption.

"I think it's time to encrypt and see if there's been any change." Mark grabbed the cassette that stored the cypher for the phone and loaded it. He entered his personal code and the phone came to life. After a few rings, it was answered with a simple, "Hello." Then, it sounded like it disconnected. "Good evening, Cliff. Are you up and running?"

Mark waited for several long seconds. Just when he was about to give it another shot he heard, "Hi Mark. We're here. I have a roomful tonight." Mark looked at Danielle and gave her a thumb's up. He knew a decision had been made. "I have JT, Ryan, and a few secret service men here with me."

"Good evening, Mr. President." Mark knew that if the secret service were there, so was the president.

"Mr. Springfield, I'm sorry it's taken so long, but we've decided to let you pass the code."

Mark glanced at Danielle with a sober look. The president's candor caught him off-guard. After a few seconds, he realized the president of the United States was waiting on him. He had been stunned into silence. He'd been in some very dangerous and nerve-racking situations, but this held a grave responsibility beyond all others.

An old memory flashed in Marks mind. It was after the First Gulf War. He had been with the CIA for ten years, and although he had been on several covert operations, this was, by far the most dangerous. Everything had gone wrong. He remembered the beach just south of the small village of Sartol, Iran. He had been helping a SEAL carry his near dead teammate through the surf. The SEAL they were carrying had been shot in the back and had a broken rib from a fall. Mark remembered the surf and how it washed his blood up on the beach. He knew the warrior wasn't going to make it home.

They had been there for one reason: to infiltrate the Iranian border and confirm that the Russian-Iranian deal to build a nuclear power plant in Bushehr was not just for peaceful purposes. The United States had planned to use the confusion created by the withdrawal of its ships and the allied forces from the busy Kuwait port of Shuwaiba to launch a smaller version of the Deep Submergence Rescue Vehicle (DSRV). Mark and his team had had a four-man mini submarine. He vividly remembered the roll of film that a near dead U.S. Navy SEAL had once pressed into his hand.

After two long days, they had been ready for extraction. All four had made it home, but only three had survived.

The memory lasted only seconds before Mark instantly refocused on the meeting. A valuable piece of hardware that would give his country a huge tactical advantage cannot be compromised. He thought again of Iran. The film he held in his hand was proof that they had more centrifuges than were required for peaceful purposes. The information had cost one man his life, but this felt different. He would have information an entire country would depend on. If he's the one who loses it, he would never forgive himself. He had prepared himself for the president's decision to carry the actual encryption, but it was a scenario he never thought would come to pass. Now that it was here, he felt uneasy. Very uneasy.

Danielle looked at Mark and did her best to appear as concerned as he was. She was already devising a way to compromise the encryption.

It was Cliff who broke the long silence. "Of course, we'll load tracking software into the delivery device. According to Mr. Swimer, we can accomplish this without detection. This is only a precaution in case the device gets out of our control."

"However, you need to be very mindful of what you have." The president was stern when he spoke. Mark had seen him on many occasions joking with dignitaries while at the podium. But this was a different side. This was all business. Mark visualized him sitting in his chair leaning in, very intent. This was the part of the presidency Mark wanted no part of.

"I'm also trying to come up with a way for the device to eat itself after being accessed three times," Ryan spoke quickly.

If he could pull that off, Mark would feel better about handling the device.

"Regardless of what we do, we will have something to you in two days." Mark sensed the president was looking around the room when he spoke, finalizing the time line.

"If I may, sir," Mark interjected, "I think it would be better for me to come get it. It may be too suspicious if they have someone watching me and all of a sudden I show up with it. When they approach me, I'll contact Mr. House and pick it up at the OSO. That'll play into what I've already told them." There was a long pause and Mark could hear movement and some conversation in the background.

After a slight pause, Cliff's voice chimed through the speaker. "Sounds good. Call me when they make contact. I'll have Ryan, JT, and a few men transport the device to the OSO, but once you leave, you're on your own.

Oh, Mark, one other thing," continued Cliff. "If they get this encryption, they can also command the satellite to self-destruct."

He understood Cliff's meaning and turned to Danielle. "No pressure," he whispered.

After ending their call, Mark watched Danielle twist the cap off the bottle of water she had retrieved from the mini fridge. Taking it from her, he gulped in down in less than a minute. "Thanks!" Without saying another word, he turned and left the room.

Danielle spent a few minutes straightening up and followed after Mark. She found him outside, leaning against a street light. "You ok?"

"Just needed some air. At least I have you to back me up. Let's get something to eat."

38

April 19th 2009
Richmond, Virginia

Mark went about his business at work, and Mike acted like nothing had ever happened. The two made small talk but never once alluded to the encryption or anything regarding the past few days. It was like it had never happened. On Friday, Mark stopped by Mike's office to wish him a good weekend. "I'll see ya Monday," was all Mike said.

Danielle hung a sign on the window of the Coffee Huut that said *Closed for Family Emergency.* They spent the next two days at Mark's house waiting. Late Sunday morning, Mark suggested that Danielle head home. He needed to do some things around the house and, he needed time to himself. The day passed quickly, and Mark was about to turn in when he heard someone pull into the driveway. By the time he opened the curtains, a green Ford Escape was coming to a stop. Cautiously, Mark looked up and down the street, then opened the front door. He didn't do it for show, but for his own safety. He had started to get an uneasy feeling the moment he had left the coffee shop. He watched Mike close the car door and then greeted him from the porch.

"Good evening Rick."

"Can I get you something to drink, maybe a beer?"

"No, I can't stay long. The wife thinks I'm out buying a pack of smokes. There's been quite a bit of discussion concerning what you have for us and frankly my bosses don't believe it. They're well-connected and haven't been able to get close to this thing. Then, here *you* are out of the blue claiming to have what we need. How will you even get near ICE? You don't work there anymore, Rick."

Mark took a step back and sat on the arm of the couch. He'd been expecting this question. He suspected their desire for this information may be clouding their good judgment and had decided early on that, if challenged, he would back away and not seem so anxious. He knew if he were too aggressive, it may not go well. Finally, he let out a long breath. "That's fine, Mike. I've been worried sick about this anyway. I'll finish up the power supply and call it good. I'm lousy at this spy thing anyway."

"Can you get it?" The caring boss was gone. The tone of his voice was almost threatening. He seemed to pay no attention to Mark's last comment. Mike was deadly serious. "I vouched for you Rick."

Mark saw the intensity in Mike's eyes. If he was ever going to be convincing, the time was now.

"They perform routine maintenance on the interface equipment every Wednesday," Mark started. "The thing about it is, it's very complex. They're always having trouble with it. Since I pretty much came up with it, I'm sure they'll be happy to see me. They'll have the encryption out to restore communication with the unit. I know those guys; they trust me." That was it. Mark put it out there and hoped it was believable. It was a simple story of people not being security conscious.

The two men stared at each other until Mike's gaze finally softened as if he had made a decision. Finally, he said, "I have something for you." He pulled an envelope from his inside coat pocket, handed it to Mark, then moved over to the La-Z-Boy and sat down. "Rick, I think you should open that envelope."

Mark pushed back a little more. "And if I hand it back to you, can we call it quits? My wife would be happier if I moved back to D.C. anyway."

"You can't offer us something then renege. It's not *nice,* Rick." In a very slow and stern voice, he continued, "Open the envelope, Rick."

Mark rolled it over in his hands a few times, then carefully pulled out his pocket knife and sliced open the top. He had never seen so many one hundred dollars bills in one place. Slowly, he looked up at Mike. "How much is in here?"

"One hundred thousand dollars."

"Jesus!" Mark exclaimed. He slumped down in the couch.

Mike leaned in and spoke softly. "Once you deliver whatever it is that we need to communicate with ICE, and it's been verified, I will hand you another envelope with the same amount *and* an offshore account worth $250 million dollars, in your name, and your name only. The cash in the two envelopes are to get you out of the country. Go anywhere you want. Deliver us the satellite and you'll never hear from us again."

Mark didn't need to act stunned. He stared at Mike with a blank look. He was moving the envelope up and down with his hand as if he were weighing it. After a long while, he spoke, "Okay, I'll do it."

Mike didn't say a word. He stood and walked towards the door, leaving Mark sitting on the couch in what he thought was, a stupor. As he reached the door, he turned back and looked at Mark. "When you acquire the item, we'll meet for pizza and beer." With that, he turned and left.

Mark heard the car start and back out of the driveway. The room became eerily quiet. He sat back and stretched out his legs and rested his feet on the coffee table. This is what he had been working towards. The fact that he was holding the envelope of money was proof that he'd been believable. At this stage of the game, he also knew that if there was one misstep, it was over. It wouldn't be long before they could wrap this up. He looked around the house. He'd grown fond of his new digs and liked the neighborhood. He almost hated to leave.

As he sat in the quiet house, it all seemed surreal. It was almost over. Except for the stack of money, it was like Mike's visit had never happened.

39

April 24th 2009
Outskirts of St. Charles, Maryland.

While Mark had waited inside the tree line behind his sister's house he had had time to think. The last few days and hours leading up to the shootings had him perplexed. Danielle had taken him off-guard. He had known this was a risky assignment, but never had he thought that someone he allowed to get so close to him would try and kill him. He fought the emotional knot in his stomach. He had killed his partner, and his family had damn near ended up the same way. But right now, more importantly, his sister was missing.

As JT drove to Dulles, Mark's thoughts went from the trees to thinking about his sister. He was deep in thought as he stared out the window. Mary's a strong woman. The only way to get her on a plane away from her family is to drug her. He wasn't sure at first if she had

209

actually been brought to California, but since hearing of the accident, he had a pretty good idea she was there. After meeting Steve Chang and his cohorts, he knew his organization was both serious and lethal enough to make people disappear.

"Airline?" JT asked while still on the 267 headed into Dulles.

The question startled him from his thoughts. He had almost forgotten where he was. "United treated me well last time. Let's stay with what works."

JT dropped Mark off at the United curb and got out to help retrieve his bag. Mark gave JT a nod, but just before he turned to leave, JT reached out and shook his hand. "Good luck."

Mark nodded, thanked him, and headed toward the terminal.

As he stood in front of the United departure monitor, he weighed his options. He decided to take the 894 leaving at ten in the morning. A quick check at the kiosk showed him he would arrive in Los Angeles at 1:00 p.m. He had plenty of time. He would wait to check in until the last minute in order to keep his firearms as long as possible. Once he declared them and checked them through baggage, they would be gone until he reached L.A. Normally, when on assignment, he would carry his firearms directly onto the plane, but this time he was not Mark Springfield, CIA agent. He was Daniel Ricci, and according to the picture in his new wallet, he had a very pretty wife.

One hour before the flight, Mark bought the ticket and checked his bag, with both firearms locked inside. By the time he went through TSA and stopped at the restroom, they were boarding. As he walked down the jet way, he glanced down at his ticket. He was in seat 3A, First Class. At 10:15 a.m., the wheels left the runway with a shudder. As Mark reclined his chair, he felt a wave of fatigue sweep over him. This was the first time in two days he felt he could truly relax without being a target. He had a long flight ahead of him, was tired, and didn't have a solid plan. He felt like shit.

As the plane leveled out at thirty-five thousand feet, Mark sat back in disbelief. He never thought that his family would ever know his true job. Now, thanks to him, they were involved. He was relieved that his brother-in-law and nieces were safe, but it was unnerving not knowing about his sister. He was mad as hell that he hadn't picked up the signs along the way. How could Danielle get so close and he not have a clue? Mike had let him off the hook too easy when he had changed the drop day. It had even felt wrong when he entered the coffee shop, yet he had gone in anyway.

The seat next to him was empty and he had more than enough room to spread out. He pulled out the note paper and went over the names. He wanted to have a plan when he arrived in Los Angeles. He circled the name of the officer that was first on the scene, Matt Hunter. He would check with him first. He needed to find out who was in the accident. He was a little hesitant about checking with the local CIA office. He didn't know how well Steve Chang was connected. He turned on his phone discreetly to avoid being seen by the flight attendant and punched the numbers from the note paper into the phone's memory, then shut the phone off. He sat back and thought about Los Angeles. *I'll get my bag, gun up, get an Avis bus to the rental agency, call Matt...* Mark fell asleep. He slept soundly until the landing gear jerked out of their wells.

40

April 20ᵗʰ 2009
Richmond, Virginia

"You'll be ready Wednesday?" Mark asked Cliff and the rest of the group as he and Danielle sat in the secure room. It was 10:00 p.m. They had been on the phone for the last two hours going over the contingency plans and what precautions were loaded into the device. Ryan Swimer had sounded the most animated and although Mark never met him, he could picture him bouncing off the walls.

"Ryan finished testing the device earlier and assures me it's ready to go," Cliff stated sternly.

"I'll start out at noon. I'll tell them I'm sick and need to go home for the day. Of course, Mike will know where I'm going. I won't be surprised if he puts someone on me. I assume Ryan will be at the facility?"

"I sure will," came a quick voice. "When I see you Wednesday, it will be clear how to dump the encryption and start the trace on the device." Mark could hear the excitement and anticipation in Ryan's voice. He sounded young and not very savvy about keeping his cool. Either that, or he was a genius and completely inept around people.

The plan was set. Mark would drive to D.C, meet the team at the facility, and pick up the encrypted device. The more he thought about driving back unescorted with the device, the more apprehensive he became. He knew anything could happen during the drive. He could be involved in an accident, have a heart attack or a stroke... anything, and the encryption would fall into the hands of a civilian. Mark hoped the precautions Ryan put in place wouldn't fail, and they would have a chance.

They already had enough on Mike to arrest him and put him away for a long time. However, they would use him for a little while longer before they took him off the streets. Mark's house was wired and JT had installed cameras and a DVD recorder that Mark had activated the moment Mike had stepped in the house.

Mark showed up for work late on Tuesday and spent the day showing symptoms that he was coming down with a cold. At noon on Wednesday, when he told his coworker that he was going home, no one blamed him. In fact, during the morning, some of them had suggested just that. As he passed Mike's office, he slipped inside and very quietly said, "I'll see you at seven," then turned and left.

The trip to D.C. was quick. Traffic was nonexistent that time of day. Mark pulled into the parking space reserved for visitors and walked up to the guard shack. The complex consisted of four buildings surrounded with a ten-foot fence that had razor wire rolled around the top. He spoke to the security guards through the glass partition for several minutes and waited. This was all an act. He had to make it look like he'd shown up out of the blue in case someone had followed him. Everyone involved was already inside watching Mark on the security cameras. As he waited, he nonchalantly looked around the building. He quickly scanned the parking lot and noticed a green Ford Escape parking in the far end of the lot.

Fifteen minutes later, Mark was met by someone he had never seen before but was greeted as if they were old friends. After several long minutes waiting for the guards to fill out their log book, he was let inside. As they walked towards the door, Mark was pulled around the side of the building to continue the ruse. His host pointed to several antennas on the roof, waving his arms as if they were having big problems. Finally, the two walked inside.

From out in the parking lot, the green Ford Escape slowly made its way out of the gate. One of the secret service agents watching the lot radioed the event inside.

A tall, skinny faced young man with curly black hair greeted Mark as he walked through the door of the fenced building.

"Mr. Springfield, nice to meet you. I'm Ryan Swimer." He shook Mark's hand vigorously.

"Mr. Swimer, the pleasure is all mine." Mark said with an extended arm.

Ryan turned Mark towards the other men in the room and said. "You remember Mr. House?"

The director of the CIA stuck out his hand and said. "Good to see you again, Mark."

"Director."

"Mark, these men are our security detail. I thought I'd ride along with them."

"Gentlemen. Thanks for seeing to it that Mr. House made it safely." Mark said with a grin. "What's next on the agenda?"

"Follow me." Ryan led Mark to an odd looking piece equipment that looked like a large handheld taser. Next to it was a digital voltmeter. Ryan, a good twenty years younger than Mark, acted like he'd been part of the group for years and spoke to Mark like he'd known him forever.

"Mark, take this voltmeter and measure between these two points." Ryan pointed to two prongs protruding from the encryption device.

Mark took the meter and probed the two test points; twenty-two volts blinked on the display.

"That's the key," Ryan exclaimed. "Anything less than twenty volts and the encryption drops out of memory; it's lost. Every time you read the encryption, you use one volt. Read it twice, you're down two; three times, and it's gone. You can also command a voltage drop just by pushing this." Ryan turned the device over, slid open a small door exposing two small spring-loaded switches, and showed Mark how to command a voltage drop. "Remember, press them simultaneously, one volt for each press."

"Is the device loaded now?"

Ryan picked up the device and plugged it into a spectrum analyzer. Immediately, a set of amber lights lit up on a separate display. "Those lights tell us that we have an up-link and reply from the satellite."

"No shit? We're talking to the actual Huntsville unit?"

"Yup, six hundred twenty-one miles over our heads."

Mark unplugged the device, turned it over in his hand and depressed the voltage drop command. Then he pressed it again. He looked at Ryan and pressed it a third time. Ryan knew exactly what he was doing and handed him the probes from the DVM. Mark took them and measured the volts. Nineteen volts blink on the display. He handed it back to Ryan and pointed to the analyzer. Ryan eagerly plugged it in and faced the group. "As you can see, the amber lights are not illuminated. Anything under twenty volts and it's gone."

Mark looked at Ryan and nodded. "Very good, Mr. Swimer. I feel better. Load it up. One more thing, how do I activate the tracking?"

"We thought it was more important to be able to clear it than track it, so the tracking battery is small. Only activate it when you leave this building. We'll be able to run it down no matter what computer it's attached to. It's good for thirty-five days. Just press these two at the same time to activate the battery. No matter where it is, if this thing's connected to anything that transmits via phone line, wireless, even over a Local Area Network, it doesn't matter what it's plugged into, in ten to twelve seconds, we'll have the address."

Mark gave Ryan a questioning look and said, "LANs? I'm not versed on the nuts and bolts of computers, but aren't LANs just that, local?"

Mark had opened Pandora's Box and Ryan couldn't wait. "Systems communicating over Ethernet divide a stream of data into shorter pieces called frames. Each frame contains source and destination addresses. Now you have the data link layer and it's concerned with local delivery of frames," Ryan paused and took a breath. He could see that Mark was having some trouble processing the information, but he continued anyway. "The data link layer is analogous to a neighborhood cop; it endeavors to arbitrate between parties contending for access to a medium. We access it by"

"Mr. Swimer, stop right there!" Cliff forcefully said. "That's a discussion for another time and place. We do not talk about capabilities that don't directly affect the task at hand." Cliff was pissed. The tension in the room could've been cut with a knife. This is the second time Ryan had rambled on about something he shouldn't have. Mark was sure Ryan would get a good reaming by the boss when everyone was gone.

Despite Ryan's youth and inexperience, Mark liked him, so he thought he'd lighten the mood. "Ryan, did you have *any* friends in high school?" The room burst into laughter.

Ryan was in his element and everyone knew it. He was the consummate nerd. He monopolized the demonstration from the time Mark had entered the room, and truth be told, he did a great job. He was talkative and extremely intelligent. Mark valued the fact that Ryan worked for them. He was truly an asset.

"Oh, one more thing," Ryan said. "If for some reason we lose the device altogether, after one month the battery eats itself and the encryption is lost. I started that clock the moment you stepped up to the guard shack."

"Ryan, I've got to give it to you. Nicely done." Mark pat him on the back, and Ryan beamed with pride.

41

April 22nd 2009

Mark drove south on the I-95 with the device sitting on the passenger seat wrapped in a paper bag. He found himself constantly glancing over to look at it. He knew there were fifteen years, countless man hours, and billions of dollars of developmental costs to the Huntsville unit. The keys to the kingdom were sitting less than three feet away. He had plenty of time to get back to Richmond and found himself driving very slowly. He had never been one to adhere to the speed limit, but now, Mark was driving like he had a nuclear bomb on his front seat.

It was 6:00 p.m. when he pulled in his driveway. Before he met with Mike, he spent the time looking around his house for a place to hide the device. When he was satisfied, he drove the familiar route to the pizza parlor.

He walked inside and saw Mike sitting in the booth with a pitcher of beer, and an older gentleman who was dressed in an impeccable suit. Mike stood and greeted Mark, "Rick Salvatore, may I introduce you to Mr. John Smith." Mark shook his hand, took a seat, and reached for the pitcher of beer.

They watched Mark pour his beer as they settled back into the booth. "Mr. Salvatore, Mike tells me you may have something for us."

"Who are you?" Mark quietly asked. Then continued pretending to be surprised. "Weren't you my chauffeur?"

"Yes, I work for Mr. Chang. He sent me to meet with you."

Mark hadn't been sure before, but he was now. Steve Chang was the head of the snake. It made sense. He only trusted himself to bring in people. He was smart enough not to leave the safety of the JPL or his core team. As important as the encryption was, he didn't make the trip. The person sitting in front of him must be the number two man. Who else could he trust with the device? He knew there was probably no way to get Steve Chang to Richmond, but he pushed a little more anyway.

"If Mr. Chang's the boss, then I'll only turn it over to him. Like I said to Mike here, if I'm going to do this, then I need to be the one who turns it over to the head guy. I'll collect my money and give him the device."

John looked at Mike and then at Mark. "Rick, will you give us a minute?"

Mark might have overplayed his hand. He stood looking at both men, turned from the table, and walked outside.

42

April 22nd 2009
Richmond, Virginia

Danielle knew that to blackmail Yuri for more money wouldn't go well for her. He knew who she was, where she lived, everything. No, she would meet Mike Vanns, offer him his freedom along with the same deal they had made Mark - enough money to get out of the country and 250 million dollars. She was certain this would work. Threatening someone with jail and branding them a spy has a way of getting their attention. But when? She had to approach Mike at the right time. Too soon and he would have her followed, too late and Mark would surely find out. She did what she did best; she waited for the right time. It was a 250 million dollar guess. While the men moved their chess pieces, she would have enough time to either copy the encryption or steal the one Mark had surely locked in the secured room. With the intelligence they had collected over the past several months, Danielle knew everything about Mike - his address, wife's name, work hours, bank account, and even his favorite bar. She would offer him freedom in return for the 250 million dollars. It was a deal he could not refuse.

Danielle was cleaning the coffee shop when Mark arrived around 9:30 p.m. He had finished meeting with Mike and John concerning the device. After brow beating each other, Mark had remitted. He knew he wasn't going to see Steve Chang, but he had played it out to the bitter end. He had to convince them that if he didn't get his way, it was over. He had left the two men with an agreement to meet on Friday, at noon, at the American Civil War Center. Mark had insisted that they meet by the cannon just off Tredegar Street. He wanted a more public spot for the exchange. He was not worried for his safety; he was doing it for show. And he was playing the worried spy.

Mark walked around the counter and started to make a cup of tea. It was his routine when no one was in the coffee shop. It was midweek, and with two Starbucks in the area, customers were all but nonexistent, exactly as he wanted it. He noticed Danielle was exceptionally quiet. She merely nodded and smiled as he made his tea. She stayed at the opposite end of the counter acting busy by wiping things down that didn't need to be cleaned. But he dismissed it as the pressures of their work. With *this* seeming to come to an end, the stress was even greater. He nodded to her as he headed towards the room, grabbing a packet of sugar along the way. After leaving the two men at the pizza place, he had devised a plan and wanted to run it by Cliff.

Danielle did not join Mark in the room. She couldn't trust herself not to look around the room for the device or not seem overly interested. She had to be cautious. Even though they had shared many nights together, Mark was an experienced agent with keen perception skills, and she didn't want to cause any suspicions.

Mark encrypted the phone and called Cliff. They had set 10:00 p.m. as the contact time before he had left with the unit. "I set Friday for the meet but I'm thinking about changing it to Sunday. I want to build in the notion of nervousness," he told Cliff.

"That might work. It'll give me a little more time to set up down there. After it happens, we'll put someone on Mike 24-7 and follow this so-called John Smith, who we know is really Martin Powell. We can't risk them discovering who we are, so we'll wait until after the exchange. Until then, it's a waiting game. Are you all set?"

"I am. As soon as they show up, I'll double check the tracking and follow my gut on when, or if, I command a voltage drop."

"The president has a lot of faith in you," Cliff began, "and your ability to read the situation. He hopes in the end we don't regret this course of action. He wanted to know if there's anything you need?"

Mark never thought the president of the United States would ever know his name, let alone ask if he needed anything. All he could say was, "I'll get back to you." If Cliff had been in the same room as Mark, he would have seen the grin on Mark's face.

43

April 22nd 2009
Richmond, Virginia

Mark had called Danielle earlier and told her to close the coffee shop and take the day off. He was going to be 'out of pocket' and saw no reason she couldn't take some time to herself. That had allowed her to be able to arrive at the bar even earlier. She knew Mike visited a bar downtown at least two days a week, one of them being Thursday. Poe's Pub was his favorite haunt. She took a chance and waited for him there. She walked through the door at 4:30 p.m. ordered a beer from the bar, and made her way to a corner table where she sat facing away from the door. Happy hour at the pub started at 4:00 p.m., but she wasn't there for that. Danielle nursed her beer, opened a magazine, and skimmed it while she continuously looked around. It was a local's bar. She could tell from the banter between the bartender, wait staff, and customers that they had long-standing relationships. Eventually, she was approached by an older, very attractive waitress and asked if she'd be having dinner. She declined, pointed to her beer, and asked for another.

Danielle was nervous. She had gone over her approach but didn't know how he would react. This wasn't the same as killing an unarmed Israeli engineer. She was up against two very experienced spies. The unknown was nerve-racking. She was perched on the precipice of ending her career *and* leaving the U.S. forever. She would *never* be able to return. A day ago, it had sounded good, but the realization of it actually happening, and happening fast, was overwhelming. There was a part of her that hoped Mike Vanns would never walk through that door. Her window of opportunity was very short. It was today or nothing. Halfway through her second beer, she started thinking about the money. 250 million dollars would last a lifetime. She could send each of her parents a small amount; but that was probably more from guilt than anything else. She didn't have much as a child and her parents' divorce had been hard on her. She was fortunate to have gotten as far as she did. As she lifted her third beer, she saw a familiar reflection appear in the mirror that hung on the wall.

Mike Vanns and Martin Powell entered the bar after they had made a trip to the American Civil War Center to familiarize themselves with the area. Mike Vanns had been visiting this hangout for years, and old habits were hard to break. As soon as he walked in the bar, he noticed the beautiful long red hair on the woman sitting with her back to him. He caught a glimpse of her reflection in the mirror that hung along the back wall of the room. The men made their way to the bar. Before Mike sat down, the bartender had his beer ready and slid it to him. The barkeep motioned to Mike's companion while he was still at the tap. With a nod, he pulled another Hefeweizen and walked it over to the newcomer.

Danielle sat a while longer and went over her rehearsed approach in her mind. When she looked over, Mike was on his second beer. It was time. She stood up and walked towards Mike. *My life will never be the same again.* "Mr. Vanns, may I have a word with you?"

Mike had been married for a number of years and the number of affairs he'd had could be counted on both hands, so when a pretty redhead walked up to him, his first thought wasn't, *Get away. I'm married,* it was more akin to, h*ow can I get you in bed?* He was a spy, and once he had gotten comfortable betraying his government, nothing was sacred. "I'm sorry, do I know you?"

"I have some information on one of your coworkers, Rick Salvatore," replied the sultry redhead.

Mike glanced at John, "I'll be right back. This shouldn't take long." He followed his new friend to her table. Rick had probably gotten involved with a married woman and she's come to his employer for help. As they sat down, the waitress appeared and picked up her glass. Danielle ordered two more.

"Mr. Vanns, Mike, if I may, I need to tell you a story about Rick. It may sound unbelievable at first, but please bear with me." She was stalling, she knew the waitress would return any minute.

"How do you know my name, young lady? Have we met?"

Danielle sat back and watched as the waitress set the glasses on her tray. She forced herself to slow her breathing and was glad she had already had a few drinks. The waitress returned, smiled pleasantly, set the glasses in front of them, and asked if there'd be anything else. Danielle shook her head. After the waitress left, Danielle leaned in and spoke in a low, hushed tone, "Rick Salvatore works for the CIA. They're going to arrest you for espionage." Danielle leaned back in her chair. She studied Mike's expression, waiting for her words to sink in.

Mike stared at Danielle with a blank expression. He didn't believe the woman sitting across from him. Her accusation started to anger him. He didn't know what game she was playing. He leaned in and asked, "Young lady, what do you want?" Danielle continued to stare at Mike. He was flustered, and she knew it. "Who are you?" he finally asked.

"Mike, my name is Danielle Minium. I work with Rick Salvatore who, by the way, is really Mark Springfield. We work for the CIA." As Danielle spoke the words, she removed her identification and laid it on the table in front of Mike.

Mike glanced down at the small black wallet. Scribed across the lower half was 'Central Intelligence Agency' affixed with their seal. The photo on the upper half was clearly the woman who sat across from him. Danielle watched Mike's mouth move as he attempted to speak. Finally, his words became audible. "This can't be happening. The CIA?" He felt like he had just been punched in the stomach. He started to experience tunnel vision. He began to lose focus. He reached out for the table. For several very long seconds he couldn't process what he had just heard. "What did you just say?" he asked. He looked around. All of a sudden, he started to think everyone must be watching him. He could not come to terms with what he had just heard.

Danielle watched his face go flush. She leaned back in towards him. "The federal government plans on taking you into custody as soon as they track down the head of your organization. You will be put under surveillance the moment you've passed the encryption." She knew that adding 'encryption,' the very thing they were waiting for, would give weight to what she said.

Mike saw his entire world collapse. His breathing quickened. He felt faint. He sat for a long while wondering what to do. Then it occurred to him. He was sitting in his favorite bar with someone who obviously was in on the operation, and... he wasn't in handcuffs.

Danielle knew she was at a crucial crossroads. She couldn't risk having him get up and run. "Mike, here, drink this." She handed him his beer. "I'm not here to arrest you. I'm here to make you a deal, one that gets me 250 million dollars, and keeps you out of jail."

"What do you want from me?" The longer he had to process what was happening, the clearer one thing became - the woman sitting on the other side of the table was, like him, a spy. All sexual interest in her vanished. His freedom was his priority.

"I want the same deal you offered my colleague, enough cash to get out of the country and the two-hundred-fifty-million dollars in the offshore account." The longer she sat there, the better she felt. She was in control of the events now. The hard part was behind her. Mike had been taken so off-guard by this encounter he had forgotten John was still at the bar. The threat of prison had momentarily changed his world. It felt like he'd been talking to this new *partner* for hours, but in reality it had only been ten minutes. Ten minutes in which he had learned a lot, most importantly that he had been played by the CIA. Rick Salvatore was really Mark Springfield. How could he have been so stupid? He had had a hunch from the start. This guy had showed up and offers him the grand prize. Mike was furious with himself and the more it sunk in, the more irate he started to become. He was now furious with this woman whom he originally wanted to bed.

"You come in here, and tell me you're CIA and expect money? You tell me you're a spy but sit there and threaten me. That if I don't give you two-hundred-fifty-million dollars, I will go to jail? Goddamn federal government has been watching me? You fucking bitch!" Mike halted his outburst. He had been gripping his schooner so hard that when he spoke, he spilled the cold liquid over his hand. He glanced around the bar and noticed several patrons starting to stare.

"Mr. Vanns," Danielle said, leaning in and taking advantage of Mike's spilled beer. "If I'm not mistaken, you have been committing espionage against the United States of America. As we both know, *Mike,* that's illegal. So, please save the high and mighty for later. Like I said, I'm not here to arrest you. I'm here to make a deal with you."

Mike didn't want to implicate John, but needed help. He started to turn in his chair, but before he turned around someone placed a hand on his shoulder.

"Everything okay over here?" It was John Smith. He smiled and stood over Mike holding his beer.

"I think you better sit down. We have a problem." He recapped what had transpired. All the while, John stared at Danielle with a blank expression.

Holding his stare, Danielle leaned in a little farther. "My colleague has the device here, in Richmond. He picked it up yesterday."

"I know. I followed him to D.C.," Mike said.

"Yes. I know. In a green Ford Escape. You were watched." She turned to John, "We know who you are too, Mr. Powell. We've had eyes on you since Mark was in California. Martin, what I don't know is how you got

235

out of California without being detected. You were being watched around the clock."

Martin's blank expression turned smug. "I'm very good at what I do." Startled, Mike turned to the person he knew as John Smith. Over the years, he'd met with him on several occasions. "You couldn't tell me your real name?"

"Part of being anonymous," Martin said as he took a long gulp of beer.

Friction started to build between the men but Danielle blew right past it. "I can't tell you how, but I plan to get the device on Friday."

"That's our meeting day," Mike spewed with an edge to his voice. He was getting nervous.

"No," Danielle corrected him, "he plans to call you and set up another day, which leaves Friday wide open. I'll get the device, verify the money, and turn it over to you."

Mike looked at Martin, then back at Danielle. It was all rather unbelievable, yet he believed it. "What insurance can you give us that you'll actually deliver the unit? And how do we know that once you get the account you won't turn us over to your friends?" he asked.

Danielle hadn't thought about this and was momentarily caught off-guard. She gave them the only thing that proved she was ready to deal, one of the CIA's top men. "I can give you Mark Springfield's address in D.C. and his sister's address in St. Charles. You can have someone check him out and his sister. Let's call her insurance in case something does go wrong." Danielle threw it out with no thought of its repercussions. She never believed Mark's sister would be harmed. She didn't know that the man sitting across from her, Martin Powell, took great pleasure in watching people suffer.

Mike Vanns was involved in selling secrets to a foreign government. He liked the intrigue and money, but he wasn't a killer and didn't like the sound of 'let's call her insurance.' He nervously shuffled in his chair.

It was Martin who spoke. "Young lady, I like the way you think," he said as he produced a notepad and slid it across the table. "If you'd be so kind as to jot down their addresses, we'll verify everything."

Danielle wrote down the address, and slid it back.

John Smith, also known as Martin Powell, had been recruited by Steve Chang not only for his brain but also for his brawn. He had no problem projecting Steve's will, and if it meant he had to hurt someone, then it made the job that more appealing. In fact, Martin Powell liked to torture people, especially women. He was paid, and paid very well. Now, potentially, he had to deal with the man from the CIA and his sister. He would enjoy it. He already began thinking of ways to taunt him and ways to get his sister to California, on his territory.

Martin's favorite drug was a mixture of propofol and sodium thiopental, two hypnotic agents he combined in his own learned portions. He never traveled without it. He could inject his victim with the precise amount of the milky substance so that it put the unwitting victim in a hypnotic state, one in which they could be led around.

Martin Powell had been put on notice with the United States Marines for not keeping his anger in check. He had been told not to re-enlist when authorities found that he had ties to a gang which he wasn't willing to cut. With his honorable discharge in hand, and background with the expeditionary force in intelligence, he had applied and was offered a job with a contractor working security at the Jet Propulsion Laboratory. Martin was working the night Steve Chang's car wouldn't start, and he had come to his aid. That chance meeting had changed his life. Steve had instantly seen a place for Martin in his organization. After several additional 'chance' meetings, Steve befriended him. And after eight months, Martin had been taken in. Chang had mentored him, and soon, Martin had nothing to do with his past life. Gangs had become a distant memory. Several years later, Steve still considered him his most loyal and capable man.

Now, here he sat in a bar on the east coast, across the table from someone who, essentially, was blackmailing them. She was a CIA agent who was no stranger to the spy game. He listened while she coolly and collectively laid out her plan and oddly enough, he trusted her. Two-hundred-fifty-million dollars has a way of ensuring trust amongst thieves.

Martin tore off another piece of paper, wrote his hotel number down, and handed it to Danielle. "When you have the device, call that number. Ask for room fifty-two. There's an offshore account set up for two-hundred-fifty-million dollars in the name of Richard Salvatore. Until we hear from you, we won't switch the names, but at best, it'll be done by Sunday."

"Gentlemen, if all goes well, you should hear from me by late morning on Friday." Danielle stood, finished her beer, laid a twenty dollar bill on the table, and left.

"Interesting turn of events," Mike said as he reached for his beer. He was going to ask why there had been the secrecy regarding Martin's real name, but the longer they sat there, the more uncomfortable he became. He watched as Martin picked up the piece of paper that Danielle had left behind and rubbed over the addresses with his fingers. Mike was now concerned about his intentions. He seemed a little too interested in their addresses, especially the sister's.

"I think I'll take a little trip, spend a little time in the big city. Mike, do you have the jade marker?"

Mike gave Martin a puzzled look. The markers were given to a select few as a communication tool and were program specific. He didn't understand why Martin would want one. "I do. I have mine at home."

Sensing Mike's hesitation, Martin looked him squarely in the eye. "I'll need it before I leave, and I'll need you to man my hotel phone tomorrow in case she calls."

"I'm almost afraid to ask, but what do you have up your sleeve?" He didn't want to know. Despite his tough demeanor, Mike Vanns wasn't a killer. He feared the worst but acted indifferently.

Martin had finished gulping down his beer. "Let's call it a contingency plan. When you get the call, go down to the lobby, use their phone to call my room, and leave a message. I'll call occasionally and check in. If I don't hear anything, we'll meet here tomorrow night, at 7:00 p.m."

Mike pushed his chair back and hesitated. He looked nervously around the bar. He looked back at Martin who was leaning back with one arm around the neighboring chair. Mike wondered how he could be so calm. Mike stood, and Martin slowly followed his lead. As Mike walked through the front door, he felt like he was under a microscope. As he drove home, he found himself praying he wouldn't be exposed as a spy. He would have to wait and see how it played out. He wondered if he would run or let himself be arrested.

From the wall safe in his small office, he retrieved the jade marker and headed to the Shell station two blocks from his house. The plan was to pass the marker to Martin and sit tight.

Danielle spent the rest of the night mentally preparing for Friday. If all went as planned, she would have the encryption and be gone from the coffee shop while Mark was still at work. If he showed up early, she would have no choice but to kill him. She had 250 million reasons. Mostly, however, she didn't want him on her ass tracking her down. There were a few things she'd learned about Mark Springfield over the past several months. One was his persistence. He would be relentless in his pursuit. She would never have any real peace.

Martin Powell would leave for Mark Springfield's house in Oakton, Virginia shortly after he left the bar. In his hand, he had the addresses for both Mark and his sister Mary. On his way to Mark's house, he made a pass by Mary and Cole's house to get the lay of the land. Then he made several slow passes around Mark's neighborhood. When he was confident that no one was home, he parked two blocks away.

He casually strolled down the street like he'd been living in the area for years. A quarter moon was shining which made it easy to slip into the backyard undetected. He froze while looking around for motion detectors that might activate the light over the back porch. He noticed one on either side of the house. He backed out and started around to the other side of the house almost tripping over a rake leaning against the garage. Slowly moving along the house, rake in one hand, he got close enough to the sensor to push it up and point it away from the back of the house. He moved back to the other side and repeated the drill.

Most locks are no match for the professional locksmith. Before long, Martin made his way through the back door as if he had the key. He methodically went through Mark's house. One thing was apparent---he liked guns. After he had accessed the second safe, he found Mark's wallet. He opened it up and studied the picture. One thing was now certain, the person he had met was not Richard Salvatore; it was CIA agent Mark Springfield. Several accommodations hung on the wall in his office, from the United States and from leaders all around the world. Martin Powell had not been fooled by many men.

Yet he had had no idea that he had driven around and sat across from a CIA operative. With admiration, he said, "Well done, Mr. Springfield. Well done." Martin dropped Mark's wallet in his breast pocket and slipped out the back as quickly and quietly as he had entered.

44

April 24ᵗʰ 2009
Richmond, Virginia
The Coffee Huut

Danielle spent the morning tearing apart the secure room. The space was small. There wasn't much to go through, but she went through everything. Nothing. The encryption was nowhere to be found. She walked through the coffee shop and looked for something, anything out of place. Nothing. "God Damnit!" She cursed to herself while looking up at the clock. One o'clock in the afternoon and still no device. She knew Martin wouldn't wait forever. "Two-hundred-fifty-million dollars... I'm so damn close, he has to have it", she spit

Yuri Kovaleskiaka had become suspicious of Danielle during their meeting at the hotel. By the time they had parted, he was sure that she was falling for the agent and wouldn't carry out the order. When she missed a prearranged drop to pass information on the California connection, he had had her followed. Now, after the reported meeting with two unknown men, he was sure she was going rogue.

Yuri made the trip to Richmond and was planning on confronting Danielle, but as he stood across the street and watched her in the shop, he decided to wait. She was rattled and unfocused. He was practically standing in the open and yet had gone unnoticed. She had been a good agent over the years. When she made the leap to passing technology, it had helped secure his own position within the Federal Intelligence Service (FIS), the new name for the old KGB. He knew it would only be a matter of time before she rose through the ranks and had access to more sensitive information in one of the most secretive agencies in existence. His investment in her had paid off. She was on the brink of gaining total access to one of the most advanced pieces of hardware ever developed. He stood there watching her and thought about the satellite. With the ability to be able to see deep within the earth, Jesus, there'd be no place to hide. The more he thought about it, the more he wanted to be the one to bring it home to Russia. Yuri decided to wait. He would continue to watch her. When the time was right, he would confront her and take whatever it was she was looking for.

Yuri watched Mark Springfield walk up to the door, then turn away. He returned moments later and walked inside. Yuri was able to watch Danielle inside the shop until she pulled the shades. He took a step into the street with the intention of helping Danielle. Moments later, Yuri heard a single gunshot followed by several more. He listened more than watched, as the sound of a gunfight filled the street. As the noise from the gun fire continued to ring in his ears, Yuri watched Mark come back out through the door. "Danielle," he mumbled, half in shock. All he could do now was follow the agent until the time was right.

* * *

Mark woke Friday morning feeling good about the plan. All he had to do was convince Mike that the meeting needed to be changed to Sunday. His end of the hunt was winding down. Once he passed the unit to Steve Chang's men, the bulk of the work would transfer to the human assets already in place. If the device was connected to a system, the guys at the NRO would track it. Mike Vanns would be arrested and eventually so would Steve Chang and his group. The government that was behind this operation would be exposed.

He drove into the parking lot of ATEC like he had every other day. He briskly walked into the lobby, paused, took a deep breath, and walked down the hall to Mike's office. He grabbed a chair and rolled it in close and took a seat. "Mike, I need to make a change. I'm not ready. I need a couple more days. I'm just not ready. I need to clean up a few things. Same place, Sunday, noon."

Mike looked him over, trying to keep his disdain in check. His inclination was to make it tough on the CIA operative. Deep down, he had known something wasn't quite right. But the amount of money they could've made had clouded his judgment. He looked at Mark in dead silence. The only thing he wanted now was to be done with the whole thing and stay out of jail. It wasn't worth the risk to allow his anger to show. The redhead would soon have the device and he could get out of the picture. Both he and Martin Powell would be gone. Mike had decided to run. He had enough money stashed. He would flee rather than take any chance of being arrested.

"No problem, Rick. I'll contact John and let him know. Sunday at noon. By the way, I'll be leaving soon, probably gone for the rest of the day."

Mark stood and nodded his head. *That was too easy*, he thought.

Mike drove to Martin's hotel and waited until well after twelve noon for the phone to ring in his room. Finally, as he was getting ready to leave for the lobby, it rang. "Hello."

"I don't have it. I'll call when I do." Danielle snapped sounding out of breath. She abruptly hung up.

He could hear the strain in her voice and decided to call Martin's room phone and leave a message he could retrieve later. He rode the elevator to the lobby and used the house phone. "She doesn't have it. Will call when she does."

Martin Powell called his own room an hour later and picked up the message. He already had a contingency plan and was happy to implement it. He checked his watch, 2:15 p.m. They would be home soon. He took out a yellow piece of paper and penned a note for his adversary.

Mark, you have one last chance.

He wrapped it around the jade marker and looked up and down the street. Not seeing anyone, he walked to Mary and Cole's house like he was an old friend, took one last look around, and let himself in. With the delays built into every alarm, he easily defeated their security system. As he made his way through the house, he noticed a collection of miniature crystal dragons. He estimated their value in the thousands. He admired it for several minutes and moved on. He took a teddy bear from the girl's bed, set it on the kitchen counter, put the jade marker on it, and left.

Cole was the first one home at 3:30 p.m. with Ashley in tow. When he saw the bear on the counter, he gave her a dirty look. "Ashley, the counter is for food, not for toys." He reached for it, noticed the yellow paper, unrolled it and read it. It must be something Mary was putting together for her brother. He pushed it aside. When Mary and Christina came home, Cole jokingly admonished her for leaving the bear on the counter. Mary looked at Cole confused.

"I didn't leave that there!"

Instantly, Cole sensed something was wrong. "Mary, that was there when we came home. If you didn't put it there then *who* did?" Cole picked up the jade piece and handed it to Mary. She read aloud the inscription written on the paper. "Mark, you have one last chance." Sensing the building tension between her parents, Ashley asked. "What's wrong, mommy?" Mary looked at her daughter and gave her a smile. "Nothing, honey, I just need to call your uncle.

Mary picked up the phone and called her brother, she asked him to stop by as soon as possible. Mary looked at Cole and asked if anything else was disturbed. They contemplated calling the police, but after a thorough search of the house they found nothing else was touched, so they waited until they heard from her brother.

Mark picked up his messages as he sat on the recliner in his Richmond house. Occasionally, he would look at, but not go near, where he had hid the device. He did not want to go to the coffee shop this close to the exchange. He couldn't risk any associations. There could be no slip ups. He went to work and back home. He was baffled as he listened to the message from his sister. He couldn't understand what could have been left for him. He called Mary. When no one answered, he sat back and closed his eyes. He'd be glad when this was over, and he was onto something else.

Bzzz, bzzz, bzzz...

The vibrating of his phone brought him out of his light nap. On the display was *Mary*. "Hello, how may I help you?" he said jokingly.

"Cole and I found something sitting on our counter when we got home. It has your name on it."

Mark could hear the urgency in her voice, and she had gotten right to the point.

"Hello to you too! Sounds important," Mark said, surprised by her tone.

"Mark, someone put something *in* our house while we were at work."

That got his attention and he sat straight up. "What is it?"

"Cole put some venison on the grill. Can you come by?"

"I'm leaving my house in five minutes." Mark got his jacket and headed for the front window. It was very unusual for Mary to call and be that short. Something had upset her. His protective instinct kicked in and he was on his way to St. Charles without another word. But before he left, Mark peered through the curtains and looked up and down the street. He walked to his fireplace, reached up, pulled the lever on the flue damper, and down dropped the device. He wasn't leaving Richmond without it.

45

All Danielle could do was wait. She was sure Mark had the device. It was clearer now than it ever had been. She had to kill him, but where? She regretted being out of the room when he was planning the drop with Cliff. She only had fragments of the plan, but she knew he would be back both Saturday and Sunday, the day of the drop, for one last communications link with the team.

When she had killed the Israeli at White Sands she had felt remorse, but it hadn't lasted long. Russia had been very pleased to acquire Iron Dome information and had paid her very well. To Yuri she was a valuable asset. This was her moment. She had no real allegiance to Russia. This would be just another hardware exchange from an asset. She was selling to an unknown, and two-hundred-fifty-million dollars was a lucrative deal. She didn't think she'd ever again have access to such a valuable piece of technology. It was a bargaining chip that comes along once in a lifetime. She would kill Mark Springfield the moment he walked through the door, retrieve the device, and complete the deal.

46

April 24th 2009
Mary Springfield's Home
Outskirts of St. Charles, Maryland
Just off Marshall Comer Rd

It was early evening when Mark pulled into his sister's driveway. Traffic had been heavier than normal. And the drive had been painfully long. Waiting for him on the porch were two of the cutest girls he'd ever seen. His nieces ran and jumped from the porch when he got close, nearly knocking him over. "You two have gotten heavy since I've seen you last. What is your mom feeding you?" The girls laughed and hung on their uncle until their mom pulled them off. Inside the house, Mary motioned him to the counter. Mark's heart sank the moment she handed him the piece of jade.

47

April 24th 2009

Martin Powell did not wait for others to act; he returned to St. Charles and took Mary Springfield. He had grown restless after not hearing from the redhead and had decided this was the only way. He knew Chang was more concerned with his standing in China than he was with the money. Martin knew that if he were instrumental in Chang achieving his goal, he would be rewarded with the money. He would never have to work again, and after looking at Mary's pictures that hung on her wall, he found his *bonus* very attractive.

Mary had just left the Barnes & Noble on Tenth Street and was on the way to pick up her daughter. While walking across the street to the parking structure, she felt a strange presence. She wasn't sure why but something wasn't quite right. She stopped and looked around. She did not see or hear anything out of the ordinary. She entered the stairwell. As she climbed the stairs to the second floor, she passed a man engaged in an animated phone call. She relaxed a bit after he passed and thought she was foolish for being worried.

Martin, the unassuming stranger involved with his phone call in the stairwell, had skillfully turned and injected Mary deep in the neck with his special milky white mixture of propofol and sodium thiopental. It was a ratio he had perfected over the years. She had flinched and started to turn away from the sudden pinch but immediately had fallen into a hypnotic state. He had slipped his arm around her waist to steady her and to appear as if they were a couple and had stood there until he was sure he hadn't been seen. When she was fully under the control of the serum, he easily led her to his waiting car. Martin sat her in the front seat and fastened the seatbelt around her. As he did, he laid his head next to hers and took in the fragrance of her hair. He stroked her smooth checks with the back of his hand. He smiled and closed the door.

For Martin Powell, getting her through an airport and onto a plane headed to California was routine. Walking a relative, who seemed *mentally challenged*, through the airport was an easy endeavor. He was fully versed on what he could get away with, and when he flashed an embarrassed smile at onlookers they offered a sympathetic one in return. The only snag he encountered was the boarding process. They boarded late so her second dose was delayed. First class seats gave him the room he needed. He partially covered her with a blanket and easily inserted the needle deep into her thigh. The other passengers were too caught up in getting settled or too polite to stare. No one had noticed.

Mary's eyes fluttered open as she heard the muffed sounds of talking. She looked around at the man sitting next to her. She knew she was on a plane. Just as quickly, her eyes closed and the fog enveloped her.

He was startled when she turned and looked directly at him. Her gaze seemed alert and very aware, but the look didn't last long. She slumped towards him, and he gently laid her back against the window. Smiling, Martin leaned his head back and smiled deviously. The hard part was over. All he had to do now was walk her out of the airport in Los Angeles with no security to worry about whatsoever.

48

April 26th 2009
Los Angeles, California

"Mr. Ricci, please put your seat back in the upright position." The flight attendant's hushed voice was enough to bring Mark out of his light sleep. He realized she was talking to him. He pulled up his seat and reached for his list and phone that had slid down the side of the cushion. He cleared the cob webs from his head and started thinking about LA. Chang's man was a day ahead, but he hoped surprise was on his side.

The wheels hit the runway with a loud chirp. When the cabin doors opened, Mark was first through the door. He headed directly to baggage claim. He was afraid his bag would be last off but when it was third down the ramp, he snatched it and headed into the restroom.

Once in a stall, he retrieved his holsters and slid them onto his belt. He then inserted a magazine into his Glock and racked the slide, loading his firearm. He slowly set his Glock into the Blade Tech holster. Mark repeated the loading process with his XD and then slipped it into the holster in the small of his back. After he secured his extra magazines in their pouches, he breathed a sigh of relief. He hated being without his firearms.

Mark sat in his rental car and called up the numbers he had put in his phone while he had been on the plane. He selected the first one. "Officer Hunter, this is Agent Mark Springfield. I work for the CIA. I just landed in L.A. and I need to talk to you about an accident the other night."

"Mr. Springfield!" Mark could hear the surprise in his voice, "Yes, I remember it very well. It was gruesome. We're still trying to sort it out. We'll need you to come by the station."

"No, that won't be possible. Not many people know that I'm in California and I'd like to keep it that way for a while. I need to ask you about the female in the car."

"If you need additional information, you'll have to contact Officer Butler. He handled the scene."

"I see from my notes that you're the one who ran the licenses," continued Mark. "Do you remember the color of nail polish on the woman?"

"How do you know I ran the licenses?" asked the officer.

"Do you remember what color her nails were painted?" Not knowing this detail was eating at Mark, though he tried to remain patient. He knew he was being short with the patrolman, but he wasn't getting the answers to his questions.

There was a long pause. "I don't remember. It was a gruesome scene. I'm sorry...I don't remember," he finally replied.

God damnit, thought Mark, *that doesn't help*! "Officer Hunter, keep the fact that I'm in L.A. quiet for a while." Mark ended the call and scrolled through his phone until he found the next number. A few minutes later, he called Officer Butler. He had to know for sure if his sister was alive. The phone rang once and went to message. "Shit!" The frustration in Mark's voice was growing.

Mark started the rental, headed for the gate, and left the lot. As he accelerated down Century Boulevard towards the I-405, his phone rang. "Hello."

"Her fingers were clean. There was no nail polish." Cameron Butler paid attention to detail and noticed everything. He knew exactly why Mark wanted to know if her nails were painted. He, himself, was still trying to identify the victim.

"Thank God. When I left my sister the other night, her nails were painted bright red. Your partner called you?" Cameron Butler heard the relief in Mark's voice.

"Mr. Springfield, we've been trying to sort this out. I have two dead and a truck driver under observation. We need you to talk to us. What's going on?"

"I'm sorry. I can't say. It's a matter of national security. What's important is that my sister's been kidnapped. I can't risk someone else trying to run in and rescue her. I need information on the deceased." Mark tried his best to be blunt but not alienate the officer.

"How am I to verify you're who you say you are?" Cameron was cautious. He'd learned one very important thing over his career. *Trust but verify*. It was a phrase made famous by the late president, Ronald Reagan. And It had saved his life more than once.

Mark paused for several long seconds. He was being questioned about his identity by someone who might be able to help. He finally said, "We need to meet."

Cameron was intrigued. In his nineteen years on the force, he had never dealt with the CIA. He'd trained with Homeland Security, the state's terrorist task forces, and the local FBI. Now he was involved with a man from the CIA who had purportedly died a few nights ago. This was an intriguing Who-Done-It complete with a kidnapping. "Mr. Springfield, I'm out of the Altadena office on Windsor, right off the I-210. If you won't come in. Let's meet"

As he was about to offer up a location, Mark chimed in. "How about Griffith Park? At the monument in front of the planetarium. 5:00 p.m.?" As soon as he had heard Altadena, he thought of the park. It was a reasonable drive, and he had previously spent hours at the observatory. It put him on familiar grounds. Cameron agreed.

"Please keep this strictly between us. Call Officer Hunter and make sure he doesn't tell anyone else I'm in California. I need discretion. It's imperative we keep this quiet." Mark was already feeling that too many people knew he was in California. He felt better about Mary but had to act fast. He had to contact Steve Chang and let him know he had something to trade.

Cameron hung up the phone and contemplated whether or not to tell his boss about this recent development. Since he was on leave, he didn't feel it was necessary. Not yet. Working for the detectives gave him a little leeway. Well, he *would be* working for them in a few days. He would give the CIA man some time, at least until 5:00 p.m.

49

April 25th 2009
Jet Propulsion Laboratory
Pasadena, California

"Richard Salvatore, Mark Springfield; or whatever his Goddamn name is, sat right in front of me! I would've had him killed then if I had known! Ken, how did this get past us?" It was a rhetorical question. Steve Chang was furious and could hardly control himself as he sat in the small room at the JPL.

Ken Benner sat patiently across from him with his elbows on the table, watching. He knew what was really driving this rant. Martin Powell, Chang's number one man had brought the woman back, the sister of a CIA operative. Martin walked a drugged Mary Springfield off the plane in Los Angeles and stashed her at the Jet Propulsion Laboratories' old test site. Ken shook his head. He had never liked the man sitting to his right, thought him impulsive. Powell had screwed up, and now they had to clean up his mess. They didn't want to find out how relentless Mark Springfield would be.

"I worked for years getting information on the Huntsville unit," Chang blurted. He knew his government was taunting the U.S. It was a ploy to get them to show their hand. Instead, they had planted their own spy. Had his government not been so arrogant, he would've eventually had ICE. It was a case of one hand not knowing what the other was doing. He blamed them for his failure. Steve Chang was furious and ordered the woman killed. They could not keep her around and risk a breach. Ken watched his boss talk to his murderous partner and a thin smile grew on Martin's face. *An innocent civilian*, Ken thought. *She would be a casualty of the Chinese military build-up.*

Ken and Martin left Chang and rode the elevator up to the lobby in silence. The two men walked outside. Ken felt the thin veil of secrecy start to tear. He knew the organization was at its end. The CIA was onto them and Chang was coming apart at the seams. Now they were about to kill an innocent woman. His heart sank as he watched the dusty Chevy Malibu pull up alongside the curb. With a slight lurch, it stopped a few feet from them.

Lorena Bean, known as 'L', was by far the prettiest in their organization and just as lethal as Martin. Slowly, the door opened and she pulled herself out of the sedan. She looked around the parking lot before moving to the other side of the car. Men always gave her the once-over. She was an unassuming petite blonde with big, beautiful brown eyes. She was the perfect person for being able to go places to which no man would ever have access. Martin relied on her heavily for his *special work*. She had a taste for murder that had started a vigilante killing spree after a rape had left her battered and hospitalized for weeks.

It had happened while she had been leaving the bank after work in which she supervised the loan department. She had been working late to help her section prepare for an upcoming audit and had left long after her coworkers. She had been alone as she walked the one block to the parking lot, never aware she was being stalked. Her predator was on her as soon as she left the bank. She was easy prey—alone and unaware. He had become more aroused the longer he had walked. When she finally looked up, she noticed the lot was almost empty. Looking around, she was glad someone else was there. He lingered next to a car fishing for keys he didn't have. Just as she swung open the door, he quickly moved across the lot, covered her mouth, and shoved her in. She had been easily overpowered and taken off-guard.

The attack was vicious. She was hit multiple times in the head as he tried to subdue her. Lorena was in the hospital unconscious for two days. When she finally left two weeks later, she swore that she would never again be a victim. Many times before the attack, she had contemplated buying a firearm but had always been talked out of it. Now, with her heightened sense of awareness and safety, she explored many options, but it always came back to what some have referred to as "The Great Equalizer." L spent many hours at the local shooting range perfecting her newly found skill, one in which she excelled. She attended shooting classes and devoured books on self-defense, anything that sharpened her awareness. She was a changed person.

Working late, and with hatred in her heart she left the bank. This time she welcomed an attack. Not being able to identify her assailant, the police had never made an arrest. It didn't matter; she wanted revenge and would kill anyone who looked at her menacingly.

L carried a Smith and Wesson snub-nosed 357 stainless revolver with mahogany grips. She had shot many firearms while at the range, but when she picked up the 357, it felt right at home. After a trigger job, it shot just as smoothly as the semi-autos, and it was easily concealed. L found herself working late and actually inviting fate. One night, when followed by two Hispanic men, she led them into an alleyway. They followed her, thinking she was an easy target. She hurried deep into the alley and feigned fear when she turned to face them. They demanded her money. One of them started grabbing his crotch and speaking Spanish to his partner. She reached into her purse. "Here, take my wallet," she cried. She thought it would be a nice touch but all she could think about was that night in the parking lot and rage welled inside her. She pulled out the revolver and the attackers both laughed, until the first two shots were fired at one of the men.

She fired another two shots from her 357 as the second man turned and tried to run. A round tore into his rib cage and another into his lower back. He stumbled twenty feet and fell, hitting the ground like he had been dropped from a building. She walked over to him. He lay on his back, his smile was gone. He looked up mouthing some type of plea. A wide smile grew on L's face as she covered his head with the front sight. She slowly pressed the trigger and watched the cylinder roll to the next round. There was a smooth break as the sound echoed off the walls.

She felt euphoria. She felt...freedom. She would've never thought the growing pool of blood under the head of her attacker could make her feel so free, so in control. She looked down at her smoking revolver and thought it truly was 'The Great Equalizer.' She raised the gun to her nose and smelled the cylinder. A smile grew over her face as the scent from the spent casings filled her nose. It gave her a sense of satisfaction no man could ever provide. Over the next nine months, she would kill seven more times, some deserving, some innocent. It didn't matter; Lorena Bean liked to kill.

She knew the killing was out of control and thought a change would help, so Lorena had applied on the Jet Propulsion Laboratory's open advertisement for a Financial Manager in the propulsion department. After a lengthy interview process, she had been offered, and had accepted, the job working for Steve Chang. It was innocent, and the two spent many hours together as she became familiar with the routine. After a few business trips, they became closer, but Steve had never made a pass or looked at Lorena in a sexual way. He was her boss during work and a friend after hours. This was a relationship she appreciated but wasn't used to. She became fiercely loyal and the two eventually developed a mutual respect.

Although the job did slow her down, it didn't stop the killings. Occasionally, she traveled throughout California visiting bars in both the worst and the most upscale parts of town. Lorena was a predator, and whoever followed her to her car, the prey. Steve started to notice a change in her when she would return from her 'mini vacations,' so he did what every concerned boss and careful spy would do, he had her followed, and assigned Ken Benner the task.

Ken reported what he had observed while following Lorena. From the inside pocket of his suit coat, he produced a small notebook and started going through it. He stopped several pages in, and looked up at Steve. "I don't know how to tell you this, but our Lorena is a killer. She is probably the one they've been talking about for the past several years on the news."

"What! Our Ms. Bean is a killer?"

"I followed her on three of her extended weekend trips. The first was up to Visalia and what unfolded in front of me was something I never expected. She drove around town finally stopping at a bar off of Mineral King, not a very nice place I might add. In fact, I thought I might have to intervene when she finally came out of the place. I sat in my car and watched as she left with this guy who was grabbing her all over. It was hard to believe.

I thought for a moment I was somehow watching the wrong person. " As Ken relived the story, Steve could hardly believe what he was hearing. "She drove over to North Cain and Goshen to a storage yard," Ken said, referring to his notes. "I was being careful not to get too close and drove past the gate. All of a sudden, I hear a gunshot. I thought, *Holy shit. He shot her!*" Steve Chang was riveted and hung on every word. "As I was turning the car around, another shot rang out. Again, I thought, *Oh my God, that son of a bitch is killing Lorena!*"

Steve cut in and yelled out, "But she's at work today!"

Ken raised his hand to stop Steve. "At that point, I got out of my car and ran towards the yard. There she was, driving through the gate. I stepped behind a junk pile or she would've seen me. I watched her drive by, she had a... uhmm...different look on her face. She looked content, maybe even happy. As soon as she turned the corner, I went in the yard and there, shot twice at point blank, was the guy." He took out his phone and showed Chang several pictures of the body. Ken looked directly at Steve. "I couldn't believe what I was seeing. Lorena had killed someone for no apparent reason and had calmly driven away. I stood there, looking at the guy." Ken's last few words trailed off as he sat back in his chair. He'd been keeping everything from Steve until he had had the full picture. Now, laying it all out, he didn't know how Chang would react.

"Oh my God Lorena?" Chang sat back and let out a long sigh.

"Same thing happened in Oakland and San Diego. Each time she seemed to enjoy it, although the guy in Oakland may have deserved it." Ken sat back and let it sink in. It had taken him awhile to process it, too. Lorena Bean, one of the prettiest and nicest women he knew, was a stone-cold killer.

Chang had been shocked to learn Lorena Bean could so easily pull the trigger on both criminally driven and innocent men. It was something he would've never guessed. He knew then that his new financial manager would fit in nicely.

Ken had showed up at her desk late one afternoon and had asked if she'd take an elevator ride with him. When she had sat across from Steve in the secure room, she had felt trapped. He had exposed her; not only did he have eyewitness accounts of her after-hours activity, he had pictures. *Oh my God! They know,* she thought. She had kept a watch on the door, expecting the police to barge in at any time, but nothing. Instead, Steve had slid the pictures and SD card in the shredder. She had been confused and a new wave of emotion had overtaken her.

She had laid her head in her arms and cried. Steve had stood, slid his chair next to her, and had tried to console her. "Miss Bean, I don't think you know what this is all about. I want you to work for me." He had known that would puzzle her, but keeping her off-guard during this time had been important. "You have a talent I can use." Her crying had weakened to a sob when she slowly looked up.

"I don't understand. I've been killing people and you still want me to work for you? I'm not going to jail?"

Steve had been delighted. She seemed to have no remorse for her victims. "How would you like to be paid for your talent? And paid very well I might add."

"What the hell is going on?" was all she had said. She had thought it possible that one day she would sit in front of the police answering questions concerning her part in the murders, never her boss.

"Let's just say I work for an agency that could use more people like you."

"The CIA?"

"Not exactly, but close." Steve had chuckled.

Lorena had sensed she wasn't getting any further so had simply asked, "What now?"

"You will be contacted by Mr. Martin Powell. You two will become friends."

Lorena had furled her eyebrows in deep thought. "Martin Powell... Martin Powell... isn't he in security?"

"Head of security for this wing. He'll be contacting you," he had concluded their discussion, "and Miss Bean, discretion is paramount."

As Lorena and Ken walked to the elevator, she began to process the meeting with her boss. Reflecting on where she worked, and the fact he didn't elaborate about the details for whom he was working, she could only come to one conclusion. As they rode the elevator up to the lobby she reached out and pushed the *EMERGENCY STOP* button just before they reached the floor. The elevator had jerked to a stop. She had faced Ken and mouthed the words, "We're spies?" Ken had reached across her and positioned his face close to hers, pulled out the red button and whispered, "Yes."

A few seconds later, the doors opened and she stepped through to the lobby feeling like a new person. An hour earlier, she had thought she was going to be accused of murder and thrown in jail, but she had been set free, free to continue this drive that consumed her.

Three days later, Martin met her at a park close to the JPL. Over the next eight months, the two worked together to perfect her skill. He taught L all he knew about the drugs he used to kill or induce catatonic states in people. Together, they had grown perfect as a killing team. When they quietly killed retired Navy Captain, Dan Rico, right in his doorway while his girls slept in adjacent rooms, they knew it could get no better.

Ken watched as Lorena smiled at Martin as she slid into the passenger side of the car.

Martin walked towards the driver's side and said with a grin. "Well, Mr. Benner, it's been nice, but we have an *appointment* with a young woman." Martin gave L a wink, and he slid into the car.

Ken rolled his hands into clenched fist, watching the two drive away.

50

April 26th 2009

Mark was familiar with Griffith Park. He had spent many hours exploring the heavens using the telescopes from the observatory. He stood far enough away from the park's monument to be obscured by passing visitors. When two men appeared together then split off in opposite directions, Mark knew they were the highway patrol men. He passed a few guys who were throwing a Frisbee. Mark had called out and motioned for them to toss it to him. In California fashion, they didn't miss a beat as they tossed him the disk. He played along while he surveyed the area to make sure there were no other suspicious looking visitors.

At 5:15 p.m., when he was sure the two men were alone, he made his move. Mark flubbed the throw of the Frisbee to the group and it flew towards Cameron. "Sorry! I got it," he yelled while chasing after it, making it appear he was part of the group. The disc almost landed at Cameron's feet. Officer Cameron bent down to pick it up and was met by Mark. "Meet me behind the observatory. Come alone. We can talk there." Mark turned and tossed the Frisbee back as he ran towards the group and disappeared in the crowd.

Cameron looked around the grassy area and wondered, *What the hell just happened? Had he been visited by a ghost?* He turned towards Shawn and motioned for him to stay put. He trotted towards the observatory. Next to the rear stairs, partially obscured by shrubbery, was the person he recognized from the torn and bloodied driver's license. Mark had watched Cameron cross the lawn and was more at ease since he had left his partner.

"Mark Springfield," he said sticking out his hand.

Cameron hesitantly offered his hand, "Cameron Butler."

"Thank you for meeting me. Is that Officer Hunter back there?"

"No, that's my partner, Shawn Davis."

"Jesus Christ! Who else knows I'm here?" Mark grumbled.

"That's it. I called Officer Hunter and told him to keep this to himself. Shawn was on the scene with me. I brought him in case we needed to pick his brain." The word 'back-up' was more appropriate, but he kept that to himself.

"Cameron, if I may, I'll be blunt. I work for the CIA. There are countries working inside the United States trying to steal top-secret technology, technology so sensitive it could change how we fight wars. I was placed to infiltrate their organization. Long story short, they kidnapped my sister. I've been shot and on the move for two days, and frankly all I care about is my sister. They tried to kill her family in St. Charles, but fortunately we were able to avert that. What I need from you is the identities of the driver and passenger. Any information will be helpful."

Cameron was shell shocked. He knew he was standing there with his mouth hanging open. Here was his first contact with the CIA, and it was not a drill, but a serious national security threat. He felt helpless. All he had were names; basic information was all he could offer. He pulled his notepad from his pocket, "I'll give you everything I have." He flipped it open and reviewed his notes. On a new page, he copied everything. Mark walked around the building to check the area, then back to Cameron who was just finishing.

Cameron tore two pages from his notepad and handed them to Mark. "We found your wallet and Mary's on the victims. After some more looking, we found theirs. I wrote my personal cell number on the bottom. Actually,

I just started with the investigators. I'm on leave for a week, but call me anytime and I'll help wherever I can."

Mark took the pages and looked them over. He recognized the name Martin Powell and shook his head. "And this Dave Quinn's the truck driver?" he asked, pointing to the name with *observation* written next to it.

"He is. He's not doing too well after killing two people. That's his address in Arizona."

"And Lorena Bean?"

"She was sexually assaulted a few years ago, other than that we have nothing on her."

"I see they were headed away from Pasadena?" He now had hope that his sister was still alive and began to feel his composure return. Mark knew he needed help. He looked up at his new partner narrowing his steel gray eyes. He had already provided valuable information. Mark decided almost instantly that Cameron could be trusted.

"I need to trust you to look something up for me and not tell anyone else, not even your partner."

Cameron looked at Mark and felt a chill run up his spine. Whatever was going on was nothing close to anything he'd ever been involved with before. *It's all or nothing*, he thought. "Name it."

Mark motioned for his notepad and wrote *Cliff House* and his phone number across the top. Then, he wrote *Steve Chang* underneath along with *Jet Propulsion Laboratory - what do they own north of the facility?* "If something happens to me, contact the person written across the top. Find out what vehicles are registered to Mr. Chang and verify his home address. I need the JPL info first and I need it quick. One more thing, and this is important." Mark reached inside his jacket and pulled out the device. "If I become incapacitated in any way, depress these two buttons three times, then personally hand this to Mr. House and *no one* else."

Cameron was uncomfortable and hadn't a clue as to what Mark was showing him. "Is this what it's all about? The crash? Them taking your sister?"

Mark studied Cameron for what seemed like an eternity, hesitant to tell him too much, yet felt he owed him a little. "The crash was a lucky break," - then holding up the device,- "and this communicates with one of our satellites. I can't tell you how important it is that it doesn't fall into the wrong hands. Can you get me that information?"

Cameron knew personal information should *not* be accessed through their database unless they were actually working a case. He was with a stranger, operating outside the box, and now he could be responsible for God knows what. He had worked with the department for many years. There were times rules couldn't always be followed to the letter. This was one of those times.

Mark sensed some hesitation and reached into his back pocket and handed him his credentials. Perhaps if Cameron saw some type of official identification it might help. Cameron opened the wallet. Written across the top was *Central Intelligence Agency* and underneath *Mark Springfield*. To the left of center was a photograph of a less disheveled individual than the one that stood before him, but it was the same person.

Cameron looked at Mark. "Why do I know the name, Cliff House?"

"He's the director of the CIA." Mark paused to let it sink in. "That number will get you his secretary. After hours it goes to his service. Mention my name and you'll be put through immediately."

Cameron let out a long sigh as he closed the thin black case and handed it back. "I'll get right on the JPL info."

Mark shook his head with acknowledged relief and the two men started to turn their separate ways when Mark turned back towards his new partner. "By the way, detective, congrats on your promotion." Before Cameron could respond, Mark disappeared into the background.

The compliment took him by surprise and he smiled. He turned and jogged back to his partner hoping he had made the right decision.

51

Ken Benner took the call from Steve Chang late in the morning. He had been notified that Martin Powell and Lorena Bean had both been killed in a traffic accident. After ending the call, he held onto the phone for a few long seconds before hanging it up. He stared blankly at the floor. Without knowing the details of the accident, he could only assume that they had killed the agent's sister. He had done nothing to stop them. Maybe if he had intervened the outcome would've been different.

He was remorseful for the agent. The team that had been sent to kill his sister liked to experiment when they had time, and they had all the time they needed. Now they too lay dead in a morgue.

Steve Chang sat at his desk contemplating his next move. After several inquiring phone calls he found out the accident had happened while they were traveling north towards their facility. The woman was probably still alive. He did, however, still need to deal with her. He had two more assets he could deploy. They were getting ready for a trip to the east coast. He had sent them to kill Mike Vanns. Chang had to cut every tie that led to him. However, killing the woman and the agent were more important. He made the call and redirected his team.

Chang was startled when the phone rang on his desk. He had told his secretary to hold his calls. Irritated, he picked it up, ready to admonish her for putting the call through, but as he held it to his ear, she immediately apologized. "I'm sorry, sir. Your brother is on line one. Says it's urgent."

"Mrs. Lindley, I don't have a brother," he sternly replied and hung up. As he sat back in his chair, the phone rang again. "Yes!" He spit into the phone.

"Mr. Chang, your brother, Mark, is on line one. He says it's urgent." She replied in a shaky voice

Steve leaned forward in his chair, hesitated, then punched line one. "Good afternoon, Mr. Salvatore, or should I say Mr. Springfield?"

"I want my sister," Mark stated coldly.

"And what are you willing to trade?"

"I have the encryption and flew all this way to give it to you."

Steve rocked back in his chair. So, the CIA was close. Steve was relieved that his people hadn't killed the women. He couldn't believe his good fortune. If she had been killed, he'd have had no bargaining power. "Family's an excellent motivator, Mr. Springfield. Are you alone?"

"Yes."

"How can I believe you?" Chang shot back.

"Like you said, family's an excellent motivator."

Chang stared at the top of his desk for several seconds. Then he asked his most important question. "How will I know the encryption you have is authentic?"

"Have one of your men test the device. There's another imaging test scheduled. You can access the satellite then. Give me my sister. I'll give you the device and you can have your satellite."

Mark laid his cards on the table the Huntsville unit for his sister. With the safety mechanisms Ryan had put in place, he hoped he really didn't have to trade one for the other. But for his sister's life, he would in a minute.

"No, Mr. Springfield, I'm afraid that won't do. Seems I have something you want. I'll give you your sister *after* I get the satellite. That's the only way I'll know for sure the encryption is authentic."

Mark sat back in his rental car and closed his eyes. He wasn't about to risk his sister's life for any piece of hardware. There had to be another way. There's always a way. His mind drifted back to his escape in Germany when Russia's Federal Security Service had had him cornered.

After Russia had discovered Ramous was a CIA operative and on the brink of receiving their sub codes, he had been intercepted and killed. On him were tickets and a location in Germany. The FSS knew it was his way out and had quickly sent agents to find his contact. The Russian Foreign Intelligence Service, FIS, were ruthless in trying to run Mark down. They employed the same agents and tactics and would stop at nothing to capture or kill a foreign agent, especially a CIA operative. If it wasn't for one of them underestimating him, he wouldn't be here today.

"Mr. Springfield!" Steve snapped.

"You need to prove my sister's alive and that she stays that way or I'll run this goddamn thing over and we both lose!"

"Very well. It's late. You'll have your proof tomorrow. I'll have my associates collect your sister and bring her to the exchange."

"Once I turn the device over, I want to be detained with my sister until you verify its authenticity and release us. I'd like to say I trust you, but I don't." Mark spoke with a controlled rage. He hated the man on the other end and couldn't wait to see him dead or rotting in a federal prison.

"Mr. Springfield, your sister means nothing to me. The Huntsville unit is worth many, many lives. I'd already given the order to have her killed once, but my good fortune has intervened. For your sake, I hope the encryption is authentic." Chang knew Springfield would never risk his sister's life but taunted him just the same. He stared across his office at the adjacent wall contemplating whether or not it was a good idea to put them together. *It makes it easier* he thought with a smile. Once he had the satellite, he would kill them both. "Someone will contact you at exactly 11:00 a.m." With that, Steve Chang hung up. He was close to having the satellite. "I will be a hero in my country," he murmured to himself, "I'll teach those stuffy politicians not to be so hasty."

If Steve was trying to infuriate Mark by abruptly hanging up, it didn't work. He was too focused on getting his sister back. He scrolled through his cell phone numbers and found Cameron Butler. On the second ring, he answered. "Any luck, detective?"

Cameron had left the station and was walking towards his car when Mark had called. He had been at the station on a ruse of following up on the accident. Since he was one of the senior officers and often worked on his off time, no one had questioned him when he had used the database to access the information.

"Mr. Springfield, I found two places. One is a picnic area close to the Hansen Dam. The other is off Paxton Street."

"I know the dam. Paxton doesn't ring a bell."

"Where Highway 118 meets the I-210. It's an area they use for testing. I looked up both places on Google maps. The dam is simply a park area, but there's a lot of excavating happening on Paxton Road. It's a large tiered area up the mountain. It's very out of the way. If it were my choice, I'd look there first. Hmm…Let's see, Steven Chang also drives a red Ford Edge registered in his name and it has a personal plate *Propel*. He lives just east of the JPL, at 228 Altadena Drive."

"First," began Mark, "Let's keep it to 'Mark' and not 'Mr. Springfield.' Secondly, Great job! That was fast." The relief in Mark's voice was noticeable. Cameron narrowed his focus and gave him a location from which to begin his search. It was a solid place to start and Mark knew it. He agreed with Cameron, if they were going to stash someone, it was going to be off the beaten path. "So, detective, how's the rest of your night look?"

52

"We're close to getting the encryption." Chang sat back in his chair. "Springfield's here in California and wants to make a trade. We're just finding out that Martin and L were on their way to the woman when the accident happened."

"She's still alive!?" Ken sat straight in his chair with such force he moved the steel table.

"It's been awhile since we've seen her." Chang quickly said. "I have to get my arms around this thing. Someone needs to run up to the old test site and make sure she's still alive. If so, we'll grab her and make the trade."

Steve looked around the room. Ken was sitting straight in his chair listening intently while Seth and Luke sat back with thin smiles on their faces. Ken Benner was a tall, formable man. He could easily control the woman but the two sitting to his left posed a more menacing threat. Like Martin and L, they both liked to kill and would jump at the chance to add another person to their dark resume. "Whether the girl is alive or not, when this is over, I want Mark Springfield dead."

Ken Benner leaned in and looked intently at Chang. "I'll go check the girl." He stood as if the decision was made.

"No! That won't be necessary. Seth and Luke will check her," Chang ordered. Ken sat down. He didn't want to appear worried for the girl. "First light, they'll head to the yard," Steve Chang continued as he looked at the two. "Get her up and walk her around. Give her water and some food. Do NOT hurt her! We'll meet the agent at eleven. Make her somewhat presentable. When this is over you, can kill them in whatever order you want."

The instructions didn't sit well with Ken. He had watched Chang's behavior change over the last few days and it bothered him. Ken had been enlightened. He had made a deal with the devil and now he wanted out.

53

April 26th 2009
JPL Test Site
Abandoned trailer

With no one left to administer Martin Powell's concoction of drugs, its effect started to wear off, and Mary became aware of her surroundings. She was strapped to a bed, and she had a pounding headache. She wondered if she had been kidnapped for ransom or the sex trade. She struggled against her restraints but it was useless. She remembered the plane ride but had no idea where she had been taken. Was she out of the country? Panic struck and she began to yank at her restraints. It was no use. Suddenly Mary thought of her brother and a phrase he liked to use, *let's man up*. She became still and made an effort to slow her breathing.

She remembered the first time she had heard that phrase. Mark used it when she fell from their tree house and sprained her wrist. Ever since, she had used that simple phrase to help calm herself. "Panic won't get me out," she almost said out loud.

Mary tried looking around. The bed she was lying on was in an older, single story building. Because of its shape, she assumed it was an abandoned office trailer. It wasn't completely dark. Some ambient light made its way through two small windows. She looked around the shadowed room and saw several tables. A briefcase lay on top of the closest. There were chairs, a refrigerator and several boxes sitting in the corner. She wasn't blindfolded or gagged so screaming was probably useless. No one would hear, but it did matter. She mustered up the strength to scream at the top of her lungs for several long minutes anyway. Exhausted, she relaxed and listened. Nothing. In the distance, she heard a piece of equipment running. Her head pounded as she lay there. Eventually, she fell into a light sleep. The lingering effect of the drugs still lurked in her system.

By the time Mark made his way through Los Angeles traffic, it was late. Cameron suggested they meet east of Highway 118 and the I-405 intersection, on Sepulveda Boulevard. But Springfield had been traveling all day and they both needed to eat and make a plan.

Cameron sat in the booth working on his second cup of coffee. When he felt he had waited long enough for the agent, he ordered two dinners. As if on cue, Mark slid in just as the waitress set the plates on the table. Cameron had begun to decipher the agent's habits and asked, "Been here long?"

"Long enough to wonder if I needed to order my own dinner." Mark picked up his fork and dove in. They ate in silence.

"Just to be upfront, I'm keeping notes on all of this for the report I'm sure I'm going to have to fill out later."

"Detective, you'll blame me for all of this. In your report, you'll tell them you've been absconded by the federal government and sworn to secrecy."

"I doubt it'll be that easy. By the way, if I'm to call you Mark, you should call me Cameron."

"But 'Detective' has such a nice ring to it," grinned Mark.

After a few minutes, Cameron sat back, tapping his fork on his plate. He liked Mark. Once he got past his appearing and disappearing act, Cameron thought Mark's team a good team to be on. The government man was growing on him. "What now?"

Truth be told, Mark was glad to have some help and thought the man sitting across from him would work just fine. "I need ammo. Then we drive up that mountain and wait. I talked to Chang. He's sending someone to get my sister tomorrow. We could head them off at the pass, so to speak."

Cameron leaned in a bit and spoke in a low tone. "I took the liberty of bringing a few things with me. In my trunk, I have five hundred rounds each of 9mm, 40cal, and 45cal. I don't know what you carry, so I just covered the bases. I couldn't draw any of the long guns from the office so I brought some personal items. I have an M1 Garand and about three hundred rounds." He sat back, waited, and watched the agent's surprised expression as he reached for his coffee. He saw the expression change when he mentioned the ammo and M1. He savored the fact that it was his turn to surprise the agent.

It wasn't an expression of surprise, however, but one of recognition. Mark casually replied, "An M1? The air-cooled, gas operated, clip-fed semiautomatic shoulder weapon? Do you know Patton called that 'the greatest battle implement ever devised'?" Mark spewed out the information as if he were reading off a card sitting in front of him. He grinned as he watched a bewildered Cameron slowly shake his head. Mark knew he had taken the wind out of his sails, but he continued anyway. "I think it became the standard service weapon in 1936."

Mark felt their relationship forge with Cameron's next two words: "*Smart Ass*"

Mark stood, dropped two twenty-dollar bills on the table, and looked at Cameron. "Ready?"

As they passed the counter, Cameron stopped and got two coffees to go.

Cameron had parked along a small embankment away from the restaurant. The two men walked towards his car. He handed a coffee to Mark. "I have a thermos in the backseat. It could be a long night."

Mark was not a coffee man, but he was happy for the extra boost. He looked at the cup. "Thanks. Why an M1?"

"I like the older guns. I also have .303 British Enfield, Mosin Nagant, and I recently added a Berdan." Cameron's excitement showed when he mentioned the Berdan.

"One or two?" Mark asked, interested.

The simple question stopped Cameron cold. He reached out and grabbed Mark's arm to stop him. He and his friends knew guns but not many of them cared about the older hardware. Who was this guy who not only knew about older firearms but was also interested in them? "Wait, most people ask, W*hat's a Berdan?* You know there's a difference?"

Mark laughed. "The same reason I know that Forehand and Wadsworth built a .44 caliber large frame revolver in the mid-1870s. I have one with *CALIFORNIA BEAR* stamped on the frame."

"You're a collector?"

"I guess, kind of. Some things just interest me. I pick'm up and tear'm apart. I like to see what the manufacturers were up to during their time period. You'd be surprised what they were able to mass produce. If you're ever in Washington, I'll show you my 1900 and older collection."

Cameron shook his head as they finished the short walk to his car. When the light came on in the trunk, Mark saw several ammo cans lined along the front, a case of water, duffel and two rifle bags in the center. "That's for you," Cameron said, pointing to a beige bag leaning against the cans. Mark looked around, reached in, and unzipped the bag expecting to find a curio. He pulled the cover back and a wicked grin grew across his face as he looked up at Cameron. "I forgot to mention," Cameron continued. "I like Mini-14s, too."

The top of the ammo cans were labeled with different calibers. Mark took the one marked .40cal and removed two boxes of ammo from the can. He scanned the parking lot before he removed the long guns and set them on the backseat along with the boxes of ammo. Then he removed the light bulbs from the dome light and the trunk. "We certainly don't need any target indicators."

54

April 26th 2009

Seth and Luke left the building at the JPL, fired up their motorcycles, and left to have a quick bite to eat before heading to the yard. They had no intention of waiting until morning.

Two years earlier, Steve Chang had been given control of Seth and Luke. They had come from the submarine base in Bangor, Washington. They were part of a spy program that the Chinese government had shut down when the U.S. became aware of the program's existence. Seth and Luke had been the muscle, and their services were no longer needed. Steve had never liked the two, but he had done what he had been told. Occasionally, he had let them follow and gather intelligence on potential newcomers or potential threats to his organization. Now, he was glad he had them. Someone needed to deal with the girl. Once the agent's sister was together with her brother, they would both need to be watched until the encryption was verified and the Huntsville unit was under Chang's control. He didn't care what happened after that. Once he reprogrammed the satellite, he would return to China a hero.

Seth and Luke turned off Paxton Street and headed up the hill. The road soon turned to dirt and the only portions illuminated were the areas washed with the lights from their bikes. The Kawasaki Ninjas made short work of the switchbacks and narrow sections of the road. It wasn't long before they found themselves approaching the gate for the JPL's test site. They knew how operations were controlled at the site. When a test was to be conducted the area would be secured two days prior to assure no unwanted traffic transited the area. It was a cost-cutting measure that allowed anyone unfettered access to the area during down times. There were many times they had found the lock cut. They stopped at the gate and killed the bikes. They sat for several minutes listening. In the distance was the normal sound of a generator that ran powering lights scattered throughout the yard. There were no other sounds that alerted them. Seth swung his leg off his bike, walked up to the gate, and keyed the lock. They slowly rode through the compound and continued up the road until they came to the old contractor's office. The office had been set up when the remote test site was built, but it was now abandoned for a newer, closer facility.

Mary had regained consciousness by the time Luke and Seth arrived. The bike tires crunched the ground until they came to a halt and the motors stopped running. "Who's there!?" she called. "Can someone help me?" She heard men talking as they walked up the wooden stairs and was relieved to hear it was in English. She strained to hear their conversation. "Hello!" she yelled again. "Why won't you answer me?"

The men stopped at the door and she heard one of them say, "She's mine first." Then they both laughed.

It became clear. The men talking in hushed tones outside the door were her kidnappers. She pulled against her restraints with such force the bed moved and thumped against the floor. Again, she twisted against the leather straps. This time the bed slammed into the wall, rattling the window above her. Looking around, she noticed two men standing inside the room. They were both wearing dusty motorcycle leathers. They looked at Mary, then back at each other; broad smiles spread across their faces.

Seth laughed out loud, walked over, and sat on the bed. "That won't help you."

"Who are you? Why am I here?"

His unshaven cheek rubbed against hers and he whispered in her ear, "Who we are is no concern of yours." He rubbed his hand down her thigh. His long, sweaty hair hung in Mary's face. She pulled her head away. With all the force she could muster, she head-butted him until he slid off the bed. The man was momentarily stunned. His partner ran across the room and pulled him up.

"What do you want from me? HELP!" she screamed, trying to sit up.

Seth slowly got to his feet, rubbing his swelling cheek. He ran his hand across his mouth and wiped the blood from his lips. "You fucking bitch!" he yelled. He yanked her hair, forcing her head to the side, and backhanded her across the face. Mary winced but refused to give him the satisfaction of crying out. Blood ran from her mouth. Seth saw the defiance in her eyes. He balled his hand into a fist and started to swing but Luke grabbed his arm and pulled him away.

"Not now! We need her tomorrow."

"God damnit!" he spit as he rubbed his bruised cheekbone. He glared at the girl wondering if he really needed to keep her alive.

* * *

Once Mark Springfield and Cameron left the restaurant, it was a quick trip down Highway 118 to the I-210. They drove up Paxton Street, slowing down when it turned to dirt. A quarter-mile up the road, Mark spotted a grove of trees. They had discussed their lay-and-wait strategy. Mark knew the trees off the road would conceal them. Before Cameron could stop the car, Mark instructed him to position the car behind the trees across the road. The oncoming headlights would light up the outside and leave the inside of the turn obscured. Without hesitation, Cameron parked his car. Mark pulled out his Glock 23 and laid it on the floor. Cameron followed suit. Mark smiled, realizing they both carried the same gun. Cameron went over the particulars of his Ruger Mini-14. It was modeled after the Military's M14 and was a very accurate weapon. His was the ranch rifle chambered in .223, and he had close to one thousand rounds of 69 grain hollow points, five hundred of which he had brought.

"I must say, detective, I was pretty happy to see that Mini-14. I have a lot of time behind one of those."

"I'am happy to finally surprise you with something," Cameron countered. He had one more surprise for the agent.

"Tell me about your M1 Garand." Mark wanted to know everything about every weapon system he had at his disposal.

"I love my Garand," Cameron started. "Never had a malfunction and it shoots straighter than I do. It's chambered in .30-06. I brought three hundred rounds of one hundred eighty grain soft points."

They had just started going over contingencies when Cameron noticed distant lights bouncing around in his rearview mirror.

"We have company."

They retrieved their guns from the floor as a precautionary measure before turning in their seats to get a better view.

"Make sure you turn away and stay down when they pass," Mark ordered.

The bikes zipped past. The dust they kicked up severely obscured the road. The riders never noticed the car hidden by the trees.

Cameron turned to Mark. "Gotta be them. There's no reason to ride up here this time of night."

"They're here sooner than I thought. Give'm about thirty seconds, then we'll go, lights off."

The half-moon gave them some light, but trying to follow two motorcycles in the darkness with the stirred up dust was challenging. The car moved at a snail's pace in comparison to the bikes. Mark did his best to call the edge of the road from the passenger's seat. When they reached the JPL gate, there was no sign of the bikes, and Mark thought it was odd that they had left the gate open. They inched their way into the compound, listening for the slightest sound. The car proceeded slowly through the compound and continued up the road.

As they started around a bend in the road, Cameron stopped the car and put it in reverse. "I think I see the bikes," he said. He backed down the road and stopped around a slight rise. Cameron put the car in park and turned the engine off.

Mark's instinct was to run into the building, throw the door open, and rescue his sister, but he knew that option was a fairy tale. His actions would have to be calculated and precise.

The two stepped out of the car with their pistols in hand. They quickly surveyed the yard. When they were confident they were unseen, they opened the back doors of the car. They slipped the long guns out of their cases. Mark looked around the yard assessing his surroundings while loading the Mini-14. He loaded and checked the weapon. It was spotless.

Cameron opened his duffel bag and handed Mark a set of electronic hearing protection. Then, he reached in and pulled out two ridged cases. He set them down on the lid of the trunk, sliding one next to Mark. "Here," he said with a smirk. "I thought these might come in handy."

Mark turned on the electronic hearing device and reached for the case. He held it up so the moonlight reflected off the inscription. Across the top was embossed *Night Owl Optics NOBG1 NVG*. A stupid grin grew on his face and he couldn't stop it.

"Well done, young man. Well done." Mark held up a set of night-vision goggles complete with an infrared illuminator; this changed everything. He quickly formulated a plan.

After one last chamber and magazine check, they walked silently to the top of the hill. They lay down on the slight rise. Mark nodded towards the building, then looked at Cameron. "What's your best guess?"

Cameron looked towards the building. "Easily, more than a football field."

"Yeah, I'm thinking probably two and a half," Mark said while laying out the last of the extra magazines. He was already mentally calculating a shot at two hundred fifty yards.

From their position, they had an oblique line of fire to the window. It was angled enough so that if someone peered out the window in the low light, they would be all but impossible to see. The old test site was not lit very well. Other than the moon, the only other illumination came from the last two pole lights on the outside perimeter of the new site. The half-moon made the lighting perfect. His night vision goggles were adjusted so he was able to see the riders moving around inside through the windows. Both appeared to be facing the corner of the room. When one of them raised his arm and lurched towards the corner, he cringed. It was Mary, he knew it. His gut told him so. He had relied on his intuition more than once. It had never let him down, and, in fact, had saved him in the past. He *knew* Mary was in that building. Since he didn't see anyone else moving around, it was a safe bet that she was bound. With the electronic amplification turned up to the max, he could easily hear the generator and every sound he and Cameron made. He had a simple plan, and when he faintly heard his sister yell for help through the electronic hearing, he had to implement it fast.

As a senior CIA field operative, Mark had trained with any organization that pertained to his work. Right now, he quietly thanked God he had spent two months training with the snipers in Fort Benning, Georgia. Mark knew the shot was tricky, and although he hadn't made any long range shots in a while, he knew the basic philosophy. *Overshoot by one inch for every one hundred yards.* Mark assessed the building. It was a double-wide mobile home converted into an office. The walls would be thinly constructed and Mary was probably sitting or lying on the right side of the building. He had to point a gun in her general direction. There was nothing else he could do. Chang's men had the upper hand; they had his sister.

Mark pointed at the lights while looking at Cameron. "I need you to take those out, first the pole on our left then the one down range, then swing that gun of yours around and shoot anyone that walks out that's not female. Go on my mark."

Cameron repositioned himself so he faced the lights. This was an easy shot for him. He had spent hours on the range making longer shots for fun. He was, however, in the prone position and felt the pressure. He couldn't let Mark down. He steadied himself, and when he felt comfortable, he simply said, "Ready."

Mark did the same. He positioned himself and worked his legs into the ground until he felt his angle and breathing were perfect. Then he quietly gave the command. "Go."

The M1 Garand bit through the still night air and rocketed the 189 grain soft point 2,700 feet per second. Because of his angle, the first set of lights were in line and both exploded when they were hit. Cameron quickly transitioned to the second set. Within seconds, the fourth light was out and the site fell into darkness.

"Holy shit! What was that?" Luke looked out of the window.

It only took Cameron a split second to finish his trigger press, then Mark heard the muffled sound of the M1. A few seconds later, the full advantage of the night vision goggles were realized. Except for the moon, the compound was in utter darkness.

55

This entire escapade rattled Mark since the beginning. His training and work typically left him emotionally unattached. It didn't include family. It didn't include having his sister's life on the line, dependent on one single trigger press. Once he made the decision, there would be no going back. In those few seconds, Mark thought of all the times he'd made difficult shots in countries around the world. He had taken into account wind and terrain, made shots over and around fellow operatives, and had never given it a second thought. His confidence and training made him one of the best operatives in the field. He was in his element and knew it. He had to detach himself if he were to succeed.

Mark twisted himself into the ground and focused on the trailer. He had to block out the fact that his sister was down range. His brow furled as he concentrated. Taking into account the minute of angle to ensure accuracy, he aligned his weapon for the two-hundred-fifty yard shot. *One inch for every one hundred yards*, he thought again. He slowed his breathing, let himself relax, and gently took the slack out of the trigger. He whispered to himself, "Identify and shoot whoever's not Mary."

Then it happened. A few seconds after Cameron's M1 roared, its blast taking out the lights, one of the riders looked out of the window. Without hesitation, Mark's Mini-14 came to life. With pressure already applied to the trigger, he only had to apply a few pounds and that rocked the gun deep into his shoulder.

The 69 grain hollow point stuck the rider in the throat slicing the carotid artery, passing through his windpipe, and glancing off his spine. It exited the side of his neck and lodged in a far door jam. Blood sprayed over the room as Luke was knocked away from the window and into Seth. The force threw them both into the corner of the room. Seth slammed into the wall hard enough to shake the trailer. Luke crumbled in a heap on top of him.

Mary let out a blood curling screamed from the sight of the carnage. Luke's blood sprayed over the walls and across Seth's chest. He scrambled to shove Luke to the floor like a leper. He pushed away from Luke and sat up against the wall. The pool was growing under his friend as his last few heartbeats pumped blood through the gaping hole. He stared at his partner dead on the floor. Time stopped momentarily before he quickly scrambled to overturn the steel tables and pull them as far from the window as possible. He was protected for the time being hunched in the corner.

Thanks to the infrared illuminator and the two windows, Mark could see heat emitting from the bodies whenever anyone got close to a window. When Seth stood and made his move for the hostage, the agent fired a burst that changed his mind. "We have to keep him away from that far corner," Mark said, pointing to the trailer.

"Don't shoot me. I'm going in closer," Cameron responded and didn't give Mark time to reply. Like a panther on the prowl, he made his way towards the trailer. The agent watched his partner as he closed the distance and hunkered in behind the only thing between them and the trailer, an old diesel forklift.

Mark needed to keep pressure on the remaining rider, so at random intervals, he fired a burst into the trailer. He could hear Mary but he had to stay focused through her terrified screams. He had ten magazines lying beside him and would use every round if he needed to, but hoped the rider would give up or try to escape through the back.

Seth sat on his heels behind the overturned tables pissed at what was happening. He had no idea who was shooting at him. No one was supposed to be here except the girl. He looked at Luke, the side of his neck gone. Seth knew his family and his girlfriend. An unexpected sense of sadness and regret snuck up on him. He shook his head and the room suddenly exploded as another volley of rounds ate into the building, throwing drywall and wood splinters across the room. Seth held his hands above his head shielding himself from flying debris. He carried a .45 caliber Colt 1911with a seven-round magazine. He had pulled it from under his jacket the moment he'd hit the floor. He stayed hunched behind the table peering around the side at the girl. He had to get to her. If he could get her, he could get out.

Mary turned away and tried to lie quietly, but every time the rounds tore into the building, she let out a scream. She knew she was going to die.

Cameron worked his way closer to the building. Not keen on being in the line of fire, he stopped short of going behind it.

Another burst, immediately followed by another, ripped through the walls and floor making its way closer to the overturned tables. Seth couldn't take it and fired his .45 out into the darkness. "Who the hell is out there?" he yelled at the top of his lungs. Mary was nearly catatonic. Pieces of drywall and insulation lay everywhere. She squeezed her eyes shut.

Cameron recognized the sound of a large caliber handgun and thought it was being shot at him. He dove behind an old set of stairs that led to the side door. Mark answered Seth's shots with another volley from the Mini-14. When his slide locked back, he deftly swapped magazines, then refocused on the room.

The fact that the assailant was blindly shooting out into the darkness told Mark that his plan was working. If he continued to keep pressure on the rider, it would work on his nerves. Seth didn't have a plan for unexpectedly being shot at from some unknown enemy out in the darkness. It was a bit of psychological warfare and had a way of driving a person over the edge. Coupled with the infrared illuminators, Mark now had an unobstructed view inside the building with half the side blown away. He clearly saw an overturned table, the edge of another, and down a short narrow hallway. But, he couldn't see the right side. Mary had to be there. He trained his gun on the tables and waited.

Cameron knew the plan - keep him pinned down and he would surrender or try to escape out the back. Either way, he was in position for both options.

Seth waited. As he began to wonder why the shooting had stopped, five more rounds tore at the corner of the table. "God damnit! Stop! Or I'll kill the girl!" Seth yelled at the top of his lungs. He looked at Mary and then down the hall as a possible escape route.

Mark let another volley rip through the trailer. He didn't want the rider to think they were there for the girl, and the more he shot through the walls the better he could see inside.

Seth only had one extra magazine. He was at his wits end and again blindly fired every loaded bullet into the darkness until the slide on his gun had locked back. He pulled the magazine and threw it across the room, yelling, "God damnit! What do you want?!" He fished the last magazine from his jacket pocket and shoved it into his gun.

Mark thought he picked up flashes when the rider fired his gun which had put him in the far corner of the room. Cameron was a few feet away on the other side of the wall. Looking down range for his partner, Mark thought, *Comms, if we could only talk to each other.*

Seth was both furious and desperate. He looked around the room and saw only one option. If he tried to make it down the hall or out the door, he would be cut down. He needed a shield and she was lying on the other side of the room.

Lying on the ground around Mark were three depleted magazines, a half-spent one in the Mini, and six full ones on the ground. He kept his weapon trained on the tables in the event the rider tried to make it to his hostage. He waited. Seconds became an eternity. Suddenly, Mark saw the rider sliding the table across the room towards Mary. Taking careful aim he let loose another three rounds smashing into the table. The rounds hit a weakened area of the steel table top, sliced through it and hammered the floor, throwing sparks and splinters around the room. Seth stopped sliding the table and pulled himself closer to the frame.

Mark couldn't risk shooting any further to his right. Mary could be in his line of fire. He had to stop the rider before he made it past the blown out walls of the trailer. Mark was so engrossed with the target, he didn't see Cameron belly-crawl out in front of the trailer. He made a quick scan of the area and caught his movement. He now saw exactly where Cameron was going. His attention turned back to the table and he laid down enough suppressive fire to give his partner time.

Cameron knew it was time to move. After the second volley of fire from the building, he sought higher ground.

He crawled across the front of the trailer with his M1 cradled in his arms. When the Mini-14 went silent, he stopped. Then, in a nonstop volley from the Mini-14, he pushed himself up to a stoop and ran to a set of old, rusted hazardous material lockers. They barely concealed him.

Mark shot over and around a partner before with great accuracy without ever giving it a second thought. He was an accomplished marksman, though he wouldn't admit it.

56

Seth was typically the person making an assault, not the one being assaulted. He carried out his assignments with pleasure. He had clearly been the leader with Luke happily following in his footsteps. They'd been with Steve Chang for two years. Their previous assignment as the primary muscle for a contractor performing maintenance at the sub base in Bangor, Washington had kept them plenty busy. The contractor had a cell, operating within itself, collecting information on the Ohio-class ballistic missile nuclear-powered submarine's Ultra-Quiet Propulsion System. They had started gathering information on the Secure and Constant Radio Communications Link and the Very Low Frequency system when they were quickly shut down. Rumors had spread through the community of spies at Bangor. It was information that wasn't supposed to get out.

The U.S. Government's Counter Espionage team had closed in on the activities by tracing encrypted communications from around the Bangor area all the way to China. When the rumors broke, they lost everything. Communications that were readily being plucked out of the air and narrowed down by the NRO suddenly stopped. They had nothing. The cell was disbanded, and Seth and Luke had been handed off to another operation.

Reassigned to Chang, they had played second fiddle to Martin Powell and Lorena Bean. However, the money was good, and after living in Washington State, racing around Southern California felt like an extended vacation. They were happy for the assignment, especially one in which they could do what they wanted. When they had left early for the yard, that is exactly what they had in mind. Seth had taken one look at Mary and knew what he wanted. Now, he wanted to survive.

He was mad as hell, but he was also just plain scared. His friend, and partner was dead on the floor. Blood was everywhere. An army was outside, firing relentlessly. He sat with a gun in his hand with only one magazine left, behind a table which was slowly disappearing. He no longer had interest in the woman except as an escape route. He had five rounds left to battle the barrage which wasn't stopping. He put his hand down to steady himself but slipped in the blood. He wiped it on his pants, smearing it down his leg. He stared at his dead friend a few feet away. He could end up the same way. If he tried to get Luke's gun, he'd be killed before he got to it. Another volley of bullets disturbed his thoughts and lit up the trailer. "Son of a bitch! Who are these guys?" he muttered.

Cameron moved from the cover of the lockers and scurried up the hill and positioned himself over the rise. He could see into the room and could almost see the rider. If he stood, he'd have him.

Mark continued to fire into the trailer. He knew Cameron had headed up and over the hill. A slight smile grew on his face. Cameron would have a clear shot into the trailer.

Seth was done. He had no fight left but didn't know how to give up. He knew these guys weren't the police. All this time, no one had said a word. He looked around the trailer. There hadn't been one bullet hole or one shot fired towards the other side of the room. His side looked like Swiss cheese and her side was pristine. "Shit, they *are* here for the girl." He peeked around the table towards the girl. Cameron saw the movement and pressed the trigger of his M1.

Seth pulled his head back but not before he had gotten a glimpse of a way out. The intuition saved his life. The round from the M1 tore away what was left of the corner of the table. The 180gr soft-point has a muzzle energy of two-thousand-nine-hundred and thirteen ft. lbs. and when it hit the corner of the table, it ripped it away from the rest of the frame and threw it across the room. It just missed Seth's face. The concussive force pushed him back against the wall and he dropped his gun. "Damnit!" As he reached for the gun, he noticed drops of blood accumulate on the floor and felt the stinging in his face. He had to act fast or he wouldn't last much longer. He blindly shot in the general direction of the new assailant.

As if mentally in sync, both men fired at the same time. The table exploded as another six rounds pummeled it from the darkness. Cameron was in position. There was not much return fire coming from the trailer. This would be over soon. When the handgun bit through the night air, he was horrified to see the rider bolt to the other side of the room - Mary's side.

Seth looked around the table and saw a small hole in the wall that had not been visible while standing. It was square and had accommodated a piece of equipment which had previously been removed. He kicked out the area surrounding the hole. Hunched behind the bed, he was safe. They wouldn't shoot near the woman.

Cameron repositioned himself and tried to get a better look into the side window. He looked over his shoulder and contemplated moving to higher ground.

Seth rolled on his rear and continued to kick out the wall. It broke and crumbled with every kick as pieces of wood and insulation shot out over the yard.

Meanwhile another shooter peered through his scope from high up on the hill. He watched as a leg kicked at the growing hole in the building. He waited, watching the events unfold, anticipating the most opportune moment. He visualized the shot.

Seth studied the enlarged hole. He could easily slip the girl through it. He crawled under the bed, cut the straps holding her feet, then returned to the hole and gave it another kick, more out of frustration than necessity. He leaned back and cut the leather strap that was wrapped around Mary's wrist.. He sat with his feet hanging out the building, then leaned to the side and cut the last strap holding her hands. She would be easy to move. She was cut free and in shock. All he had to do was grab her, shove her through the hole, and use her as a shield. He had been right, not one more shot had been fired since moving to her side of the room.

The man on the hill smoothly cycled the bolt of the Savage 111. With it nestled deep in his shoulder, he slid the safety off. Through the Nikon scope, he saw legs appear and disappear. He would get one chance to make this work. He risked getting shot at from the men already engaged in the fight, but at this distance, even Springfield and his partner would have a hard time hitting him. He had been impressed with what he had seen so far. He had thought it was a done deal until Seth had suddenly crossed the room. Now, both men were out of position to deal with him. They would both have to move and cross over into the open. It didn't matter. He didn't like Seth anyway and was glad to help, something he should've done days ago. He was in line with the window above her bed. When he had seen Seth kicking out the wall, he knew what he had to do. For him, it was an easy shot.

Mary had no idea what was going on, but she had, at some point, made the decision to live. She was ready to fight back at the first opportunity. She tried moving her arms after the straps were cut, but they both locked up. Her muscles screamed with pain. She'd been in one position for hours and her entire body was cramping. *If only Mark were here.* She thought of her brother, always her protector. *He would know what to do.*

Seth jerked the bed closer to him. He grabbed Mary by the arm and tried to drag her off the bed, but she pulled away. He laid his gun on the floor, reached up with the other hand and forced her to the floor. She twisted her arm and easily broke his grip. Her body screamed when she spun around, drawing both legs in close. With all the strength she had left, she kicked him in the chest. Seth jerked to the side and was knocked into the adjacent wall. Since both legs were draped through the hole, his body bounced back and he gasped for air. Mary's kick was hard, but in her weakened state, it didn't have much effect.

Seth maintained control. He had all he was going to take and grabbed the gun lying next to him while holding his chest and gasping for air. Mary glared at her attacker. When she saw him reach for the gun, she moved. But before she could finish her thought, he reached out and grabbed her ankle. She reared back aligning her foot with his face. At the same moment she was about to smash his face, his arms flew in the air and his body was thrown back against the floor. The sound of a gunshot rang in her ears.

57

The shot rang out somewhere behind Cameron. Both men looked in the same general direction. Mark swung his gun around and searched the area above his partner. He looked down at Cameron, then back up the hill. Nothing.

Seth rose and made a grunting sound Mary had never heard before. She tasted the bile in her throat. The front of his shirt and jacket were soaked in blood. The floor behind him was covered with dark red pieces. He flopped backwards and thumped onto the floor. His left arm twitched uncontrollably. Then, there was no movement at all. Mark heard her bloodcurdling scream. She became lightheaded. The trailer began to spin, and she passed out on the floor next to Seth.

Ken Benner had never liked Chang's men. When Luke had been killed in the first few seconds of the fight, he felt no remorse. He had arrived at the JPL's old test site shortly before Luke had been shot. He had been there many times and knew exactly where he needed to wait for the riders. When he saw the two lawmen arrive, he decided to let it play out. He had moved to higher ground to watch. He wasn't going to allow the agent's sister to be harmed. He had a second chance. When he sent the single .270 caliber round down range, he knew it would hit its mark. It cut through the trailer with little deflection, hitting its unseen target dead center, just below the chest. He worked the bolt, ejecting the cartridge into his hand. When he saw the legs shoot straight out and go limp, he knew he wouldn't have to chamber another round. When he had been in the Rangers, he had been considered the best long range shooter in his company. He and his fellow Rangers would routinely compete to make shots out to 1000 yards to hit suspended Iraqi coins. He had learned to shoot well and had developed the mental skills necessary for a gun fight. He had no desire to engage with the lawmen, so he remained motionless on the hill. He was too far for them to see even if they were looking high enough. According to his range finder, he was 678 yards away. Ken Benner felt redemption. He'd killed for his country. Now he killed to protect an innocent civilian.

Mark and Cameron continued to scan the hillside. With the exception of the generator rumbling in the distance, the site was eerily quiet. Whoever was shooting was positioned high enough so as not to be seen. He saw Cameron lying in position scanning the hill, so he quickly made his way towards the trailer. Mark sprinted in a random zigzag motion for a little over two hundred yards. By the time he reached the old forklift, he was out of breath. Kneeling, he brought the Mini-14 out and kept it ready while scanning the grounds. He swapped out his magazine for a full one.

The urge to run into the trailer was overpowering, but years of training and experience had kept him alive this long so he stayed put, listening and watching for any movement on the hillside. It gave him time to catch his breath and to decide whether or not he should step out in the open.

Cameron had been getting ready to change his position when the shot rang out. The unexpected round of fire startled him, but he realized that he wasn't the target. The round had done little damage to the trailer, but it had stopped all movement inside. He turned and trained his M1 on the hill as a precaution, but from his angle, he couldn't see very far. He looked in Mark's direction and saw him moving towards the trailer. Immediately, he returned his focus back to the hillside.

From his comfortable position high on the hill, Ken knew the men could not see him. He could stay this way all night if he had to. The men had just been in a gun fight and needed time for their adrenaline to subside. He waited. It gave him time to think. This was going to end Chang's organization and he had no delusions of escaping the fact that he would be hunted down. He was part of it and considered approaching the agent and offering information that might help him make a deal.

Mark checked his watch. It had been four very long minutes since he had made it to the forklift. He was giving it five minutes before he made another move. There'd been no movement from the trailer nor any shots fired from the hill. It was time to move closer. "Detective," he said in a conversational tone. The electronic hearing would easily pick it up. Saying Cameron's name could put him in jeopardy if it was overheard by someone else.

Cameron turned back towards Mark but kept his M1 pointed towards the hillside. He raised his hand in acknowledgement. Mark motioned for Cameron to join him at the forklift. He shouldered the Mini-14 and swept it over the hill while Cameron slid down the hill on his rear. It wasn't long before he was standing next to Mark.

There was much to say, and when this was all done, they'd sit down and drink a gallon of beer. Right now, however, it was all business. "I don't know who that is, or where, exactly, that came from, but I think he's after the rider. Cover me. I'm going to the trailer."

Cameron nodded while scanning the darkness. Mark turned and within seconds was standing at the trailer door. "Federal agent," he yelled. He kicked it in, tearing the knob and latch away from the frame.

With his Mini-14 up, he moved through the doorway, swept the room, and headed towards the far corner. He recognized the body dressed in leathers lying in a pool of blood. He scanned the room for the man's cohort. He saw Mary first, then the rider, both lying on the floor. Mark was sure the man was dead. The body, which was half stuck through the wall, was surrounded by what looked like nearly eight pints of blood, and the smell of death lingered in the air. He moved towards Mary while keeping an eye on the man lying next to her. Half of him stuck through the wall.

Mark checked his wrist watch. It had been seven minutes since he had been leaning against the cold forklift, enough time for the blood of the rider to migrate towards Mary. He placed his finger on her carotid artery and let out a sigh of relief when he felt the pounding of her pulse. He moved his hand under her nose and felt a slow and steady exhale. His shoulders slackened. The strain and tension of the last two days left his body as he put his hands under her shoulders and rotated her away from the blood before it reached her hair.

A ferocious fury crept in as he thought of Chang and all he had put her through. But he set it aside. He had to tend to her first; his fury could wait.

"Everything okay?" Cameron asked as he backed up to the door.

"We're good. My sister's unconscious. I think she fainted. I'm going to move her to another room." Setting down his Mini-14, he took off his night vision goggles and tossed them on the bed. He scooped up his sister and carried her to the adjacent room. He wanted Mary to wake up in a room free from death and gore. He gently laid her against the wall propping her up in a corner. Softly rubbing and lightly pinching her cheek trying to get her to come to. "Hey, are you going to sleep all day?"

When she didn't come around, he stood and went to the front of the room while checking his watch. It was a habit he'd gotten into years ago, one he had picked up from a now retired agent. Tracking time and watching its consistent movement kept him grounded during high-stress situations. It had helped him to focus. It had been sixteen minutes since he had been at the forklift.

Cautiously, he walked outside and stood next to Cameron. He kept his Mini-14 out and ready as he scanned the hill. "Couldn't bring her around," he stated. "Just need to give her more time."

"She'll be alright," Cameron assured him.

Mark lowered the Mini-14 slightly, turned to Cameron, and said, "I think we're done here."

Cameron nodded his head. They walked back into the trailer. Mark knelt by his sister and stroked her hair. As he asked Cameron for help to carry her out to the car, she lifted her hand and grabbed his.

She heard voices but couldn't quite bring herself to open her eyes. Gradually, they fluttered open. She stared up at her brother and seemed not to recognize him.

"So, this is our damsel in distress," Cameron said, standing in the doorway. His M1 rested on top of his forearm and his night vision goggles were flipped up over his head.

Mary looked at him for several long seconds, then back at her brother. "Mark?" She mouthed in a barely audible whisper. Then her recognition returned. "Oh my God! Mark!" She reached up and threw her arms around his neck. Tears flowed down her cheeks.

"I'm sorry, Mary. I am so sorry," he choked as he fought the tightness in his throat.

"What happened? Why am I here? What's going on?" Mary asked as she looked around the small room. "Why are you here?"

He held her shoulders and looked into her eyes. "First, you're okay. Do you understand that?" He needed to be sure she was coherent.

"Of course, I do. I'm sitting on my ass on a cold floor."

Mark turned to Cameron and laughed. "Yup, she'll be alright."

"What happened? What are you doing here?" she asked with a distant glaze in her eyes. "I was kidnapped, Mark. I was kidnapped! Oh my God! What about Cole? And the girls!?"

"They're fine," Mark replied and pulled her close. "You're safe now, Mary. Everybody's alright."

"But, how did you know where to find me? How did you know where I was?"

"Mary, I'm sorry, but you're here because of me." Other than giving her the news of their parents' death, it was one of the hardest things he'd ever had to say. To admit that he was the cause of her suffering ripped apart his insides.

"What are you talking about?" she asked, startled.

He didn't care anymore if she knew. He owed her the truth. "Mary, I work for the CIA. This assignment caused me to cross paths with some very bad people. They tried to use you to get to me."

"The CIA? The CIA, CIA!"

"Yes," he chuckled, "the CIA, CIA!"

"You're a spy? Mark, you're a spy!?" She was repeating herself; it was hard to grasp what she was hearing.

"Well, for now, let's not get into any of that. We need to get you out of here."

Mary motioned her head towards Cameron while trying to stand up. "Who's that?"

"Probably one of the best decisions I made today. His name is Cameron Butler. Works for the Highway Patrol. We teamed up earlier. You can thank him for your rescue."

Mark hadn't yet taken the time to cut the straps still hanging from Mary's arms. As he helped her up, he pushed the straps up her arm and rubbed the red welts on her wrists. Mary looked at Cameron and gave him a bewildered but warm smile. "Thank you for helping my brother, *the spy*," she said, looking at Mark with a grin.

"I wasn't doing anything tonight anyway. You're welcome," Cameron told her, a little embarrassed. He hadn't expected to be given credit for the rescue.

Mark pulled out his Kershaw that was clipped to his inside pocket and cut the straps from his sister's arms. "I'll never forgive myself for getting you involved with all of this." He bent down and started cutting the remaining restraints from her legs.

"Did mom and dad know their son was a spy?" she asked.

Mark paused for several seconds. He turned and looked up at Mary. "Mom didn't, but I think Dad had an idea. I wasn't sitting in an office all day. When I was gone for a while, he liked to ask me about it, kind of put me on the spot, but I think he was screwing with me." Returning to the straps, he smiled at the memory.

When she was cut free, the men picked up their weapons and night vision goggles. Mark glanced out the windows to make sure it was safe to leave. "It's time to go," Mark said to Cameron. He looked at Mary. "We'll go out first and I want you to follow close behind. There is still someone out there." Mark took a step, then turned back to Mary. "One more thing, don't look to your left when we pass through the other room. It's not pretty."

"Mr. Springfield." The voice came from their left as they approached the old forklift. The voice sounded familiar, but Mark couldn't place it.

Mark cursed and stuck out his arm and moved Mary close to the forklift.

He and Cameron stepped in front of Mary, raised their guns, and scanned the hillside.

"Mr. Springfield." The voice didn't sound far away. Mark stepped halfway around the forklift and swept his Mini-14 in its direction. A very tall man stood before him with a rifle pointed towards the ground.

58

"Drop your weapon, step to the left, and put your hands behind your head," Mark ordered. He kept the forklift between them.

"There's no need for this. I could've shot you in the trailer." He stooped down and laid his Savage 111 on the ground, stepped to the left, and raised his hands. Mark moved from around the forklift and lowered his gun. Ken Benner, a member of Chang's group was here and, he quite possibly had saved his sister's life.

"You're under arrest. Detective, if you would do the honors."

Cameron laid his M1 against the back of the forklift, presented his Glock, and approached Ken.

"Place your hands behind your back interlacing your fingers," Cameron commanded. Once Ken complied, he re-holstered his Glock. As a precaution, he held Ken's lower few fingers in case he needed to exert control. He produced a pair of handcuffs and cuffed him. Cameron went through Benner's pockets and patted him down. He glanced at Mark who was within twenty feet pointing the Mini-14 directly at the big man's chest. Cameron led him by the forearm back towards the forklift and sat him on the fender. Ken obeyed without resistance and stared at Mark the entire time.

Even though Mark had used them a hundred times, Mary could not believe the words 'You're under arrest' came from her brother. His tone was nothing she had ever heard before. She felt helpless as she watched her brother hold the man at gunpoint.

Now that he was in custody, Mark began to relax, and for the first time sensed the chill in the air. "Why did you come out here? More importantly, why did you stay?" Even though Mark had the upper hand, he maintained a safe distance. While Mark addressed Ken, Cameron walked over and picked the rifle up from the ground.

"Please be careful with that," Ken said still staring at Mark. "I came out to right a wrong. There's no need to kill civilians." He looked over Mark's shoulder at Mary. "I'm sorry you were put through this."

Mark felt his sister walk up behind him and with his left hand moved her away. Cameron walked towards Mary while still scanning the hillside.

Looking back at Mark, Ken continued, "I have information you may find interesting, but it doesn't come free."

He wanted to make a deal. He wanted out. Mark wondered if he should hear him out or haul him in and be done with it. There were people who would make him talk no matter what, but the truth was he owed Ken a chance. Mark took a couple steps towards Cameron. "Detective, please take my sister back to the car. Give us a minute." When he was sure the other two were out of earshot, he asked a simple question, "Who is it?"

Ken waited. He did have a person and the agent had obviously determined that from Ken's simple statement. He didn't, however, want to show his hand. "Do you suspect someone?" he asked the agent.

"Mr. Benner, we can play this game all night or we can cut to the chase. Here's what I'll offer, since you saved a family member of a federal agent, helped apprehend the two in the trailer, and gave us a lead on whoever's really behind this..." Mark had made deals with criminals who had little to offer many times. But this was different. Mark was quite certain Ken Benner *could* offer more than a little, and he had saved his sister. He knew he'd cut Benner a break. Mark lowered his weapon as a show of trust. "I'll personally vouch for you."

Ken needed a minute. He never thought he'd ever find himself leaning against an old rusted piece of equipment handcuffed in front of a federal agent on a cold night. He looked at Mark and sensed he could be trusted. He had fired one single .270 caliber round and saved an innocent woman's life. It was his redemption. He was ready to come clean and ready to pay the price for working with Chang.

"You've been to Chang's room at the JPL. The cabinet in the corner houses a piece of communication equipment, the one thing I don't have access to. About thirty days ago, I let myself into the room. Chang was on the phone and in a heated exchange with someone. He ended the call shortly after I walked in. All I heard was, 'You'll get your money, and I don't care what you do for the government, you'll have to find a way to get here.' It was a woman."

"You know this how?"

"After the call he referred to her as 'that bitch,' very uncharacteristic of him." Ken looked at the ground and shifted his feet, deep in thought. "Then, a few days ago, the same thing happened. We met to talk about Danielle approaching Martin, and again he was agitated, like I've never seen him before. He could hardly focus on our conversation."

"Could've been from finding out I wasn't who he thought I was," Mark said as if trying to piece it all together. The image of Danielle lying on the floor flashed into his mind.

"No, it was something else. He wanted the encryption. He didn't care who it was coming from. Whoever it was, told him that they knew the next test date, the time the Huntsville unit was programmed to power up. He thought Martin was going to bring the device back, but instead he brought your sister. When the accident happened, he was furious. Then, when you called, it all fell back into place. In fact, he was so sure of himself, he made plans to leave. He didn't know I knew, but when his secretary handed me his travel plans thinking it was just another trip, I took the liberty of looking at them." He stopped and looked at Mark. "We didn't know Powell was going to take your sister. I'm sorry for that. He was telling us that he had a federal agent's sister stashed up here. I thought 'you dumb ass.'" Ken paused before continuing. "The closer Chang thought he was to actually getting the encryption, the more irrational he became. I think he panicked and sent them to kill her." The explanation sounded more like he was talking to a colleague not a criminal confessing to a federal agent. He had gotten lost in the conversation and had meant to stop himself before the last statement had slipped from his mouth. Too late.

Mark's stomach tied in knots with Ken's last words, but he forced himself to put it behind him, for now. He was looking at someone who had made a bad decision years ago and was now ready to pay the price. Thank God Ken had decided to do it now. Mark pondered Benner's potential candidacy for SLIPP - a program similar to the Witness Protection Program that relocates people throughout the country. The Secure Location International Protection Program is a top-secret organization set up for people who, on their own accord, change sides and aid the federal government by infiltrating spy rings or bringing down high-level dignitaries. For their part, they're moved out of the country and given a stipend as a type of reward. The catch is, once the person is relocated with their new identity, they can no longer return to the United States. Mark thought the acronym appropriate, and knew somewhere there was a room full of people making them up.

Ken continued. "When you called and offered a trade, Chang wasn't sure if your sister was still alive. That's why he sent these two." He nodded towards the trailer. He shook his head, stared at the ground, and said, "He was going to have you both killed. I couldn't do it anymore. This was my second chance. That's why I'm here." Ken knew this was the only way. Saving the girl and confessing made him feel…clean. A weight lifted from his shoulders.

Mark listened to Benner's explanation. He needed time to think and he couldn't do it holding someone at gunpoint. He wanted to close his eyes and sleep for a week. In the past few days, he'd killed three people. Six were dead, and for what? Money? In his wallet he carried a small laminated card with the simple phrase. *If all you feel is recoil, take your finger off the trigger.* It was a reminder. Shooting someone, taking a human life, is an emotional act. When it stopped bothering him, it would be time to stop. He was almost there. First, Danielle. He knew he would never forget the nights they'd shared, the love he'd felt, the betrayal and her lying on the floor staring up at him, dead. There was the shooter behind his sister's house and now one of the riders, both for whom he had little regard. He was looking in Ken's direction but really wasn't looking at him. He was deep in thought. When Ken leaned forward to stretch his back, Mark reflexively leveled the Mini-14 at him.

"I'm just stretching a bit," he said cautiously.

The move surprised Mark and even though it was harmless, he was taken off-guard. That convinced him he needed to think someplace else.

"Will anyone miss you tonight?"

Ken simply answered, "No."

"Let's go," Mark said as he motioned his gun towards the car. They walked to the car in silence. Mark followed twenty feet behind. Ken had shown remorse but Mark still thought it prudent not to let his guard down.

The car started and slowly headed in their direction.

Mary sat in the front seat. Draped over her shoulders was a blanket Cameron had given her. Some water bottles and a few energy bars, which he had gotten from the trunk, sat on the dash. She thanked him and drank a bottle and a half of water. She reached for the energy bar and asked, "How did you get involved in this?"

"I responded to an accident a few days ago. At first, it looked like you and your brother were killed, but as we investigated further we found, of course, it wasn't true. Two other people lost their lives. I don't know how he found me so fast, but he did and enlisted my help. He can be very persuasive," he added with a smile, nodding in Mark's general direction. "I don't want to say too much without your brother here."

Mary reached over and took his hand. "Thank you, Cameron. Thank you. If my brother asked you for help, he must have seen something in you. He has a short list of friends. I'm still trying to digest the fact that he is a spy."

"Well, I don't know about that, but whatever he does, he's pretty damn good at it."

Mary muttered, "My brother the spy," and chuckled at the thought of it.

Cameron donned his night vision goggles to have a look around the compound. It took a few seconds to locate them, but he could see Mark and Benner walking towards the car.

"When do you think I can call my husband?" Mary knew the answer, but had to ask.

"Well, your brother's headed this way. Let's give him a lift and you can ask him." Cameron wasn't going to let her make a call. He had no idea what the agent had up his sleeve. It was a moot point; as he looked down at his phone it showed the same thing it did the moment they had entered the canyon - *No service* - Cameron pressed on the brake and stopped about thirty feet from the men. He got out, stood by the car, and waited for direction from Mark.

"Mr. Benner, wait here," Mark said. He sidestepped Benner while keeping an eye on him. He walked to Cameron's side of the car. As he passed in front of Mary, he flashed her a thin smile.

She took one look at her brother and knew this wasn't over.

59

"Detective, the person responsible for this has no way of knowing his guys are dead. In fact, he'll have no way of knowing until tomorrow when they had planned on riding out of here and into cell service. We have until tomorrow morning. We have to keep him on ice. We need a hotel, some place we can get out of the elements, eat, and put together a plan." From the short time it took to get from the trailer to the car, Mark had a loose plan, but he wasn't beyond listening to Cameron if he had any ideas. So far, Cameron had performed just as well as any agent, given the circumstances, and Mark was actually looking forward to his thoughts.

"There's a Best Western over in Mission Hills. The rooms are set up so they can be entered from different parking lots. That will keep him out of sight," Cameron said, half pointing at Ken. "We can probably be there in twenty minutes."

Mark walked back over to Ken. "You're willing to cooperate?"

Ken looked Mark straight in the eyes. "I'm done with those guys. I won't give you any trouble."

"Keep an eye on him," Mark said as he looked back at Cameron. "I'm going to get their cell phones from the trailer. I think they'll come in handy." He laid his rifle against the fender and walked to the trailer. He went through the pockets of the two dead men and retrieved their wallets and cell phones. The light was dim but he could see the ashen color of their faces and thought –*Touch my sister* – He turned and left the trailer.

Cameron and Mark stowed their long guns in the trunk. They asked Mary to step from the car as they sat Ken in the backseat and zip tied his feet together. He didn't resist and was almost helpful as they secured him in the back.

"Detective, shall we?"

Cameron slid into the driver's seat, Mary got back into the front seat, and Mark sat behind his sister with his Glock in hand. He didn't expect any trouble from Ken, but if Benner had a change of heart and somehow broke free, he'd wreak havoc in the small car.

Cameron drove out of the test site. Mark stared at the back of the front seat wondering what woman, of the small group of participants, would know the actual test date. He occasionally glanced at Ken to let him know he was still being watched. The words, continued to reverberate in his head. *I don't care what you do for the government...* Hmm. Was someone trying to flex their importance? There was the nicely dressed auburn-haired lady who showed up in the oval office to brief him on the Huntsville unit who had also shown up to brief Danielle. *Very unassuming*, he thought. He would have Cliff pull the names of all the people who knew the test date and separate out the women. *But how to flush her out?* He almost said it out loud. However, his plan for Chang was simple, so simple it had to work.

Thirty minutes after they left the dirt road, they arrived at the hotel. As they pulled into the hotel parking lot, he leaned forward and pointed to the far quad. Cameron nodded and eased the car into the furthest available spot. Mark glanced at Ken who returned a smile of reassurance.

"Mark, I'll get us a room," announced Cameron. "Maybe I watch too much TV, but I wouldn't want you tracked by their security camera."

If it wasn't for his knowledge of the NRO's Advanced Facial Recognition and Camera Location Software, Mark would've laughed out loud at Cameron's paranoia. He knew, however, any video that touched the internet could be collected, tracked, and passed on without the subject knowing. Something he'd keep to himself. "Sounds like you do watch too much TV," he said with a chuckle, "but that's not a bad idea. You never know who may drive by."

The three waited in the car without saying a word. Mark heard his sister lightly snoring in the front seat and smiled to himself. She was safe. She startled awake when Cameron returned to the car. "Got two adjoining rooms," he said, pointing to the third and fourth door to the right of the car.

"Detective, take my sister to her room. I need a few minutes with Mr. Benner."

"She gets her own room?" Cameron quipped. The joke was small, but it brought smiles to both Mark and Mary. Cameron stepped to the other side of the car to help Mary, but he was too late. She was out and had the door closed before he made it around the car. He watched as she started towards the walkway, ready to help if she needed steadying.

Mark watched from the car as Cameron swiped the keycard. They both disappeared through the door. He shifted in his seat to face Ken. It was now early morning. He was exhausted and knew everyone else was tired as well, so he kept it short. "If we get through this and are able to flush out this mystery woman, I'll see to it that you're dealt with fairly. But if you cross us, I'll make your life a living hell." Mark took the knife that was clipped to his pants pocket and motioned for Ken to slide his legs across the car. He sliced through the Teflon straps with the serrated blade. He took the blanket that Mary had left behind and draped it over Benner's shoulders covering his cuffed hands. He looked for Cameron, who was opening the door to the adjoining room.

Before Mark slid from the car, he looked back at Ken. "Mr. Benner, you and I may someday end up on the same plane. If that day should ever come, you'll have to tell me how you made that shot." A thin grin flashed across his face.

Once inside, Mark told Ken to sit in the chair. He pulled out the cell phone JT had given him in St. Charles. Cameron kept an eye on Ken while Mark walked outside. At the other end of the parking lot, he placed a call to Cliff and briefed him on the situation, going over a few details of his loose plan. As they spoke, the plan started to take shape. "Two more things," Mark added. "First, Ken Benner. I think he's a good program candidate. As I said, he came in on his own and saved my sister. He's not been a problem since he's been in custody." Mark took precautionary measures on the phone to talk around the relocation program which wasn't well known. "Secondly, I'm most impressed with the highway patrol man," Mark continued. It was well known among his peers, especially to Cliff, that he did not trust people and rarely mentioned someone outside the agency. He did not easily hand out compliments. They talked for a while longer and ended with Cliff's assurance that he would call Mary's husband, Cole.

Mark walked back to the room and sat in the chair by the desk. He felt every muscle of his lower back. He reached in his pockets and pulled out the cell phones and wallets he had recovered from the riders. He laid out both driver's licenses on the desk. "Let's see. Who do we have? Seth Robinson and Luke Rivera. Detective, what's our plan?"

Cameron sat on the corner of the bed with his Glock 23 resting on his knee. He reached for an open bottle of water and turned back towards Mark to speak, but Ken spoke first.

"Chang's not expecting to hear anything until the morning. Seth would've made the call to set up the meet."

Mark nodded. Without that bit of information, he would've had to guess which phone to use first.

There was a light knock. The three men looked towards the adjoining door. Mark opened the door. Mary was holding a hotel robe. "Ok to jump in the shower?"

"Of course, then I want you to try and get some sleep. My boss is calling Cole, so don't use the phone. This will be over soon." He stepped through the door and gave her a hug.

"How long have you been with the CIA?" Clearly still processing that he was an operative for the CIA.

"Oh, for a while. You know, on the application there's a paragraph. It's in bold type. I'll paraphrase - *Knowledge by non-Agency personnel of your association with the Central Intelligence Agency or the Intelligence Community may limit your ability to perform or preclude you from certain assignments.* I didn't want to be precluded from anything. Now, go shower." He started to step back through the open door, but then he reached out and gently held her arm. "I'm really sorry."

"Don't be. I thought I was being trafficked for the sex trade. But it was even worse. I was being sequestered with a bunch of spies," she teased.

"Sequestered! Lawyers," was all he could say as he walked back through the door, shaking his head.

Steve Chang's phone rang twice before he picked it up. Looking at the name of the caller, he smiled, "Yes?"

There was no reply, then the phone went dead. Again, the phone rang. He answered, and there was no reply.

After several minutes, it rang yet again. This time the name 'Luke' appeared as the caller.

Irritated, Chang raised his voice "Yes!" No reply. He hit 'End' harder than he should've and tossed the phone on his desk.

The smirk on Mark Springfield's face indicated that he was happy with the results. He picked up Seth's phone, punched in a text, and hit 'SEND.'

60

April 27th 2009
The White House
Washington D.C.

Cliff contacted the president after Mark's call and briefed him on the plan and how he thought they should proceed. The president agreed and called a partial cabinet and select members of the upcoming test, to the oval office.

The president mingled with his guests while Cliff prepared his notes and looked around the room. He saw many wide eyed stares. It was clear this was the first time most of the participants had been this close to a president. When he was ready, he nodded. The president cleared his throat and addressed the group. "Ladies and gentlemen, I would like to introduce the director of the CIA, Mr. Clifford House. I believe Mr. House has something for us."

"Thank you, Mr. President." Cliff turned and addressed the group. "I have a bit of bad news. Several months ago, we became aware of a spy within the Huntsville organization." Cliff paused. "We planted one of our own to flush them out, and in doing so, we used a copy of the encryption as bait." Cliff looked around the room while studying the small crowd. He somberly continued, "Early this morning, we lost contact with our agent who had the copy of the encryption." Several gasps were heard and murmurs arose amongst the crowd. Cliff went on. "As everyone in the room knows, 'the huut' is scheduled for another test. It is at this time I think it prudent that the test be cancelled." The room became louder with questions. "I've advised the president to send the command to shut down the satellite." The room burst into objections; 'the huut' would be useless. Cliff motioned with his hands to quiet the small group of engineers and technicians. He looked at his notes and asked for Richard Avila to raise his hand.

"Yes, that's me," came a shaky high-pitched voice from the back of the room.

"Mr. Avila, please explain the power sequence of the satellite."

Richard was 'the huut's' head power distribution engineer and had worked on the project from when it was a drawing. He wasn't used to public attention. He looked around the room and his face reddened. "The Huntsville unit powers itself up at predetermined times. It sends a warm-up and power-on voltage to the ICE which primes it to receive a matching encryption, then it waits for a command. The last command we sent were coordinates positioning it over Iran. When it powers on again, it will be waiting for us to tell it what to do."

"That's exactly why I've decide to shut it down," the president spoke firmly. "We can't risk anyone else communicating with it. We have to assume the encryption was compromised." The final decision had been made.

Cliff added one more bit of information. "There is one piece of the puzzle they don't have, the time of the next power on. That's why it is critical we do this. As all of you know, Tuesday, at 2:00 p.m. Eastern Standard Time, the unit will power-up. Eight minutes later, it will complete its self-test, then we'll send the command to shut it down." He saw many long faces as he scanned the room and reminded them. "The X-37B is scheduled for another maintenance flight in two months. We'll change out the encryptors and move on."

Everyone there knew the date and time of the next test. It was the elephant in the room no one saw. Working the security piece at the door was the woman Mark suspected. Shannon sat close to the door. She controlled access by checking everyone's ID against her list.

Close to the president another woman smiled to herself, then almost laughed out loud. *You're going to follow a checklist and wait eight minutes? We'll have plenty of time.* She was certain Chang had the device and needed her more than ever. If the agent was, indeed, missing, that was one less thing to worry about. This was the last time she would ever be inside of the oval office again.

Chang's phone buzzed with an incoming text. *In the canyon with the woman. She's alive. Where do we meet?* Chang sat back in his chair looking at the name 'Seth' displayed on the screen of his phone. *This could be anyone*, he thought. The canyon had poor to no reception at all. Chang became suspicious. He sent back a question.

Who was your previous employer?

Mark looked directly at Ken, "Mr. Benner, do you know who Luke and Seth worked for before Chang?" Mark asked, nodding towards the wallets.

"They both came from the sub base in Bangor, Washington. I have no clue who they worked for and I doubt Chang does either," Ken answered, accepting his fate. He had no way of knowing, but one day he and the agent would be sitting on an airplane headed to Oslo, Norway.

Mark locked eyes with Ken for several long seconds, then formed his next text.

A smile crossed Steve Chang's lips as he read the message, *Bangor, Damnit. Now where do we meet?* The sender was irritated, and that fit Seth's personality.

Mark glanced at the alarm clock sitting next to the bed. 9:12 a.m. He knew time would pass quickly. He hoped Cliff and the president's meeting in the oval office went well. He hoped they were able to motivate the woman.

Steve Chang sat in the secured room at the JPL and opened his communications bureau with the intent of sending a message to China, but was greeted with a blinking light. He hesitantly reached for the phone, certain she had left the message. *Impatience will get you nowhere,* he thought as he encrypted, then punched in his code.

"I hear you finally got what you're looking for. I'm on my way." She sent the message from her apartment and then waited. But she couldn't wait long, she had the 10:35 a.m. flight out of Dulles.

Chang sat back with furrowed eyebrows on top of a slightly twisted face and wondered what she knew. He checked his watch and thought she would more than likely be in the air. He punched in her number and got his answer; it went to message.

61

April 27th 2009
CIA Headquarters
Langley, Virginia

C liff was starting to think about lunch when his secretary buzzed his phone. "Sir, Agent Hollister for you."

"Thank you, Bethany. Show him in." Cliff had put together a small group to tail the women after they had left the oval office. They had all gone to work preparing for Tuesday, all but one. Agent Mike Hollister was assigned to Shannon May.

Mike Hollister had joined the CIA two years before Mark Springfield. A master's degree in computer programming was highly sought after by the agency. Hollister swore his allegiance to the United States with six other clandestine service trainees after a recruitment drive had left him wanting more. Back from a rare vacation, he was spending time in Washington, D.C. After finalizing the plan with Mark, the director had gathered agents and assigned each one of them to a woman to tail. It was a nice change for Mike; normally he worked overseas. He liked being back in Washington and he hoped this mundane shadow job lasted a while. He, too, was beginning to think about getting out of the field. Mike Hollister followed Shannon home to her apartment. He parked half a block away. He could easily see her front entrance and the back alley. Occasionally, he got out to stretch his legs. He strolled down the sidewalk and walked across the street window shopping. He kept watch by looking over his shoulder and through the reflection in the glass. On his fourth and last trip to the corner, he saw a familiar woman watching a cab driver load bags into the trunk of the cab.

Mike had been briefed on 'the huut' shortly after its inception. He had stumbled upon it while accessing an engineer's home computer during a routine sweep. Richard Avila was doing some preliminary designs in the early phases of the program and would continue his work on his home computer long after he would leave his office. Mike had reported Avila's activities and now that he knew, he had to be *officially* told. The engineer had been disciplined for working on a top secret design on his home computer and had been re-educated on the protocols for handling top secret information. He never again worked outside the office.

Mike continued to observe the woman by the cab. He saw no other agents around. From inside his coat pocket, he pulled the list of suspects he'd been given. Her name was not on it. He strolled back to his car. His instructions had been simple, report any suspicious activity. While he Contemplated his next move, Mike adjusted his earpiece. Raising his right arm, he spoke softly into the small microphone clipped to the inside of his sleeve. "I need an agent to watch Ms. May. I have an additional suspect on the move." After a short pause, he heard.

"I'll be in place in fifteen." Ten minutes later Mike heard. "In Place."

He took one last look down the alley and at the front entrance of Shannon May's apartment. He slid into the front seat of his car, started it and drove to his office.

At his desk, he accessed the Yellow Cab Company's database. He typed in the number written on the side of the cab, 1708. The screen displayed the driver's name, registration number, pick-up address, name of client, and drop-off location. The contract carrier the government uses for Dulles is American Airlines. He accessed their database and typed in the woman's name. Nothing. He backed out of their system. With several other airlines to choose from, he tried Delta. He got the same results and moved on to United's data base where he got a hit. Flight UA1402 departs Dulles _IAD_12:21 p.m. Arrive_ LAX_ 2:42 p.m. Travelers-1.

Mike wrote her name on a piece of paper, folded it, and headed to the director's office. Outside the office, he asked to see Mr. House. But since the two had known each other for so long when they were behind closed doors, Mike was on a first name basis with the director.

Cliff gave Mike a hardy handshake and motioned for him to take a seat. "You know, Mark had a hunch it was Shannon. Your presence makes that son of a gun right again," Cliff said.

Mike laughed and couldn't stop. He knew this was serious, but reveled in the fact that Mark Springfield was wrong. They were close friends, and he knew Mark was an intelligent, almost gifted agent with an unmatched sixth sense. For him to be wrong about Shannon would go a long way. Mike sat up, leaned in towards the desk, and rested a forearm on the edge. Raising an eyebrow, he began, "Do you know who lives down the block from Miss Shannon May and is probably at the airport waiting on, if not boarding, United Flight 1402 to Los Angeles?"

Cliff returned a confused look. "No, who?"

Mike held the folded paper, shook it in front of the director, then reached across a small stack of papers and laid it in front of Cliff, who snatched it from the desk.

"Jesus Christ! I didn't put anybody on her! How did you know?"

Mike started to explain, but Cliff suddenly held up his hand. "On second thought, tell me later," he said as he picked up the phone. "Beth, get me the 486 th." He looked at Mike, "Do you have an overnight bag packed?"

"Always do."

"Get it." Thirty seconds later, the phone rang. "Yes?"

"I have Colonel Haley on the line, sir."

"Colonel, I have a location. Los Angeles, California."

"Ready in thirty minutes, Director," replied the colonel.

Earlier, as a precautionary measure, Cliff had the colonel in his office at 7:00 a.m. briefing him on a potential flight that could happen at any time, to any place. Haley headed the 486th Flight Test Wing used to fly U.S. State Department and Federal Emergency Management Agency personnel around the country. The unit was also used covertly to fly the CIA around the world. That was not the first time Colonel Haley had sat in the director's office.

One hour after Cliff placed the call to the colonel, the men sat in comfort in the 757 cruising at 35,000 feet. The two Pratt and Whitney turbo fans produce over 43,000 pounds of thrust for an airspeed well over 400 knots. Under current conditions, they would be in Los Angeles in less than five hours. They ate lunch, and then went to the communications bay to call Mark. He needed to know they were on their way.

Mark had just stepped outside his room to have a look around when his phone buzzed. The display read *Unknown Caller.* He walked across the parking lot. He took the call but stayed quiet giving the party on the other end the opportunity to speak first. "Scotch or whiskey?" Mike asked

Mark laughed, "I'd take an ice cold Carolina Blonde." Twenty-five years ago the answer would've been "tequila." Mike's voice was a welcome relief. Cameron had been a capable, partner, but nothing beats thirty years of working together.

"Glad we got that cleared up. How would you like a visit?"

"You traveling solo?" They kept the conversation generic. The sixty-five million dollar 757 could both transmit and receive encrypted communications, but Mark's phone operated in the clear.

"The boss and I are on the company jet," Mike said. "We'll be in your neck of the woods in three hours."

Mark put it together. Since they were headed his way, they were chasing someone. "I take it the boss was convincing."

"Your plan worked, but the client isn't who you think it is."

Mark was careful with his next request but knew Mike would get it. "I need you to do your magic. The person we're meeting is going on a business trip. Can you call his secretary and find out the details? It would be nice if you joined him." He was effectively telling Mike to find out where Chang was going.

62

April 27th 2009

Mark had to do two things - position the cavalry and trust Benner. Chang planned on running as soon as he got the device. He purposely set the meeting close to the airport in a very public place, Freedom Park, just off the 710, thirty minutes from LAX.

Chang's phone buzzed as he was walking through the lobby of the JPL. His face twisted in disbelief.

Benner killed the agent, was waiting for us, Luke's been shot."

He stopped dead in his tracks. He read the text again, walked over to a small group of chairs across the lobby and sat down. He didn't know what to think. *Did he have the device? Will this delay my departure? Where's the girl? What about Luke?* The last two he didn't care about

363

as long as they weren't going to the authorities. Then another text popped up.

Benner's found what you're looking for.

"Benner? I knew you wouldn't stay away," he muttered to himself. Under the circumstances, he was damn glad he hadn't.

The transaction had to be believable. The only way was to have Ken Benner deliver the device. Mark's boss would never let it out of his hands, so asking permission was out. It was a risk he would have to take.

Chang stared at his phone. Things were spinning out of control. He liked being in control. Perhaps he should stay put, but there was too much in play to stop now. He had already sent a message to his handlers in China and his contact, who had an important piece of the puzzle and would be in LA soon. He wasn't going to stop now. They could meet and leave the country together. He didn't like doing any of the heavy lifting, but there was no one else. He would have to trust Benner to deliver the device. "This will work," he told himself. "I'll get the device, meet her at the airport and we'll leave. It's that simple. The agent is dead. It gives me plenty of time. I'll be long gone before anyone finds out." Chang picked up his phone and sent a text to Ken.

Entrance to Freedom Park. Be there at noon. Bring the device.

Mark was holding Ken's phone when it buzzed. The message came in quicker than he thought it would. He hadn't had time to approach Ken, so he typed the reply. *I'll be there.*

Mark had barely sent the text when Seth's phone buzzed.

I'm done with the girl. Do what you want.

Mark seethed at the coldness in the text, but it meant that Chang had taken the bait. Mark walked into the hotel room and sat on the bed facing Ken. "Interested in helping?"

Ken had accepted the fact that he would be spending a lot of time in prison. Helping the agent couldn't hurt. It took him thirty seconds to join Mark's team. His relocation in the SLIPP program was a done deal.

"When the time comes, I need you to pass this device to your boss. If he asks, you killed me, Seth is somewhere with the girl, and you have no idea the condition of Luke. Anything else and you'll have to wing it. After you're done and Chang is gone, wait there. You'll be taken into custody and brought back here."

Ken simply nodded his head.

Mark stood and faced Cameron. "Do you think your partner can help? I need someone to watch Mr. Benner and bring him back here after the drop. Can you two take care of that?"

"I think he can be talked into it." Cameron took his phone from the night stand and placed the call.

Mark slipped into Mary's room and handed her his back-up gun, the Springfield XD 9. No stranger to firearms, she checked it and laid it on the night stand. He glanced at his watch. It was time. He turned, kissed Mary on the forehead, and told her to stay put. As he walked through the door between the rooms, Cameron stood up and announced, "He's on his way."

"Detective, I can't thank you enough. Take Mr. Benner. Stage him in the car and wait for Chang. Once he passes the device, bring him back here and wait. I can't risk anyone being seen or any questions being asked. I'm going to run an errand."

"We'll be here waiting for your call," Cameron assured.

Mark reached behind his back and removed the device. If Cliff knew he was turning it over, he'd be furious, but he had no choice. He had to make it to the airport in case Mike couldn't. He flipped it over and stared at it, then slid open the cover and pressed the switches commanding a voltage drop. The device could be used two more times and then the encryption was gone.

Chang drove to Freedom Park and waited by the entrance. He realized his nerves were on edge when he caught himself shifting in his seat. Fifteen minutes later, Ken pulled into the lot and parked next to Steve so their windows were in line. There were only two other cars in the entire lot. Chang didn't know there were two men watching him from a block away. Cameron and Shawn were out of their car looking through a set of binoculars.

"I have it," Ken said as he looked around nervously.

"Pass it to me," Chang demanded. He was anxious. Ken could see he was sweating. "Mark Springfield, is he dead?"

"He was there waiting for your guys when they left the trailer. He shot Luke and had Seth pinned down. I had driven up to check the girl. I didn't think anyone else was there. I heard the gun fire and went to the offices. I came up behind the agent. He never knew what hit him."

Ken wasn't sure if it was believable, but then he saw the smile grow on Chang's face. He looked over his shoulder and to each side then handed the device over.

Chang anxiously took it and stuck it between his knees. He measured the voltage with the meter he had brought with him.

According to his contact, the device had been loaded at the facility. If it still had a voltage greater than twenty, it still held the encryption. He watched the digital display blink twenty-one volts. Finally, after years of digging, he had the prize. It didn't end as cleanly as he would've liked, but it didn't matter. He had the encryption. There was only one obstacle left: getting it through airport security.

Steve Chang handed Ken Benner a thick white envelope. It held the money he'd been stashing over the years. He needed to give Benner something. "When I get settled, I'll send more. This should hold you over for now."

Chang was full of shit, and Ken knew it. Once Chang made it to China, Ken would never hear from him again. He knew Chang only gave him the envelope so he wouldn't cause a problem and try to stop him. Benner opened the worn envelope and thumbed through the cash. There was no less than two hundred thousand dollars. He looked at Chang, satisfied.

Ken held out his hand. Steve hesitated, but extended his arm and reached out and barely took Ken's hand for a brief light handshake.

Chang couldn't drive out of the lot fast enough. He maintained his composure for the thirty-minute drive to Los Angeles International Airport. Like Mark, who had driven from Washington with the device sitting on his front seat, Chang drove as cautiously as if he were carrying a nuclear bomb. The closer he got to LAX, however, the more difficult it was for him not to speed. The urge overpowered him. He had done his best to stay focused, but his speed increased anyway. He exited on Central and drove around the terminals with some relief. He pulled into a parking spot in the structure across from the Bradley International Terminal, sat back, let out a heavy breath, and smiled.

He carried only a small duffel. He stopped at the ticket counter to show his passport and finish his check in. As he walked through the terminal, his fingers went numb from his grip on the bag. He laughed and tried to relax. Inside the men's restroom, he stood in front of the mirror and saw beads of sweat running down his forehead. Placing the bag between his legs, he wet a paper towel and wiped his face. It was imperative to stay calm going through security or he'd be flagged and searched. He was an hour and a half away from being en route to China. He took several deep breaths and left the restroom. The line through TSA was long, and the closer he got to the front, the more apprehensive he became. He did not want to be the reason his items were searched. He stepped up to the conveyor and stripped himself of anything that could possibly alert the machines or agents. He took every precaution.

He went through the metal detector without a hitch and was waiting for his bag to roll off the belt when an agent asked him if he owned a brief case. He turned and the TSA agent held up a soft-sided case. The man in front of him claimed the item. Chang's heart raced. The thought of trying to explain what he had was nerve-racking. His heart pounded so hard he could feel it in his ears. He was sure everyone around him could hear it as well. The belt stopped for a few seconds, then started again as quickly as it had stopped. His bag appeared and was conveyed into his waiting hands. He had cleared security. It was as if the sun had shone through the ceiling. Steve Chang turned and started towards his gate. He floated through the terminal.

Across from the gate was a woman he'd never met but recognized, nonetheless. Scanning the terminal, he crossed the crowded walkway and took a seat beside her.

She had seen photos of Chang during security briefings, so when he approached, she removed the bag from the seat next to her and motioned for him to sit down. Chang spoke first. "What do you know?"

"Springfield is reported missing," she said a little nervously.

Chang sat back and smiled. "Is the time still the same?"

"Nothing has changed. It was confirmed this morning."

"Excellent." He knew not to ask the time. She wouldn't give that up until she had been well taken care of. He turned and looked at her as if he'd known her for years. "You realize you can never come back?"

"There's nothing left for me here anymore, hasn't been for a long while. If this is what I have to do to live in comfort, then so be it," she said tersely – with no reservations in her voice.

They sat in silence and watched people hurry through the terminal. When Chang looked at her again, he noticed the corners of her eyes were wet.

By the time they heard the first call for boarding, airport security was a distant memory. They held first-class seats, and after the families were boarded they moved towards the agent at the podium. As they walked through the jet way, Chang knew he had pulled it off. In forty minutes, he'd be wheels-up and on his way home.

Before they were seated, they were offered champagne and eagerly accepted. It was a long flight. A celebration was in order. A quick conversation with a fellow passenger provided an easy seat change and they were able to sit together. After everyone was seated and the cabin door closed a male steward proceeded down the aisle refilling glasses and chatting politely with the passengers. The mood was light as they settled in for the long flight.

"Mr. Chang, may I refill your glass?" It wasn't unusual for the crew to know the names of the first-class passengers. When Chang look up, he recognized the same steward who had poured their first glass.

"Yes, thank you."

Mike Hollister stood holding the champagne bottle with a towel draped over his arm. He smiled at them, wondering how they were going to take the news. "Madam Secretary, thank you for joining us this afternoon."

Jordyn Kennedy was delighted to be recognized and gave Mike Hollister a warm smile as she held up her glass. Mike carefully poured the champagne, playing out his part all the way to the end. He pulled the bottle back and allowed her to take one final drink. "Madam Secretary, Mr. Chang, if you please, my boss would like a word with you," Mike said as he motioned with the bottle, pointing behind them. They graciously turned to address the steward's colleague.

Mike had seen many people arrested, but never before had he ever seen the color drain from someone's face so fast. Jordyn Kennedy turned and stared directly into the eyes of Cliff House.

From the look on Cliff's face, Chang knew something was wrong. But one look at Jordyn and he knew something was *terribly* wrong.

If Mike hadn't reached for it, Jordyn would've dropped her glass. "Mr. Chang, allow me to introduce you to my boss, the director of the CIA, Mr. Clifford House."

Chang sat motionless as he comprehended what had been said. Then, he twisted furiously in his seat and screamed at Jordyn.

"You bitch. You set me up!"

Mike firmly placed his hand on Chang's shoulder in case he tried to lunge at Jordyn. She sat stunned, white as a sheet. She mouthed a few inaudible words to Chang and then, without warning, threw up between their seats. Chang made no attempt to move. He felt the crushing hand of Mike's powerful grip.

With his other hand, Mike handed the bottle and glass back to a young female stewardess. He reached under Chang's seat, took his bag, and then allowed him to slide away from the vomit which had been spewed on the arm rest. He looked at Jordyn who was sobbing uncontrollably and handed her the towel that was still draped over his arm. "Mr. Chang, Madam Secretary, you're both under arrest for the act of espionage against the United States."

Except for the few who had heard Mike say "Director of the CIA," the passengers in first class didn't quite know what was happening. When he spoke his words, they knew the men standing in the aisle were law enforcement.

The cabin became silent. Passengers were twisting in their seats trying to get a good look. A hushed chatter grew throughout the cabin in both Mandarin and English as the passengers pointed and reached for their cameras.

Cliff, quite aware of his surroundings, identified himself and instructed everyone to put away their phones and cameras or they would be confiscated.

"The cabin door, if you will," Cliff said as he turned towards the flight attendant.

From the 757, Mike had easily searched the databases of several airlines until he found the one with Steve Chang and his co-conspirator. He had interpreted Mark's request for him and Cliff to play the intercept team. The only way to convict all parties was to have them on the same plane getting ready to leave the country with the device in hand. Cliff had met the crew as they were preparing the aircraft for the upcoming flight. He informed the captain that they would be making an arrest aboard his aircraft before take-off. Arrangements had been made to assure the safety of the other passengers.

After the 757 had touched down at LAX, Cliff was met by the head of airport police. Though they didn't know the details, they were happy to help the director of the CIA. It had worked perfectly. Mike was more than happy to serve champagne and chat with the passengers until the time was right.

As they led a very irate Steve Chang and almost catatonic Jordyn Kennedy from the plane, airport police waited in the jet bridge that had never been retracted. Mark Springfield leaned against the far wall, his right leg bent at the knee and his foot flat against the wall as the entourage exited the boarding area. He watched the police lead them to the security door. Chang started yelling obscenities at Mark across the terminal but was forcefully pushed through the door before he could say much.

Mark pulled the phone from his pocket and placed a call to Cameron. "It's over, detective. Bring everyone to the airport police office." Mark walked through the door and towards Mike. The two shook hands and as Mark reached for the bag, Mike pulled it away.

"This is evidence," Mike kidded. He smiled and handed it over. "Well, my friend, that's an arrest I won't soon forget. She threw up all over the seats, almost got your Steve Chang."

With a satisfied grin, Mark took the bag, unzipped it, and retrieved the device. Flipping it over, he commanded a voltage drop, five times. It completely dumped the encryption. "Now, I feel better," he said as he tossed it back in the bag.

"You look like shit," Mike said, looking over his friend.

"Thank you," he said, as they walked towards the group.

Mark applied pressure to the right side of his lower back. "I think my back needs some more time off."

63

April 27th 2009
Los Angeles, California
LAX International Airport

Mark Springfield and Mike Hollister stayed outside the airport police office to catch up. Cliff handled the details and made the call to the operatives who were surveilling Mike Vanns, who was immediately taken into custody.

Mutual respect between both Mark and Mike had developed over many years of working together and their friendship was unshakable. Even though Mark had stopped the loss of the Huntsville unit, he would never take the credit. "I was just the one the director happened to see in the hallway," he'd say. Each knew the other to be a very capable agent and thought the CIA was the most well run and lubricated machine in the world.

Cameron pulled into the police parking lot at LAX. The head of the department met him curbside and took Ken Benner into custody. Cameron was escorted towards the office at Cliff's request. Mary was helped from the front seat and stood with Shawn, Cameron's partner. Eventually, they were all escorted into the building.

Before Ken was taken to the small room they used for holding, Mark introduced him to Cliff. The introduction was brief and they both knew Benner wouldn't be locked up for long. Cliff turned to Cameron and Shawn and thanked them for their diligence.

Mark walked over to Cameron and stuck out his hand. Cameron spoke first. "Some night. Remind me, why did I take a call from you?" They chuckled as Mark shook his hand.

"Detective, I had a feeling about you when I met you at the observatory. I couldn't have picked a better non-agency partner. Thanks again."

"I'm guessing this is one of those things I can't tell my friends about?"

A thin smile spread across Mark's face. "Detective, welcome to my world." Mark walked to the director to finalize his trip home.

Mike walked up to Cameron, took his hand, and shook it vigorously. "Mike Hollister."

"Cameron Butler."

"A compliment from Agent Springfield, I see," Mike said with a raised eyebrow and a twisted smile.

"His friends call him Mark." Cameron had a quick wit and wasn't going to let the events slow his humor. The exchange started Mike laughing.

"I can see why Mark picked you," he said. As they continued talking, Cameron relived the events of the past day.

Mary, feeling out of place, stood off to the side while her brother engaged the other men. The only thing she really wanted to do was talk to her husband and the girls. An officer approached her and asked for her statement, but Mark materialized by her side. "Officer, that won't be necessary," he said and pulled Mary to a quieter side of the room, handing her a phone. "Here, five minutes. There'll be more time later." Walking away, he looked over his shoulder. "One more thing, no CIA talk."

Twenty minutes later, six agents from the LA office crowded into the office of the airport police. They would accompany Cliff and Mike back to Washington and process Chang and Kennedy. Mark pulled Cameron and Mary outside. "Detective, would you like to join us for dinner tonight?"

"It's the least we could do," Mary added quickly.

"Thank you both, but I think I'll take a rain check. If I ever make it back to see your collection, we'll do it then."

"Deal," Mark said as he held out his hand. Mary stepped in and gave him a hug. Mark knew he would be seeing him again.

"If you'll excuse me, I need to have your boss call my boss, but before I go, let me give you my home address and phone number. If it's ok, I really would like to stay in touch. Not many of my friends like the older hardware." Cameron had felt a kinship and hoped he wasn't out of line.

Mark chuckled. "That won't be necessary. I think I can find you."

"Of course you can," Cameron said, shaking his head as he smiled. He turned and disappeared through the doorway.

"Well," Mark said as he turned towards his sister. "How about we take a short trip up the coast? An hour, two at the most. There's a place north of Ventura that sits on the edge of a cliff that overlooks the ocean. The view is beautiful."

Mary didn't know why he didn't want to jump on a plane and fly home. She gave her brother a confused look. But she could see and hear in his voice that they were going to do this. So, with a surrendered smile, she asked, "Can we eat first?"

"Nope, they have some of the best food south of Santa Barbara."

As they walked to the car, Mike yelled from the door, "Mark, phone call."

"Take a message," he said, half looking over his shoulder.

"I think you'll want to take this," Mike insisted.

Mark apologized and begrudgingly walked inside. Ten minutes later, he reappeared at the car. Mary was already in the car. Her head was leaned back and her eyes closed when Mark shut the door. "Sorry about that."

"Important?" she asked with her eyes still closed.

"I guess when the president calls, you have to talk to him. Oh, by the way, he's invited us to dinner next week."

Mary's eyes shot open and stared straight ahead. "Of the United States? Jesus, Mark! What else do I need to know?"

"That's it. I work for the CIA and the president's a friend of mine."

Mark pulled onto Century Boulevard . Occasionally, he glanced at Mary. It would take a while for her to register it all. She'd been through a traumatic event. She would need time to process the last few nights. She was a strong woman, but she would need some space before she went home.

He chose Highway 1. The constant view of the ocean would be far better for Mary than the crowded I-405. She could stare at the ocean and enjoy the calming effects of the Pacific almost all the way to the inn on the cliffs. There they could spend the night eating and drinking wine.

64

April 28th 2009
The Inn on the Cliffs
Just north of Ventura, CA

Mark opened the door of the hotel room for Mary. She walked out into the bright Southern California sunshine. They glanced around as Mark slid on his sunglasses. "Up for a road trip?" he asked.

Mary looked at her brother and tilted her head. "Where to?"

"Arizona. Gotta see a guy."

"Ok. Can we get something to eat first?"

"We'll grab a bite on the way." He tossed his sister the keys and headed for the car. He opened the driver's door and stood straight as an arrow while she slid in. She chuckled while he pulled the seat belt over her shoulder.

As they traveled south on the 101, Mark made a few calls - one to Avis, letting them know he wouldn't be returning the car at LAX, and one to Cliff. Mary kept her eye out for a place to eat. Nothing looked good. Mark pointed to a Jack in the Box and gave Mary a nod as he finished his call to Cliff. "Pull in there and I promise we'll find the best restaurant when we get to Phoenix."

"Deal." She took the off-ramp. After a short wait in the drive thru, the two were back on the road. In between bites, Mary broke the silence. "Phoenix?"

"I want to introduce you to someone. He saved your life," he said as a matter-of-fact.

Mary's face reddened and her eyes welled up with tears. Her anxiety broke his heart. He leaned over and gave her a hug. Even though the ordeal was over, they were both still emotionally charged.

"Now don't get all sappy on me," he said as he sipped his coke.

They drove without speaking for over an hour, their thoughts drifting over the last few days. Mary was the first to break the silence. "You know, I saw you in Mexico."

"When was I in Mexico?" he asked a little sheepishly.

Mary glanced at her brother and rolled her eyes. "Oh, the same time we were there with the girls."

"Why didn't you say anything?"

"Thought I'd let you have your fun."

Mark was a heartbeat away from telling his sister what had really happened in Mexico. Without him "having his fun," their trip would've turned tragic. He paused and looked out the window and swallowed the lump in his throat. "Boys will be boys." He laughed.

Mark volunteered to take over at a rest stop off the I-10. They were a few hours from their destination. She complained but gave up the wheel. Mark had the address he had copied down. With the directions he had pulled from the computer's mapping program at the hotel, he drove straight to her savior's house.

They parked along the curb. Mary noticed the name on the mailbox – Quinn - and looked questioningly at Mark.

"He's the truck driver." Mary started crying. During dinner, he had briefly told her of the accident and Cameron's part in the affair. He left out the gory details.

He took a few napkins from the Jack in the Box bag and handed them to her. She wiped her eyes as he rubbed her back. Jokingly, he said, "Come on, let's man up."

She turned and gave him a little laugh.

Mark rang the bell. When no one came to the door, he knocked lightly. His heart sank after a few minutes when no one had answered. He reached inside his jacket pocket and fished around for his notebook when he heard the lock on the door. Cautiously, it opened.

"May I help you?" came a soft, demure voice.

"Yes, we'd like to see Mr. Quinn."

"Are you from the paper?" Her soft voice became stern. "My husband's not taking visitors."

"No, ma'am. My name is Mark Springfield, and this is my sister Mary. We have some information regarding your husband's accident." Mark's frame almost filled the doorway. He reached in his pocket and pulled out his ID and showed it to Mrs. Quinn. She glanced up, giving him a twisted look when she read CIA. She was a very attractive woman. Barely five feet tall with short, curly light brown hair. Her deep brown eyes held his gaze. Mark sensed her protectiveness of her husband. He knew the only way they were getting through the door was to tell her the truth. "Mrs. Quinn, your husband saved my sister's life and I want to thank him."

"Two people died in that accident!" she spouted defensively.

"Yes, they did, and they were very bad people. May we come in?"

She gave both of them a long look, but slowly opened the door. "Only if you quit calling me Mrs. Quinn. Jodie will do."

Mark was relieved when he walked through the doorway, but he sensed quickly that the mood in the house seemed dark. He hoped this hadn't been a bad idea. She walked them down the hall and into the living room. Dave Quinn was sitting on a loveseat. Mark took one look and saw the anguish in his eyes. It had only been a few days since the accident. It was obvious that it had affected him immensely. Mark walked over and stuck out his hand.

"Mr. Quinn, my name is Mark Springfield. This is my sister Mary."

Dave stood up and took Mark's hand in a defeated grip as he gave it a light shake. "Call me Dave. Welcome to our home." He turned to Mary and gently took her hand. Mary's hand disappeared inside Dave's as he shook it.

Jodie motioned for them to take a seat. She had been so focused on what Mark had said at the door that she hadn't thought to offer them anything.

"What do you want to know about the accident?" Dave asked skeptically.

"Dave, I think it's what I can tell you about the accident that might help."

"Might help? I killed two people," he said, leaning forward and dropping his head in his hands, grief stricken.

Mark looked at Jodie, then back at Dave. "I work for the CIA. Some very bad folks pulled my sister into the middle of one of my assignments. She was kidnapped from Maryland, drugged, and flown to California. Here's where you come in. When the situation turned bad for them, they decided to kill her." Dave and his wife looked at Mary. "The two people you hit were on the way to kill my sister. The driver was Martin Powell, the passenger, Lorena Bean. They're both enemy spies and ruthless killers." Mark paused to let what he had just said sink in. Then he continued. "Dave, if that accident hadn't happened, my sister would not be sitting here today." With those last few words, Mark felt himself choke up.

Disbelief shrouded their faces. They glanced at each other and stared at Mary. It took several long seconds for them to fully understand the ramifications of the accident. As the realization settled with Jodie, she stood up and pulled Mary from her seat. "Oh my God!" she murmured. She locked Mary in a bear hug and started to cry.

Dave looked at Mark with a blank expression, still processing what he had just heard.

"Mr. Quinn, you saved my sister's life. The individuals killed were very, very bad people. Your accident was our saving grace."

Dave understood, but it took an extra minute for the emotional transfer to happen. His utter despair turned to elation.

Dave stood and reached for Mark's hand and arm. He pulled him up from the chair. Mark was trapped in a crushing handshake. "Thank you. Thank you for coming. You have no idea. You have no idea what I've been going through. I couldn't sleep. I can't eat..." Dave continued to shake Mark's hand as he continued to talk. Tears streamed freely down his cheeks. "Thank you," he repeated. "Thank you."

Dave retrieved a few beers from the refrigerator and they continued talking for a few more hours. When it became late, Mark insisted he buy dinner.

"The best place in Phoenix!" Mary exclaimed.

Epilogue

Seven weeks later, the governor of California, the State Senator, and the head of the highway patrol received certified correspondence from the Central Intelligence Agency. Detective Cameron Butler's presence was requested, with travel expenses paid by the United States government, at CIA headquarters, in Langley, Virginia, where he would be presented an award from the director of the CIA.

Cameron was told of the request during a routine staff meeting. He was called before his peers and harassed about his pending trip to Washington.

Not many knew the details of Cameron's involvement. He thought it best to keep it to himself. His boss had been called and brought to the LAXPD office, by two agents from the CIA's Los Angeles office, for a face-to-face meeting with Cliff, who had outlined the importance of what had transpired. He was told only what he needed to know, but it was clear that officer Butler had been instrumental in the outcome.

When the news had been plastered everywhere that the Secretary of Homeland Defense was being detained for questioning, he had kept quiet. After Jordyn's husband had left her for a younger woman, she had become bitter. With no real friends in Washington, she had thrown herself into the Huntsville project. When events had started to unravel, she'd seen the potential and had taken a chance. Like Danielle, she had known it was a once-in-a-lifetime opportunity. She had contacted Chang and explained that even if he had the code, he would only be able to access the satellite at predetermined times, and at most, he would only be able to make three attempts before losing the pre-loaded encryption. She had also told him he was being watched and would have to shake his tail before heading to the airport. She had been clear. She was contacting him to offer him his last chance. It had infuriated him. They would meet and flee the country after Springfield turned over the encryption. She would be paid handsomely. It was a little extra she felt she deserved. She would defect and never look back. She had had no idea that the director's speech that morning had been a ruse to get the co-conspirator to run. If it had not been for Mike Hollister watching Shannon May, she may have gotten away with it.

Cameron had been involved in events that only happened in movies. He had gotten a look at how things worked with the folks he'd always known as 'spooks.' He was excited to make the trip east. When Mark had called with an offer to stay at his home, Cameron was pleased and accepted graciously.

When Mark returned to Washington he started the paperwork that would take three days to finish. He had kept notes throughout the assignment, but the last few days, he got as precise as he possibly could. There would be indictments. If Mark had his way, every last one of them would die in the deepest hole of a federal prison. Everyone would be charged with espionage and he tied kidnapping and attempted murder to all their charges.

Two days later, Mark pulled out his legal pad and started what he thought was the best part of the assignment. A monitor stared at him, but for this, he wanted to sit and scribe on a sheet of paper. He would transfer it to his computer later, formalize it on company letterhead, and send it up the chain to be signed by the director of the CIA and the president of the United States. It was a request to bring a civilian into the agency and to present an award seldom given to anyone outside the department. Mark looked forward to the day Cameron would stand to receive the accolades. He had little tolerance for men who blew off their responsibilities, but would bend over backwards for someone who went above and beyond the call of duty. Cameron had been thrown into a situation of which he had no prior knowledge, made a decision to help, and pulled out all the stops to do it.

Mark rolled back in his chair and rested his feet on an open desk drawer, interlocking his fingers behind his head as he reflected on the events. After several minutes, a wide smile grew on his face. He knew exactly what the detective needed as a personal gift. Mark picked up the phone and called JT.

On Monday morning, Cameron boarded a plane bound for the nation's capital. He touched down at Dulles International Airport late that afternoon. With the map from the rental car agency next to him and the directions Mark had sent, he easily found his home in Oakton, Virginia. Mark met him in the driveway with a welcome handshake. Once he was settled, Mark treated his guest to dinner. Cameron spent the rest of the night looking over Mark's firearm collection and reliving the events of the past two months.

On Tuesday, Cameron spent the day walking around Washington while Mark helped prepare for the ceremony that was to be held on Wednesday. A light rain fell towards the end of the day as Cameron drove back to his host's house. He couldn't keep the smile from his face.

The next morning, the two men arrived early at the CIA headquarters which gave Mark time to show the detective around. Cameron was in awe as he approached the building. He walked through the entrance and was greeted by a huge skylight ceiling. "This is the newer section of headquarters built in the mid-1980s." They walked through the lobby. Cameron tried to soak it all in. Before him was Kryptos, a large bronze sculpture fashioned after an ancient scroll and printed in code." It began at the entrance and continued to the northwest corner of the courtyard. Mark explained the theme was "intelligence gathering." They passed Sculpture Hall, a modestly sized room that held numerous statues. Shaking his head in wonder, Cameron turned to Mark. "This is fantastic."

Mark smiled. "Follow me."

They walked into the courtyard and passed several tents which had been set up for the occasion. As they walked up to the older part of the building, Cameron suddenly stopped. Carved in stone at the entrance were the words, "And Ye Shall Know the Truth and the Truth Shall Make You Free." Cameron took a step back. *All the secrets*, he thought. *All the secrets that have been whispered in these halls*. He looked around, wondering what decisions had been made because of all these people.

"It's our Motto," Mark said, leaning in.

Cameron was overwhelmed with his private tour. If he was taken with what he now saw, he was going to love what lay ahead.

Cameron stepped through the door and before him was the most identifiable symbol of the CIA. The floor was inlaid with the large granite seal measuring sixteen feet in diameter. He studied the eagle, shield, and the sixteen point compass star.

Mark stepped up from behind and pointed to the star. "That represents the convergence of intelligence data from around the world at a central point, and the shield is the standard symbol of defense, and, of course, the eagle is us."

"*Us?* Meaning agents?" Cameron asked.

"No," he said, shaking his head. "*Us,* as in every single American." Mark said it with an intensity that caused the hairs on the back of Cameron's neck to tingle.

Cameron stood looking around the room, absorbing the magnitude of it all. Finally, he turned to Mark. "You work here with all this history. There are decisions made by world leaders based on what the United States tells them. You people are a major part of that." Cameron continued pointing around the room. "*This* is where it happens!"

Mark lay a hand on his shoulder. "It's like working next to the ocean. Eventually, you don't notice it anymore." Mark was being modest. He felt the power and the history of the building every day he walked through the doors.

The courtyard was set between both the newer and older buildings. Today, it was set up with a small viewing area centered in front of a podium and flanked with the American flag and a flag with the symbol of the CIA.

At 10:45 a.m., department heads, support staff, and agents not assigned overseas, started to fill the courtyard, mingling amongst themselves. Cameron looked around and noticed everyone seemed to be in a light and festive mood. At exactly 11:00 a.m., the director approached the podium, carrying a large manila envelope and a black case. Cameron and Mark occupied the first two seats and listened as the director talked about duty, honor, and courage. Cameron, in a partial daze, realized his name was being called.

"He's calling you," Mark said as he nudged him. Then the clapping began.

Cameron stood, very embarrassed, and walked to the podium. Everyone stood. He was sure that the lump in his throat was noticeable as the director shook his hand. He looked out over the crowd, then at the photographer who flashed several pictures of him and the director shaking hands.

He never expected to be at the headquarters of one of the most secretive agencies in the world, let alone standing in front of its director receiving recognition for simply doing a job that he felt was his duty. Yet here he was, in front of a sea of strangers staring at him and nodding their heads in approval. Cameron was speechless.

After the ceremony, while most of the people were milling around the tables of food, Mark walked up and introduced JT to Cameron. "This is the detective I told you about."

Cameron stuck out his still shaky hand. "Hi, nice to meet you."

"Jeremiah Thompson, but please, call me JT."

Mark walked over to a table and retrieved a box. He handed it to Cameron. "I have something for you, thanks to JT."

As he reached for the box, Cameron felt his eyes getting moist. He had never quite felt this way. He couldn't explain why he was choked up now. He fought the feeling, walked back over to the table, set the box down, and pulled off the Sunday comics that Mark had used as wrapping paper. He looked at Mark. "Nice touch." Inside were two black cases. At first he thought it was firearms. It wasn't until he removed them that he understood. He laughed as he pulled them from the box.

With JT's advice, Mark had gotten him two two-way radio tactical kits. Cameron looked at Mark. "I don't know what to say."

"We needed those," Mark said jokingly.

They had hardly said anything else before JT swooped in, anxious to explain the new toys. Pulling out the plastic-wrapped pieces, he held them up to Cameron. "These are Raven-4's Two-Way Radio Tactical Kit with bone conduction speakers. It allows you to hear clearly by positioning the speakers on your facial bones. You can hear through the bones in your head leaving your ears open for optimal situational awareness."

"Bones in my head?"

"Bones in your head, my boy. It also employs a noise cancelling boom microphone so you can operate in chaotic, noisy situations."

"You know, like when someone is shooting over your head," Mark said with a grin.

At that moment, the courtyard speakers boomed, "Let's eat."

Cameron and JT put the kits back in their boxes. Mark stuck out his hand. "Thank you, Cameron. Thank you for saving my sister."

"Mark, I was just along for the ride. Thank you for all of this," he said, motioning around the yard.

The men turned and walked towards the tables. When they were out of earshot from JT, Mark looked over at Cameron, "Don't think for one minute I didn't see that tear almost fall on my nice wrapping job." Mark normally wouldn't have called attention to it, but the atmosphere was light and he, himself, was in a rare mood.

Cameron shook his head and said, "Spooks."

They finished their luncheon and the tour of the building. Mark pointed out memorabilia along the way which included a walk around the Berlin wall display. They finished the day with a stop by Mike Hollister's office where Cameron watched with amusement as the two harassed each other.

The next day, Mark saw Cameron off with a promise to stay in touch. As Cameron backed out of the driveway, he waved goodbye to the agent. Pointing his car towards the airport, the events of the last nine weeks rattled around in his brain. Once he was out of sight from his host, he pulled over and removed the plaque and certificate from their cases. Running his hand over the plaque, he breathed a deep sigh. A highway patrolman honored by the top spies. It gave him a new respect for their organization. He took one final look at the framed certificate. Then, he did something he hadn't thought to do during all of the commotion. He flipped it over. Written on the back was a simple note - *Detective, you performed admirably in the face of adversity. Thank you for saving my sister.* Signed in two different hands were *Mark and Mary Springfield.*

Cameron looked up from the writing and out at the surrounding countryside. Three weeks ago, he had been presented a letter from the governor of California. Yesterday, he had been to Langley. But it wasn't until he read the simple inscription that he truly grasped the implication. It's what the agent had said all along. He really had been instrumental in preventing the loss of whatever it was that was worth dying for. But more importantly, he had helped save Mary's life.

Cameron looked down at the plaque again and ran his hand along its edge. The lump he had felt in his throat yesterday returned. His face felt flush. It would have embarrassed him had he been in front of his colleagues. Then it happened again. A single tear rolled down his cheek and splashed just under Mark's name.